Critical Acclaim for The Heap

"Mixing centuries of mystery and intrigue, Albarelli weaves a chilling, stunningly cinematic story with street children at the heart of the action. The author fleshes out fascinating characters drawn from Biblical and Apocryphal literature, as well as Christian mystics and "heretics" from the Middle ages. *THE HEAP* will stick with you long after the last page."
—**Elizabeth Black,** author of *BUFFALO SPIRITS*

"H.P. Albarelli Jr. skillfully turns his investigative reporter's mind to the imagination in *THE HEAP*, an absorbing and inspiring book that blends mystery and meditation in a thriller about children who make a place for themselves in a world gone senseless. Albarelli braids politics, religion, history and fantasy in such novel ways, you'll read *THE HEAP* with urgency—and be sorry when it's over." —**Carlo Wolff,**
freelance book critic to *The Boston Globe* and *San Francisco Chronicle*

"Albarelli has given us a mystical tale of hope and humanity amid savage brutality—a haunting allegory as old as history itself. *THE HEAP* is at once a mesmerizing literary carnival—surreal, seductive and wicked— and an introspective yearning for something higher."
—**Susan Edwards,** senior editor, *Tampa's Weekly Planet*

"The far reaches of Biblical storytelling—and beyond—become the well-traveled terrain of *THE HEAP*, a gripping and mesmerizing tale of unattached souls that quickly attach themselves to the reader. Jump into *THE HEAP*, and you'll find it hard to extricate yourself."
—**Edwin Black,** author of *IBM and the Holocaust* and *Format C*

"I couldn't put *THE HEAP* down. It reads like a modern day *LORD OF THE FLIES*, with generous helpings of Biblical heresy to rival *THE DA VINCI CODE*. Albarelli's writing is hypnotic and provoking; *THE HEAP* is a dazzling book of amazing power and imagery."
—**Paul Wolf,** historian and critic

The Heap

H. P. G.

The Heap

H.P. ALBARELLI JR.

Preface by Nicole McDonald Albarelli

PEREDUR PUBLISHING, LTD.

NEW YORK, LONDON, AND PARIS

THE HEAP

The epigraph by Talking Heads is from the song
"Life During Wartime" written by David Byrne, Chris Frantz,
Jerry Harrison, and Tina Weymouth. Used with permission
from Index Music, Inc./Bleu Disque Music Co., Inc. (ASCAP).

The epigraph by Arthur Lee is from the song "You Set the Scene"
written by Arthur Lee,used with permission from Trio Music
Company, Inc. (BMI) and Grass Roots Music (BMI).

The epigraph by Faithless is from the song "Liontamer" written by
Zoe Johnson, Maxi Jazz, Sister Bliss, and Rollo.
Used with permission from Faithless.

ISBN: 0-9761044-0-7
2004097986

Printed and bound in the United States of America
by Peredur Publishing, Ltd., New York, London, and Paris.
www.peredurpublishing.com

First Edition
Cover and book design by Jen Huppert.
Front cover artwork by Justin Walters.
Front cover photograph by Don Farrall.

Visit author H.P. Albarelli Jr. online at www.albarelli.net

This book is for my children Damien, Nicole, and David;
my parents, Henry P. Albarelli Sr. and Nancy O'Neill Albarelli;
Phyllis and John Nolin; Helen McDonald;
and most especially, it is for my loving wife,
Kathleen Rose McDonald.

It is dedicated to the late Robert Moore Williams,
a prolific author, who decades ago took the time to teach a
young boy much of what he knew about writing.

In loving remembrance of Jason Edwards and Jacob Yager:
Who is the third who walks always beside you?

Table of Contents

Acknowledgments

The author would like to express his special thanks to Nicole for finding Father Gabriel Olivier Surin; to Cali; to Wallace Green; Gladys Colburn; Nick and Natalie Piacun; Ben Cook; Amanda Sager; Christina and Isaiah Burris: Leah Soon Gardner and Daniel Gardner; Keese and Sylvana Lane; David R. Cromer; J.P. Mahoney; Molly Jarvis; Nolan O'Neill Albarelli, Kathryn Nolin Albarelli, and Michael Hefflon Albarelli; Siraaj Knight; Jen Huppert; Justin Walters; Marcia Schutte; Bob Spear; Cody Davidson Nolin and Kathleen Ann Nolin; and most of all, to Amber Lauren Smith, a remarkable writer, who faithfully stood by as friend, muse, critic and editor.

There be many shapes of mystery,
And many things God makes to be,
Past hope or fear.
And the end men looked for
Cometh not,
And a path is there where no man sought.
So hath it follow here.
                    —Euripides

This ain't no party, this ain't no disco,
This ain't no fooling around,
No time for dancing, or lovey dovey,
I ain't got time for that now.
                —Talking Heads

Everything I've seen needs rearranging ...
                    —Arthur Lee

This Child wise beyond words
Whose tears flow without seize.
                    —Faithless

You shall gather all the spoil of it into
the midst of the street of it, and shall
burn with the fire the city, and all the
spoil of it every whit, to Yahweh your
God: and it shall be a heap forever; it
shall not be built again.
                —Deuteronomy

What is life other than a series of stories?
That these stories portray more than a banal
journey to Death's door is not for the one that
has lived them to declare, but for the one who
hears them and decides they have taken him
to places that transcend Death and make the
journey worth repeating.
                —Urbain Grandier

Preface

first encountered Father Gabriel Surin, wholly
unexpectedly, in a dimly lit pub in London's West End.
It was an unseasonably warm October evening, and I
had gone there with friends after a long day of classes
to unwind with a pint or two. I didn't notice the darkly
clad figure hunched at a corner table until I excused myself and
crossed the room to go to the loo. As I passed his table, he looked
up at me. I nodded and he smiled and said, "Hello," as if we'd
known one another all our lives. His smile conveyed that rare sort
of world-weary wisdom and warmth that is all at once both
disarming and mesmerizing.

Returning to my table, I once again had to pass by him. This
time, lost in his thoughts, he did not look up. Something about his
demeanor made him seem singularly solitary and sad and, for
reasons I still don't understand, I was concerned for him. I
stopped and asked, "Are you okay?"

He looked up and said, "Yes, I'm fine. Just thinking, is all."

"A mind is a fire to be kindled," I said, quoting a line still fresh
from a philosophy course.

He smiled again and finished, "...not a vessel to be filled."

I nodded toward his almost empty glass. "Speaking of which, can I buy you another?"

"Thank you," he said, "but one is my limit."

Suddenly I felt very foolish. "I'm sorry, I'm bothering you."

"No, no, please," he said, standing. "It is I who should apologize."

He motioned to the empty chair across from him. "Would you care to join me for a moment?"

I looked at my friends across the room thinking that perhaps I had acted too impulsively. I didn't know anything about this person, and it was very unlike me to approach any stranger in this way. Yet somehow, I knew there was no danger in this and it was the right thing to do.

He extended his hand and said, "My name is Gabriel Surin."

I introduced myself and, in deference to his Roman collar, which I noticed when he stood, called him Father.

"Please, Gabriel will do just fine," he said.

He was tall and gaunt yet appeared quite fit. I judged him to be no older than his early forties. His eyes were a remarkable shade of blue that in the pub's dim light seemed incandescent. His thick prematurely-white hair was several weeks overdue for cutting. After I sat down, I saw how deeply tanned he was. "There are people who spend small fortunes trying to achieve that color," I remarked.

My comment served as a good segue into our ensuing conversation. He told me he had just that day returned to London from abroad where he had been working as an archivist and historian for the Church. He specialized in apocrypha and pseudepigrapha literature, works deliberately excluded from the Old and New Testaments. Several years ago, he explained, he journeyed to an obscure monastery where he discovered several long lost books sitting dust-covered on a shelf as if patiently awaiting his arrival.

"They must have been very important books," I said, noting how intense his eyes became when he spoke of them.

"You can't imagine."

He went on explaining that he had intended to only spend a few months at the monastery, but then due to circumstances beyond his control, his stay abroad had lasted nearly three years. A little over two of those had been spent living among a large group of street children.

"That must have been fascinating work," I said.

He looked away for a moment and then answered, "It wasn't really work, but yes, the children were wonderful."

When I remarked that he must miss them an awful lot, he nodded and his eyes grew misty.

"Tell me about them," I said.

"I don't know that it would be wise to say much."

"But, why?" I asked, surprised at his response.

"Something happened," he said softly. "Something that many people will not believe."

"You can't tell me anything?"

"Do you really want to know?" he asked.

"I wouldn't have asked otherwise."

He looked about the room. "Well, perhaps a little."

What Father Gabriel told me about the children both intrigued and repulsed me. I marveled at their ingenuity in finding ways to cope and survive with the hand life had dealt them, yet I found it uncomfortable to be reminded of the levels of cruelty inflicted on them. Like everyone, I knew these things still happened in the world, but found it easier to pretend they didn't.

That evening in the pub, Father Gabriel said nothing about what had ultimately happened to the children he lived among, but his hesitancy in sharing his story, and the way he spoke around some of my questions, left little doubt that something of great import had occurred. Listening to him talk about both his scholarly work and his time with the children made it easy to realize that he had great passion for both, but at the same time he seemed distracted by something. Talking, his voice would trail off mid-sentence; he would look away and become momentarily absorbed by some thought. Only later, after he was gone, did I learn about the terrible knowledge consuming him.

Nonetheless, that first evening, I was so enthralled listening to him that I didn't notice the closing bell had rung until one of my friends and flatmate, Sasha, was standing over me hesitantly asking, "Nicole, are you ready?"

I told her to join us for a minute and introduced her to my new friend. As a barmaid hurriedly cleared the table, I asked Father Gabriel if he was staying somewhere nearby hoping that we could get together again to talk more. He said he didn't know how long he was going to be in London and would most likely take a hotel room for the night before deciding.

"Our place is only a short walk away," I told him. "We have a foldout couch and it's late. Stay with us, and we can talk more before you decide."

"That's very kind," he said, "but I can't impose."

"Nonsense," I insisted.

"It would do our place well to host some holiness for a change," Sasha joked.

Father Gabriel stayed with us for only two nights, but in that short time I was able to learn more about his time abroad. I continued to be shocked to hear him tell about the horrendous lives and living conditions of the street children, but that shock was soon eclipsed by the rest of his story.

During Farther Gabriel's first night with us, I awoke in the darkness to hear him in the next room thrashing about in bed, mumbling odd sentences and calling out what I soon learned were the names of children. On his third day with us, while Father Gabriel was out for a walk, there was a hard pounding on my flat's door. I opened it to find three men dressed in dark suits who all looked remarkably alike. They showed me official looking credentials that identified them as being with branches of the British and United States governments and then one of them asked if Father Surin was available.

When I said that he was out, another of the men, in an accented and phlegmy voice, asked, "Would you mind if we came in and looked around?"

I sensed right away from their demeanor they already knew that Father Gabriel wasn't there and had taken his absence as an opportunity to knock.

"What is it you're looking for?" I asked.

"We'll tell you when we see it," the third man said brusquely.

I stepped aside and they purposefully moved into the flat spreading out as they did. Their search was quick and thorough. As I anticipated, they found nothing that provoked any curiosity. When they were finished and about to depart, one curtly said, "Tell the good padre we'll be back."

Upon his return Father Gabriel wasn't surprised to learn about our visitors. "I should have known they'd find me here," he said.

"What do they want?" I asked.

"I'm sorry that I've involved you in this. I should go now and not make it any worse."

"There is no reason to apologize, or to go, really."

"No, I must go."

I continued to protest but it did no good.

Shortly after he left, I found a worn black and white photograph and a thick, tattered, leather-bound journal resting on top of an end table in our living room. The photograph was of a group of seven children, all smiling for the camera. Tucked into the center of the children, seated on its haunches, was a big, dark-colored dog. Lying on the ground, in front of the group, was a large, rectangular metallic case. The sun, invisible overhead, cast a majestic glare off the case. On the back of the photo, were the handwritten words: "And a path is there where no man sought." Inside the journal, written in a hand often difficult to decipher, was an account of what happened during Father Gabriel's last seven days of his two years in the place called the Heap. I began reading it and hours later sat stunned by what it said.

I know that many people will say the following story is not true, that no incident like the one described by Father Gabriel ever occurred, and that indeed he never existed, or if he did, he was simply a delusional man victimized by his own mental afflictions, but that does not offend me. I understand why people would be skeptical or disbelieving given that we live in a world where any such story is best relegated to the realm of fiction, a world where nothing of any real import occurs unless fully sanctioned by television and the newspapers. Be that as it is, however, please know this story is true and that I remain forever thankful that Father Gabriel came into my life and shared it with me. Wherever he is, I hope he is safe and at peace with himself.

—Nicole McDonald Albarelli
London, October 2004

The Heap

Day One

rom my perch high atop the mangled steel and chrome, I could see the Tire Boys going through their daily routine at the northern corner of the Heap. Like always, everyone carried their share of the morning's bounty, tires large and small, meaty black orbs that had given their best to the asphalt and hard gravel that ultimately destroyed them.

But on this day, the day it all began, something was different.

This day, unlike others, rotund Raoul, with several oversize tires encircling his thick shoulders, instead of leading the group, was walking alongside Warranty and Humbatter, two of the younger boys. Each boy held one of the handles of a large metallic case they were carrying. Humbatter, the taller of the two, shortened his gait to compensate for Warranty's game leg as he strained with the weight of the case. Raoul appeared to be guiding the boys around the various piles of refuse and offering words of encouragement. Behind them, followed the remainder of the group, with Pockets bringing up the rear, lugging two tires that nearly touched the ground, both looped around his small shoulders. As the group neared the entrance to the Burrow, Raoul again broke protocol and stepped aside allowing the two boys with the case to enter first. Then he glanced about and motioned to two of the other boys to remain outside and stand guard before disappearing himself into the Burrow.

Scanning the Heap southward, I saw that I wasn't the only one observing the Tire Boys. Three children from the Bottles and Cans Cabal, the girls Phaedra and Sayu and the boy called Maxi, were crouched by a tall pile of cardboard observing their movements. Nameless, his tongue hanging loosely, sat panting next to them. Maxi lowered the small binoculars he held and said something to Phaedra who nodded in response. The girls then picked up their collection sacks and the three of them began moving in my direction. When they passed beneath my spot, Phaedra looked up at me, her placid green eyes catching mine, her mouth forming a calm, deliberate smile that brightened my day in no way the sun ever could.

"You want to be careful, Mr. Fantasy, too long out of shade on a day like this, and you'll burn to a crisp," she said, tossing me one of the delicate metallic flowers she made from scraps of copper and aluminum.

She was right. It wasn't quite mid-morning and already the temperature was hovering in the high thirties Celsius. For the past few weeks it had been unseasonably hot even for that place where the temperature rarely is anything close to pleasant. Not long after coming to the Heap, I conjectured that heat had a way of stifling productivity, but you would never have concluded that from watching the children that dwelled there. There in the Heap, regardless what whim Mother Nature decided to serve up, enterprise was always pursued with passion.

Before I go any further with my story, it is only proper that I explain my objectives and introduce myself. My aims are simple and straightforward, yet the facts, as often the case, are complex and convoluted. Perhaps this is a result of my jumbled state of mind, but I think not. In recent years, as I will attempt to reveal, my life has taken odd twists and turns, but that is not my primary subject. Here, my intent is to relate the events of my last seven days spent in the place called the Heap. There, I was called Mr. Fantasy, but my real name is Gabriel Surin. To be precise, from the age of twenty-two on, it was Father Gabriel Olivier Surin. You might find it helpful to know, perhaps even a bit hard to believe, that I was once considered a rising scholar in the obscure area of ancient written works deemed not genuine, or apocrypha, by the Church.

Perhaps you are unaware of the great number of errant scriptures and books that the early Church methodically purged from existence, countless volumes, many forever lost to the flame, destroyed by official decrees of bishops and emperors alike. These were no ordinary books. They were poetic and spellbinding accounts of differing cosmogonies and apocalyptic finishes filled with intriguing hints of Nirvana, glimpses of Hades, and possible truths. In 333 A.D., Constantine gushed that these were the impious and wicked works of heretics and enemies of piety. So he, and a complicit clergy, ordered that their authors be branded contemptible forever after and their scriptures be consigned to the flame. But, as you shall see, not all of these books were lost. Some secretly survived obliteration.

It may be as much a mystery to me, as to you, what pushed me into this obscure and labyrinthine line of work so rutted and riddled with arcane remnants. As a youth, I was like any other boy who daydreamed through the more rote moments of adolescence of life as a cowboy, a pirate, fireman, policeman, or soldier. Maybe it was my attention to detail, my childish obsession with wanting to know more than those around me that led me toward my chosen profession. Cowboys wore spurs and chaps, but why, I asked? Pirates flew the Jolly Roger, but why? Who was Roger? Why was he jolly? Those most irritated with my need to know would inevitably warn me that curiosity killed the cat, but my response only made matters worse: which cat and why? The unknown fascinated me and fed my youthful zeal for life. Where others my age feared what they could not see, I found comfort. The things that went bump in the night, odd rustlings in an empty closet, strange scratching under the bed made me feel alive and invigorated. That life held untold secrets and intrigues was mere grist for my intuitiveness.

In my teens, I envied those around me who possessed that beguiling combination of extroversion, charm, and quick thinking, but that mixture was the opposite of me. I was always the person in the corner of a crowded room, by himself, making an impression by not being noticed or for what I didn't say. Whereas some people were happiest surrounded by others, I was most contented alone; where others were at ease with a rush of exotic experiences, I favored slower samplings that could be savored and completely appreciated. I was one of those people who could linger before a work of art for a long period of time, lose myself in a book for hours on end, given to introspection but never unduly absorbed by it. I understood my interests and needs and appreciated that they weren't those shared by the many. I liked things to be orderly and to come in arrangements that could be fathomed and if they didn't come that way, I was compelled to make them so.

As I grew older, I remained insatiably curious about subjects that seemed to interest nobody, asking why about matters that others seemed quite content to accept. Perhaps it was only natural that I was drawn to the study of history. I believed that history could give shape to a misshapen world, that it could provide a semblance of order and reason to things that needed rearrangement. Little did I realize in my zest that history is scarcely more than play dough to be manipulated and shaped in any way its handler chooses, or more kindly put, that it is a problematic discipline which even the best and sincerest practitioners tie themselves up in knots over. Eventually I came to the understanding that history was not "the story of events," as one of my professors would say, but one of egos and opinions of events, an abstract, acquired skill, cloaked in time's occurrences, intended to advance arguments and philosophies. But still, I was indelibly tainted with idealism in my passion for history. And I felt I could be, would be, the one to uncover lost particles of time that would serve to replace mere play dough with true building blocks for truth that nobody could dispute. That I would fail on all counts was inevitable, but I am getting ahead of myself here, and you must wait a bit longer for that to be explained.

During my early university studies, before entering the seminary, I had been singularly drawn to John's Biblical passage, "En arche en ho Logos, kai ho Logos en pros ton Theon, kai Theos en ho Logos." *In the beginning was the Word and the Word was with God and the Word was God.* For me, this verse, in numerous ways, formed the basis for my pursuit of the certainty and knowledge provided by history. For me, the Word was history.

Of course, I was aware of the Church's interpretation of this haunting line, that the Word was the Logos, or knowledge, imparted from God through Christ. But, given my tremendous curiosity about ancient esoterica, from my studies I had also become well aware that knowledge of the Word long pre-dated John's writings and of the more mysterious meanings bestowed onto the perplexing verse. I had been intrigued to learn that at one time, and perhaps still in certain circles today, there raged great debate over what the Word actually was. The debate comprised one of the world's oldest and most perplexing mysteries. To better comprehend this mystery, one must go back to ancient texts, written long before the birth of Christ. These texts maintained there was a mystic, secret Word that was variously regarded as "unspeakable," "unutterable," "indescribable," and "ineffable." Somehow this Word had become lost to man. There were many accounts as to how this had happened, with perhaps the most widely circulated one being that Adam, who knew the Word while in the earthly Garden of Paradise, had it removed from his memory after God expelled him. Thus the Word became the Lost Word. The followers of Moses taught that if anyone were to speak aloud the Word, all of time and matter would come to an instant and catastrophic end. The ancient Egyptians built huge temples within which knowledge about the Word was hidden in hermetically sealed containers. It was common to find written in hieroglyphics the statement, "The Word creates all things. Nothing is before it has been uttered in a clear voice." The goddess Isis, eldest daughter of Kronos and sister to Osiris, was said to embody the Word, which Isis said stood between man and Truth. Isis claimed that she obtained the Word after having conjured the god Ra, who taught her that through its means she could command the unseen forces of Nature, but that its utterance would bring down everything below and above the Sun. Still, said the Church, "Jesus Christ, the interpreter of the divine mind and will, is the Incarnate Word," but others differed or weren't so sure. For me, the maturing youth who was drawn irretrievably to mystery, I was perfectly content to accept all claims as I continued my search for certainty.

I came to this country from London nearly three years ago to pursue my work at a little-known monastery that housed several collections of rare books and documents. In return for the privilege to conduct my research there, I had agreed in advance to minister in my spare time to what the monastery's good friars called the "ubiquitous street urchins" who populated the nearby city in large numbers. But, as fate would have it, I never had the opportunity to fulfill my obligation.

Shortly after my arrival at the monastery, a special police squad was surreptitiously formed to rid the landscape of street children by conducting citywide sweeps. Overseen by Colonel Daihen, better known to the children as "Colonel Dreadful", the sweeps were designed to provide the area's tourists with an environment in which to frolic, devoid of any reminders of reality, guilt free, undisturbed by some sad-eyed adolescent thrusting out a grubby palm for alms. Due to Colonel Dreadful's unconventional and incredibly harsh tactics, the initial sweeps were much more effective than anyone anticipated. But soon he went too far.

Frequently, in the middle-of-the-night, the Colonel would lead roundups that proved most economical for apprehending large groups of huddled, sleeping children. Roughly roused, the groggy youths were herded into vans that delivered them to dank jails where they would be held for days on end without food or care. But jail was the least of the children's fears.

A favorite tactic used by the Colonel was to separate the older children from the younger and then transport them to a large rubbish and scrap yard outside the city limits. Here, where nobody but Dreadful and his men could hear their screams, the children would be mercilessly abused and tortured.

One morning, workers at the dump found the mutilated bodies of four children. The timing of the discovery could not have been worse. Some of the world's most prestigious humanitarian institutions were holding a huge assembly in the city's grandest hotel, and prominent on their agenda was the plight of the world's street children. I am sure you can imagine what followed next, the both real and feigned reactions of outrage, the indignation that a "few bad apples" had spoiled an entire police force, the inevitable "never again" promises from the very politicians who supported the sweeps to begin with.

As you may have guessed, the local press was delighted with the story. It was the classic good versus evil, David and Goliath tale that the press so relishes. The children were an archetype of everyone's worst dreams, the embodiment of there-but-for-fortune, fine fodder for the most gut wrenching, conscious-soothing copy and conversation, but ultimately a cause for fear and alarm. They represented one part of an age-old perpetual relationship with those who could only feel sorry for them from a respectful and safe distance. It was the common emotional response that makes all of us uncomfortable, and the children understood this remarkably well. People would emote sympathy and compassion for them from afar, but disown them up close where they were a bit too real—and perhaps even threatening. The press's fleeting attention to the story focused on its immediate and more grisly aspects. Nobody wanted to devote the time and trouble to uncovering and revealing the root causes of what had happened. No reporter had any interest in peeling back the multiple layers of the onion for fear of getting a difficult stink on his hands. Within a few short weeks, the story was gone, and reality and the current of complacency that it rides upon quietly wound their place back to dominance.

But some of the street children took stock of the hard lesson learned and, taking advantage of the short lived attention, they abandoned the city and took up permanent refuge at the very scene of the crime—the refuse dump that had been colorfully dubbed "the Heap" by local journalists. There, the children, over two hundred in number, reconstituted themselves and established what any anthropologist would deem a tribal-like, self-reliant community. Rarely, after its formation, did anyone leave the confines of the fledgling community except to occasionally venture into the city's vast outdoor marketplace to purchase clothing or other necessities unavailable in the Heap. Thus was I relieved of my commitment to occasionally work among the children.

Perhaps, kind reader, you are now wondering how fate did eventually bind me with the children, and this seems as good a place as any to explain. Two years ago, my life was inexorably changed by the sudden and unexpected event of what I think of as my mind imploding. I had been working rather feverishly at the time, and one day while sitting at my cluttered desk in the monastery, my vision suddenly began to turn cloudy. It was as if I'd entered a bank of low-lying fog from a perfectly clear day. I stood from my chair and groped my way to the door, but my feet felt heavy and sodden like one experiences in a nightmare where you want to run but your legs feel as if they are moving through a deep bed of wet concrete. Fumbling about, I grasped the doorframe to keep myself from falling.

Gradually, the fog began to give way and I saw strange shapes illuminated by strobes of light followed by a fierce whirling sound in my head. My vision turned inward with incredible geometric patterns filling my head. It was as if I was peering through a giant kaleidoscope; twirling hexagons of neon blue, green, and red evolving into ever-expanding super novas melting into slow-moving solar storms, tossing up lava-like eruptions.

Eventually, everything gave way to what appeared to be an enormous and elaborate grid system that spanned to eternity, superimposed over a many-branched tree with transparent green leaves. Somewhere way in the distance, or deep inside my head, a voice whispered, "A leaf is good. Everything's good ...but what is the Word?" As I gazed upon the tree and grid, every pore of my body, as if in response to a silent cue, opened up and drenched me in sweat. My sudden loss of fluid, and overwhelming sensory overload, caused me to collapse to the floor. My last thought while gazing at the grid was here finally was the solution to everything that had eluded me in my life and work; here was the answer to all the inexplicable mysteries that life and the universe held. And that answer was so simple, yet so overwhelming, that it had escaped mankind for centuries. Everything was irrevocably interwoven into an ultimate answer—a truth stunning in its simplicity, stunning in that it had remained unseen, unrealized, and invisible for so long.

I awoke a full day later to find myself strapped tightly to a bed in the local hospital. A nurse was hovering over me like an angelic apparition. She smiled when she saw my opened eyes and said, "Goodness, you're back."

"What happened?" I asked, trying to sit up.

"Don't fret, now," she said, undoing the straps, explaining that they had been for my own safety. "Freshen up some, if you'd like, the doctor will be in to see you soon."

About an hour later, after I was astounded to discover that every hair on my head had turned completely white, a doctor wearing a drab lab coat, flanked by two eager interns, asked me to recount what had happened.

When I finished relating my disjointed recollections, he mumbled, "Only a participant can be a profound observer," and told one of the interns to make a notation on my chart.

He then withdrew a small penlight from his lab coat's breast pocket. Leaning over me, he brought the light close to my right eye and then to my left. I smelled curry on his breath.

"What's wrong with me?" I asked.

He gently lifted my left eyelid and peered more closely. After a moment he moved the light away and said, "Seizure by aberrations."

"Apparitions?" I asked, mishearing him.

"No, no," he said, "aberrations."

He moved the light back to my right eye. "Some of my colleagues call it episodic disorder. It's a dysfunction in the cranium's electrical system, so to speak."

He leaned closer examining my right eye.

"You've been working very hard lately, no?" he asked.

"Yes," I said.

He leaned back and slipped the penlight back into his lab coat. "I can see that."

Later, the nurse told me that what I suffered was an uncommon epileptic-like seizure caused by electrical discharges in the brain. "Small, but violent upheavals in the limbic system," she said, "thought to be brought on by stress or overworking, but nobody really knows for sure what causes them."

"Brainstorms," I pondered aloud.

"You can think of them that way," she said.

That I had experienced fever seizures as a child apparently contributed much toward this diagnosis. And, while I was curious, I knew nothing about the limbic system and thought it best to leave it that way given it was an area of my body to which I had limited access.

"How uncommon?" I asked the nurse.

"Well, let's just say you're in good company," she replied. She explained that a good number of renowned artists had also experienced episodic disturbances. She recited a list of names, "Van Gogh, Edgar Allen Poe, Artaud, Virginia Woolf, Strindberg, Emily Dickinson, the list goes on."

"But I'm not an artistic savant," I said.

She made a face that said, what can I say?

"How long will I be here?" I asked.

"At least a few weeks, but don't fret; we'll keep you occupied."

True to her words, I was discharged after twenty-one days, but while I was recuperating, a series of events that would transform my life took place. During my second week, I was awakened from a slumber one afternoon by a loud commotion in the hallway outside my room. I got out of bed and peered through the small square window of my door. Two uniformed policemen were struggling with a small boy who couldn't have been any older than five or six. Despite that his hands were bound behind his back, the boy was doing everything he could to get away from the men. An orderly and a nurse stood watching as the men tried to force the boy into the room across from mine. The orderly held a tray containing a syringe and a small glass bottle. I watched as the policemen finally pushed the boy into the room, but not before one of them pulled a black baton from his belt and clubbed the boy hard across the back of his neck. Later, I woke up again in the middle of the night to the tinny silence of the hospital thinking about the boy. Looking out my door's window again, I thought I saw a small set of luminous eyes in the window across the hallway looking back at me.

"He's from the Heap," the nurse said the next morning in response to my inquiry about my new neighbor. "He says his name is Pockets."

Seeing my expression, she quickly added, "And don't ask me why. These children call themselves all sorts of odd names."

"Why is he here?" I asked.

"He was picked up in the marketplace. When the local jail is full, they bring them temporarily here sometimes."

"And he'll stay on his own?"

"If he's like all the others, he'll be gone before they come back for him," she said.

Later, at breakfast in the cafeteria, I watched him, sitting alone at a table nearest the room's large single window. He devoured the food on his tray like he hadn't eaten in days. When he finished, he turned his chair to face the window and sat staring at the glass, his little feet inches above the floor, legs swinging back and forth.

He didn't look like most of the region's children. His hair was lighter in color, eyes a light shade of green, cheekbones well pronounced with a splash of light copper freckles across each. Like most children his age, his build was slight, yet the muscles of his dark legs and arms were well pronounced. When he turned my way and saw that I was looking at him, he locked eyes with me for a moment before turning back to the window. I didn't know it at the time, but the window squarely faced the direction of the Heap.

That afternoon he sat in the same place for lunch. I walked from the serving line to his table, sat down across from him, and introduced myself. He looked at me without speaking and nodded his head slightly. When I offered him my two slices of baked bread, he shyly accepted them and told me his name was Pockets.

"Why do they call you that?" I asked.

"It's what I call myself; it's my name," he said.

"But, how did you get it?"

"When I was in the city, before leaving there, my only pants had no pockets," he said, as if that were explanation enough.

"So you named yourself Pockets," I persisted.

"Yes, and that way I had them."

Over the next five days, before he vanished one night, we developed a cautious friendship. At first, apart from his understandably suspicious nature, he seemed like a fairly normal child, however, the more time we spent together, the more I became aware of his feral like qualities. I remembered when I was a boy not much older than Pockets; I had been enthralled by accounts of children raised by packs of wolves. I was well acquainted with the stories of the Wild Boy of Aveyron, Peter of Hanover, and Kasper Hauser, but had always been most intrigued by the so-called Wolf Children of Midnapore.

In 1920, a man named Joseph Singh, the head of an orphanage in Northern India, was informed by frightened villagers of a pack of ghostly, half-human wolves that emerged nightly from a huge mound near the jungle's edge. Skeptical but curious, Singh went out one night when there was a full moon to observe the mound from the safety of a tall tree. There, in the moonlight, he watched in amazement as several wolves came out followed by two small girls. In his journal, Singh described the girls, soon learned to be three and five years old, as "hideous looking and walking on all fours ... their faces nearly completely obscured by matted, thick, filthy hair, their eyes unlike human eyes, glowing brightly in the moonlight."

A few days later, Singh returned to the spot with a hunting party and captured the girls after being forced to kill the she-wolf, which fiercely defended her cubs. Still, the girls, howling and fighting ferociously, had to be pried from the protecting claws of two cubs that held them. They were taken to Singh's orphanage where they were cared for and slowly exposed to the ways of civilization. Incredibly, Singh soon learned that the girls were not sisters as he had thought, but instead had been taken by the wolves at separate times from different villages.

Singh, well intentioned, worked hard to wean the girls, whom he named Kamala and Amala, from their lupine habits, but he had little success. Both children hated life in captivity and grew ill. Amala, the youngest, died, and Kamala curled herself in a corner of her room where she mourned for months. She survived her illness, and Singh was able to make some headway in making her more comfortable around humans and in teaching her to speak simple sentences, but she was locked into the conflicting minds of a young child and a wild beast. One can easily imagine her unhappiness. Singh reported that when she died at the age of sixteen her, last words were, "Papa, I hurt."

In certain situations, Pockets' feral qualities manifested themselves in stark ways. At meal times, he always shunned utensils, hovered protectively over his food, ate with his hands, often poking and prodding items that were obviously foreign to him, but he always consumed everything on his tray. At the end of each meal, he would take a slice of bread and meticulously mop up every smidgen of food.

On his third afternoon at the hospital, we were given Jell-O for dessert. Pockets gazed down at the square green cube holding several bits of pineapple and cherry with a look of utter amazement. Curiously, he leaned down closer to examine the suspended pieces, sniffed them, and then carefully poked the cube with a finger causing it to quiver slightly. He looked at me and asked, "How did that happen?"

In the day room, where patients gathered to watch television or to read, he rarely sat in a chair or on one of its several couches, but instead would stand or squat with his haunches inches above the floor. Remarkably, he had no interest whatsoever in looking at the television. Instead, he would stand for long stretches staring out the window toward the indiscernible Heap in the distance. Once while standing like that, I noticed him lift his head and begin sniffing in a canine-like fashion, his nostrils moving up and down. He turned to me and said, "They're peeling potatoes for lunch."

If not looking out the window, he would read one of the few books available from the hospital's cart. One of the orderlies remarked that while making his late night rounds, he found Pockets reading. The incredible part of what he said was that despite the hospital's firm midnight lights-out rule, reading in the dark seemed to be no problem for Pockets. It was like he had the vision of a nocturnal animal, the orderly said, surely exaggerating his account. He added that instead of sleeping in his bed at night, Pockets slept under it, on the floor.

The few times that he exhibited any signs of youthful delight were particularly disarming. I remember the first time he laughed in the day room. The sound froze everyone in their place, causing every nurse and attendant within earshot to come running. Something in the book he was reading had apparently struck him as humorous and he threw his head back and emitted an unearthly low howl, which grew in intensity before quickly changing into a series of short, sharp hoots. It was as if an excited primate had invaded our midst.

Through our conversations, bits and pieces of Pockets' life prior to going to the Heap emerged. He remembered living with his mother in a small one-room shanty near the center of the city. He described her as having been very beautiful. At home at night, he said, she would read books to him taking the time to point to certain words, cooing the sounds and asking him to repeat them. He said that she would take him in her arms and softly sing to him while lightly rocking back and forth. When he was about four years old, he explained, his mother began bringing him every morning to her new job in a small factory that assembled shoes for export. There, Pockets recalled, he would have to sit quietly beneath her workbench and devise ways to amuse himself.

I knew that women providing alone for their children in the region faced near insurmountable odds and those who sought work were frequently cruelly exploited. After about a week of coming to the factory, a foreman told Pockets he would have to begin routinely carrying water to all the other workers if he was to be allowed to stay. At first the work was fun, but soon it became a situation where he was lugging all sorts of things about and if he weren't prompt about it, the foremen would hit him on the backs of his legs with a switch to speed his movements. When his mother complained about her son's treatment, she was given more work to do and was told that if she didn't continue to bring Pockets to the factory, she would be fired. I knew that a regular workday in such a place lasted ten hours with one unpaid break for lunch; a workweek consisted of six days, but despite these long hours worker's wages amounted to little more than enough to purchase a subsistence amount of food.

Pockets said that life went on like this for what seemed like many months, until one night at home he and his mother were awakened from their sleep by the sounds of many people yelling and screaming on the street outside. When his mother got up and opened their door to see what was happening, she was pulled into the crowd. When the crowd had passed and once again it was quiet, he went outside and called out for his mother, but there was no answer. He stayed awake the rest of the night waiting for her to come back, periodically going outside and looking for her, but she never came. The next morning, Pockets went to the factory, but his mother wasn't there. He spent the next three days walking the streets looking for her. On the fourth day, a man and his family came to the shanty and told him to leave, that the place was now theirs. He went back once more to the factory to look for his mother, but she still wasn't there. He began living on the streets and never saw her again.

I remarked to him one day about how much he obviously enjoyed reading.

"Where I live I have all that I want to read," Pockets said.

"How is that so?" I asked.

He looked hurt, and I was embarrassed that my thoughtless question had betrayed my knowledge of his living situation.

"You'd be surprised at what people throw away," he said. "Books of all sorts."

"And you read a lot of them?" I asked.

He looked at me suspiciously and then looking down at his little hands folded in his lap he asked, "Do you know the story of the one-eyed men?"

I shook my head saying I didn't think so and he looked surprised at my response.

"Where I live, I read it almost every night to the others."

"And where you live," I said, deciding to come completely clean with him, "that is the place you call the Heap?"

He looked at me with challenging eyes, his lips pursed. "That is what a lot of people call it, but not me."

"What do you call it?" I asked.

"Home," he said.

"Do you know what the ocean is?" he asked me one afternoon.

"Yes, I do."

"Have you ever seen it?"

"Many times."

His eyes widened at this and I realized the basis of his questions, that he had never seen the ocean or for that matter any large body of water, despite that some were not far away. For many people, the world is growing remarkably smaller at an alarming rate, I thought, but how easy it is to forget that there are still people who know little more of it than their immediate surroundings.

"Do boats really move across it?"

"Yes, they do. And planes fly over it, and people even swim in it."

"With the fish?" he said, unconvinced.

"It's very large," I told him. "Very large, with plenty of room for everyone."

"Bigger than here?" he asked motioning toward the great expanse outside the dayroom's window.

"Far bigger."

"Someone told me that the ocean sometimes drowns in its own waves," he said.

"That is an interesting way of putting it," I said.

"You've really seen it?"

"Once, I even sat in it and read a book."

He eyed me somewhat suspiciously.

"I would be happy to see the ocean," he said.

It was amply apparent that Pockets enjoyed having someone to converse with. I assumed it had much to do with the fact that I made every attempt to speak to him as an equal. I also thought his enjoyment might have been all the greater because I was an adult. I had gathered from our conversations about the place he called home, that no adults lived there. I assumed, in some way my attention to him took on a patriarchal role that filled a void in his life. Despite his enjoyment, however, Pockets would inevitably withdraw at any given point in our conversations. It was as if an invisible hand would arbitrarily reach out and yank him away from me.

I asked him about it. "You don't completely trust me, do you?"

"I'm not sure what you mean," he replied.

"Do you know what trust is?"

"Giving yourself to someone," he said, without hesitation.

This answer surprised me, and before I could think of anything to say, he said, "It is stupid to give one of the only things that I have."

I still wasn't sure about the story of the one-eyed men, and after dinner one evening, I asked Pockets about it. It was clear he thought it utterly remarkable that a man with my level of education wasn't familiar with it, but nonetheless he patiently summarized the story telling me it was about a brave sailor who became shipwrecked along with his crew in a dangerous, lawless land ruled by monstrous one-eyed men. After one of these monsters killed several of the crew and ate their brains, the sailor blinded the one-eyed murderer with a heated oak spear.

It was at this point I realized that he was relaying a section from the larger story of Odysseus and the Cyclops Polyphemus, but I said nothing. After he had finished, I asked him what he liked most about the story. The promptness of his answer told me that he had thought a lot about it. "It tells me that there are other places, besides here, where men who cannot fully see rule," he said.

"Are there other stories that you especially enjoy?" I asked him.

"Do you know the story of Alice and the rabbit?" he asked.

"Ah," I said, "now that one I know."

He grinned widely and recited, "Will you, won't you, will you, won't you, won't you join the dance."

He threw his head back and began to make his unusual sound. I began to laugh with him and, as I did, I remember thinking I had never felt happier in my life. Then suddenly my head was filled with excruciating pain. I grabbed my temples, began gasping, and crumpled to the floor. The last thing I heard, before passing out, was Pockets yelling for a nurse.

Hours later, after I had been sedated, the doctor, accompanied by the same two interns, paid me another visit and repeated his earlier routine of examining my eyes with his light. When he leaned over me this time I smelled after-shave lotion.

"What do you see?" I asked.

"The world and all its splendor," he muttered.

"What?"

"Shhh," he said, concentrating harder on my right eye.

After a while he stood up straight and nodded slowly to himself while jotting something down on my chart.

"What is it now?" I asked.

"The same, only more of it," he said.

"Am I going insane?" I asked.

He handed my chart to one of the interns. "Do you know who Gerard de Nerval is?" he asked.

"Beyond that he was a French writer, absolutely nothing," I said, becoming irritated with his allusiveness.

"Over a century ago," he said, "Monsieur de Nerval strolled down a Parisian sidewalk with a live lobster on a pale blue ribbon. 'Have no fear,' he told astonished passersby, 'he doesn't bark and he knows the secrets of the deep.'"

"That's insane," I said.

"Some people would certainly draw that conclusion," he returned.

"And?" I asked, confused and more irritated.

"Have you ever considered adopting a lobster for a pet?" he asked.

"No," I said. "Never."

"Then you're on safe ground."

After this second episode, I began having periodic headaches, sometimes quite severe, almost always preceded by odd precursor sensations. The headaches were debilitating to the point where I could do little more than lie in bed with a wet washcloth draped over my eyes so that no light could intensify my pain. My temples would methodically throb to a beat all their own, and a dry, nauseous sensation would spread through my nostrils and sinuses.

The slightest movement of my head would have the effect of producing little bouts of dizziness and disorientation. Lying as still as possible and, unable to concentrate on the simplest of thoughts, I would gently squeeze my eyelids tightly shut and while away the time observing the cascading luminous phosphenes and entoptics, my only form of diversion or entertainment. Inevitably, my headaches would follow the premonitions.

It always went like this: I would begin the day feeling fresh and remarkably lucid, and then, out of the blue, I would be struck by a crushing headache, but not before I experienced some sort of strange moment of precognition where I strongly sensed that something was going to happen.

Beyond a layman's simple awareness, I knew little of the merits or marvels of precognition. Perhaps like you, gracious reader, I had heard tales of remarkable synocratic occurrences and had experienced my own gentle hints at their alleged fantastic reach. Out of the blue, one thinks of a long forgotten schoolmate only to pick up a newspaper hours later to see his face in a photograph. Or, more commonplace, a cliché, one suddenly thinks of a close friend and moments later the telephone sounds, and it's that friend on the other end. These instances, of course, placed me in line with everyone who has wondered whether these little flukes were products of chance or design, and, if by design, whose design and why? But now, seemingly overnight, such fortuities, what some baptize small miracles, were occurring with increasing frequency and were taking on greater significance that made them impossible to take lightly or ignore. While reading a newspaper, I noticed a photograph of a ferryboat filled with regaling tourists and I felt a foreboding sense of imminent tragedy. The following week the same paper's headlines blared that the ferryboat had struck a submerged object and quickly sank, taking half its crew and all passengers to the bottom. Conversing one afternoon with another patient, a woman who was being treated for a relatively minor problem, I sensed strongly that she was about to die. As much as I tried to force the feeling away, it persisted, and two days later the woman passed away in her sleep from a long, undetected ailment. Other instances were less catastrophic. Sometimes what I sensed would be relatively simple, minor events. Two nights before Pockets disappeared, I had a vivid vision while talking with him of the two of us sitting amidst a huge pile of twisted metal. We were sharing a divided pastry and Pockets was grinning widely, his mouth covered with the pastry's fluffy crème filling.

Each such occurrence seemed to meld itself into an emerging pattern in my life. It was as if some unseen force was diligently directing the acts of my life and formatting them into a mysterious scheme that was leading to a secret, but grand, finale.

In hindsight, I now see that it all began several weeks prior to my becoming ill, but locked into my feverish work pace that allowed for little focus on anything else, I had taken no notice of it. The first such event occurred several weeks before my first episodic attack. I was sharing an austere dinner of boiled potatoes and green beans with the monks at the monastery. Evening meals, under the strict rules of their order, were one of the few times conversation was allowed. One would think that the laxity allowed would produce an aural state bordering on glossolalia or speaking in tongues, but this was not the case. Conversations, if you could call them that, were stilted and consisted of odd threadless utterances that seemed to originate from nowhere, having minimal connection to what was said before or after. It was weeks after having come there before I realized the monks, most of whom were elderly, were simply acting at doing what was expected of them, and that they had no actual interest in talking to one another.

That evening's dinner had come near the end of what had been an especially intensive work session for me, and I was nearly nodding off at the table. Outside, the wind was dying down from a fierce but brief thunderstorm that had blown through the area. I sat chewing a bite of hard, half-boiled potato thinking I had to get some sleep soon when someone said something like, "Well, one person's trash is another's treasure," to which another monk replied, "In every heap of misfortune, there is a dash of luck." But what I heard in my weary awareness was, "In that heap of trash, there is an unfortunate treasure."

Confused, I asked, "So, what is this unfortunate treasure?"

Amid blank looks of equal confusion, I thought it best to excuse myself. I went straight to my room where I intended to sleep. To let in the fresh night air, I opened the room's sole window and as I turned to undress I noticed in the distance, beyond the edge of the city, an incredible rainbow. The more complete end appeared to be centered directly over the location that I would come to know as the Heap. Dusk was fading into darkness and the lines of the sinking sun served to sharply accentuate the rainbow's colors. I watched them fade in sequence with the sun and then I lay down thinking how ironic that the proverbial pot of gold be positioned in a refuse dump.

The next morning, rested and refreshed, I sat down at my desk eager to resume work when the lamp that rested atop it, an old gooseneck fixture with a chipped, cobalt blue shade, began sporadically going off and on as if the power were about to fail, not an uncommon occurrence given the monastery's ancient electrical system. I sat back in my chair waiting for the inevitable, but the light remained glowing normally. When I leaned forward to begin working, it started flickering again. This process repeated itself several more times and I thought, Okay, what? What is going on here? The light blinked once as if acknowledging my question. I stood up and leaned over the desk and checked the cord leading into the fixture base and the wall, but found nothing out of place. As I was about to sit back down, I happened to look out the window situated high over the desk and I saw a dark colored, narrow plume of smoke rising from the spot that the rainbow had touched the previous evening. I watched as the smoke slowly rose higher and then curved downward forming a large question mark over the Heap.

At the same moment, the desk lamp began acting erratically again, this time in a repetitive, syncopated series of long and short flickerings. I counted them, three short followed by three longer ones, over and over, the international signal for distress and help. Within minutes, the questioning smoke plume dissipated and the flickering stopped. I sat back down at the desk thinking about what it meant, if anything at all.

The day after Pockets fled the hospital, I sat in the day room thinking again about the rainbow and the smoke. At this point in time, I had become keenly aware of such seeming random manifestations and their possible hidden meanings, and I felt more strongly than ever that something hugely significant was occurring in my life, but I hadn't a clue what. For weeks, the chain of coincidences and premonitions had been happening with regular frequency. Each morning, I would arise with a certain degree of apprehension about what the day would bring.

As I contemplated all of this, I looked out the dayroom's large window and again saw that smoke was rising from the same spot in the Heap. This time the long, tapered plume rose higher before curving downward and forming what appeared to be an arrow pointing squarely at the Heap's center. Somehow, I felt this was a signal, a secret sign that something hugely important was pending, and that I should be there where the arrow pointed. A week later, when I was discharged from the hospital, I went straight to the monastery, packed my few belongings, and called a taxi to come and deliver me to the Heap.

Day Two

This was a highly unusual day in the Heap. For the first time since my arrival, nearly two years ago, the Tire Boys failed to make their daily collection and were nowhere to be seen. From sunup to sundown, there was no movement about the entryway to the Burrow, except for the changing of the Watchers, and even that wasn't normal. Rather than the usual two Watchers, an extra had been added so that, regardless of rotating breaks, there was always a dual presence. Equally unusual, nobody from the Bottles and Cans Cabal or the Newspaper Nasties ventured outside to work all day. By midday, only four Ragpickers, a fraction of the usual number, somnambulistically moved about, but the other twenty or so remained inside. Even the Gardeners and Kitchen Krewe operated with far less than their customary numbers.

Something was amiss, but I didn't know what.

A little beyond midday, I went below to the Kitchen Krewe's tent for lunch. Because of the heat, I wasn't that hungry, so I helped myself to only a plump Asian pear and a small sprig of green grapes from one of the fruit trays. In line, with only a few children ahead of me, I asked for a single scoop of mashed potatoes and passed on everything else available.

"You need to eat more, Mr. Fantasy," said one of the servers, a boy called Blue, who I knew Pockets had been teaching to read. "You'll turn to nothing but skin and bones," he said, holding up another generous scoop, which I politely declined.

I poured myself a glass of apple juice from a dispenser at the end of the line, and walked to one of the many picnic-style tables, where I saw Humbatter and Fly, a member of the Tin Clan, sitting across from one another.

As I approached the table, I heard Humbatter say, "Right now, it's really none of your goddamned business. When we're ready to tell what we have, we'll tell everyone at the same time."

Fly, with his back to me, started to say something, but Humbatter caught his eye and then raised his toward me.

"I'm not interrupting anything, am I?" I asked.

"No, please sit with us," said Humbatter.

I joined them and began slicing the pear into sections. Humbatter had a sheepish look on his face and Fly fidgeted nervously with his fork.

"Not many people out working today," I said, biting into a juicy slice.

Neither boy said anything in response to my remark, and Humbatter began setting his utensils on his tray, preparing to leave. Fly looked over his shoulder, as if searching for someone in the tent.

"I haven't seen any Tire Boys out all morning," I said to Humbatter, and then turning to Fly, added, "Or anyone from the Tin Clan."

Both boys shrugged and nervously looked about.

"It doesn't take a genius to know that something's going on," I said.

"See, what'd I'd tell you," Fly said to Humbatter, smirking. "The entire Heap knows that you've found something."

"And what did I tell you?" Humbatter shot back. "I don't talk out of group. You know that."

Humbatter stood and picked up his tray.

"I've got to get back," he said, and then looking at me, "I'm sorry for what I said earlier."

"It's not a problem," I told him.

Under the unwritten rules of the Heap, work was conducted from sunrise to about noon. Then everyone sought shelter from the heat until the sun began its mid-afternoon descent. As the temperature became less intense, another four hours of work were accomplished. This went on like clockwork, six days a week with only Sundays set aside for personal chores and time off. Here, kind reader, you are probably wondering about religious observance—the short answer is that, in the organized sense, there wasn't any, but, like anywhere, the subject was not that simple. I had a brief conversation about it with Raoul not long after coming. He explained that while nobody in the Heap discouraged religious belief, neither did anyone encourage it. When I asked why, he said there was an unspoken consensus among the children that religion was a private, personal matter that was best practiced alone because some of the children had seen and experienced its destructive elements and lost family and loved ones in religious-inspired conflicts. "Some of us don't want to believe that God would allow hateful acts," Raoul said. "I mean no offense," he added, "but true religion is found in the heart and doesn't need a name or roof over it."

At another time, I spoke with Maxi about the subject, and he revealed that a good number of the children were too occupied with lingering past fears and wrongful things that had happened to them to give any real thought to religion. "A lot of us are more concerned about evil than we are God," Maxi remarked. He told me he believed evil came from demons that entered our world by attaching themselves to bad thoughts. "That's their doorway in," he explained. "It's the demons who come through that cause people to do bad things."

Holidays in the Heap were unknown, vacations unheard of. It was doubtful that any of the children adhered to any sort of printed calendar or that they would have understood their particulars. In the Heap, marking time revolved around the ancient practice of observing the sun. Without fail, the sun performed like a bell knelling or a whistle sounding workers to and from the job. While a good number of the children wore wristwatches, many which had ceased working long before they were strapped on, it was the path of the sun across the sky that dictated their routines. Like the Babylonians and Egyptians of long ago, the children divided daylight and nighttime into twelve sections each. During my many months there, I observed that productivity always rose sharply during the summer months because daylight hours were longer by a full hour or more.

Work was practically everything in the Heap. The Heap's entire social structure revolved around it, depended upon it, was synonymous with it. Work in the Heap was not divided along lines of class, caste, age, or sex. What was good for one child to do was good for all to do; there were no jobs that were above or beneath anyone. Nobody intentionally worked harder than anyone else; nobody intentionally worked less than anyone else. Work was shared equally and everything that came from work was shared in the same manner. The aim of work was not livelihood, advancement, mobility, or eventual retirement; it was simple survival.

Private possessions among the children were not discouraged or limited by design or any expressed political dictates, but by the needs of each child. If, for example, a child wanted to use his share of any proceeds from work for the purchase of an article of clothing from the city, that was the child's choice, and the article was his or hers to do with as he or she saw fit. Because the children had little exposure to the more overt elements and impacts of mass commercialism and consumerism through television, entertainment, and related peer pressures, material wants were few.

Work and survival in the Heap depended entirely upon the essence of the Heap itself, waste. Everything that was transported to the Heap was obsolete—things, large and small, in the eyes of their owners that were no longer useful, practical, needed, desired, or wanted. I'm sure by now, dear reader, that the supreme irony of the Heap has struck you—that the children nobody wanted were those who made best with and survived on the products that nobody wanted.

In my first few days living there, I observed that each child belonged to a tribal-like group organized around each particular enterprise it engaged. These groups over time developed fixed names. In all, there were seven. Of course, there were the Tire Boys who busied themselves with the seeming endless supply of discarded tires that arrived at the Heap. Daily they would scour the several drop off points and collect tires, separating them out by passenger and commercial, or heavy truck, grades, and by natural versus synthetic rubber. Certain tires, deemed unusable for any recycling route, would be painstakingly stripped of the two or three pounds of high carbon steel and bead wire. For reasons never explained, the Tire Boys, unlike any other group, had no females as members. Some of the Boys went about their routine wearing old shoulder pads so as to facilitate carrying multiple tires. Others among them, perhaps as a lark, wore salvaged crash helmets, many with dark-tinted visors, and old military helmets. Besides tires, the group also handled car and truck batteries, old refrigerators, heat pumps, air conditioning units, and infrequent deliveries of scrap metal and steel.

The Copper and Tin Clan, generally identifiable by the small straight cuts and slashes on their hands and forearms, were charged with one of the Heap's most labor intensive enterprises. It was not at all uncommon to see Clan teams of three or four children devote entire days to stripping out the copper from surplus wire and cable. Copper prices fluctuated wildly, but were nearly always a steady source of income. The Bottles and Cans Cabal, which was overseen jointly by Phaedra and Maxi, routinely gathered the massive amounts of plastic and glass bottles dumped at the Heap each day. Plastic bottles were separated out for processing through a large, antiquated, gas-driven compacter that noisily spat out square blocks that were stacked for recycling.

The Ragpickers, or Simple Sisters as they alternately called themselves, were informally divided into two sub-groups: one that scavenged and separated out the loads of used and discarded clothing, the other that, through the use of a dozen revamped sewing machines, either repaired some of the clothing or refashioned material into apparel that would be sold to merchants who came weekly from their marketplace operations. Perhaps, because of their specific enterprise, or for some other unknown reason, the Ragpickers group had several transvestites as members. Few in number, they were all in their mid-teens, and it was always entertaining to see them about the Heap dressed to the nines in colorful and outrageous clothing they had selected out and remade for themselves. The other children, with only a few minor exceptions, accepted the transvestites as fully-fledged members of the community and were always quick to come to their aid when delivery drivers would make fun of them and shout out cruel remarks.

The Newspaper Nasties, dubbed as such because of their ink

stained hands, operated one of the Heap's more lucrative businesses. Three times a week, huge deep-well dump trucks would arrive from the city filled with discarded newspapers, magazines, books, and cardboard. The trucks would back up beeping onto pitched concrete ramps and empty their loads into a row of six large metal bins situated at the Heap's southern-most corner. For reasons unknown, the Nasties tended to be more aggressive than the other groups. Disputes among them, minor or major, were almost always settled through physical means, often through boxing or wrestling matches conducted in accordance with rules set by the group itself. Many of the Nasties sported tattooed faces and arms, and they tended to dress, whenever possible, in leather, with black as their preferred color.

The Gardeners, the second smallest group numbering about fifteen, took care of the Heap's nutritional needs. Their expansive growing plots, situated on the northern end of the compound so as to take full advantage of the shifting sunlight and shade, consisted of multiple rows of tomatoes, potatoes, various melons and squash, and other vegetables. Flanking the squash rows were grapevines that were formed over arched, walk-through wooden trellises that ran about fifty meters in length. Running parallel with the grapevines were three rows each of apple and pear trees, and flanking them, but separated by a four-foot chain link fence, was a small pigsty that generally held no more than four or five snorting swine at a time. The Gardeners kept the sty delightfully mucky with waste-water and garbage from the cooking tent, and the contented, fly-haunted pigs, always caked in mud, never appeared a bit concerned about their pending fate. Easily identifiable by the large-brimmed straw hats they wore, the Gardeners were the most conservative of the Heap's groups. They tended to keep to themselves, and when they did mingle among others, rarely did they have much to say.

Out of necessity, the Gardeners sometimes worked closely with a group of about twenty-five children who referred to themselves as the Burners. They were the Heap's largest group and were responsible for preparing, cooking, and serving meals three times a day. The Burners, often called the Kitchen Krewe by others, were notoriously temperamental and volatile, but rarely did their angry outbursts move to the stage of physical confrontation. They were easily recognized by the paleness of their skin in comparison to the other children. This was because their work was performed out of the sunlight under the cover of three large canvas tents pitched together in a cluster. More often than not, the tents' side-flaps were rolled up so as to allow for natural ventilation. At the center of the main tent, which was where food was served and everyone gathered to eat, was a high, open canvas gable supported by corner and ridge posts. It was through this gable that the venting for three commercial-sized, propane-powered cooking stoves ran. The tents were within easy eyesight of my spot, about one hundred yards away, and sometimes I would watch the Burners go about their chores. Frequently while they worked, mostly in the morning hours, the Burners would spontaneously break out musically in a shout-and-call routine. The routine went like this: One child would kick it off by shouting out an impromptu, rap-style line, something like, "Oh, the stoves are hot, I say the stoves are so hot." And another child would then pick up the line by calling out, "She says the stoves are hot, so hot, but I say they're not," and several Burners would add a rhythm section to the chant by beating on pot bottoms with ladles and wooden spoons and add to the verse until soon the whole group was moving about Broadway-style, chanting and making a joyful noise while still accomplishing their culinary work.

Besides working together, each group also lived together in housing that was distinctively theirs. Overlooking their earthly enterprise, the Gardeners lived in an elaborately painted series of three-story dwellings from which they could survey their growing plots at will. Fashioned out of a dozen stacked twenty-and-forty foot transport and sea containers, each level of living space was connected and accessed by metal ladders attached to outer walls. The second and third levels had extended, thatched-roof verandas that held a wide variety of salvaged porch and beach furniture, and atop the third level of containers were four huge metal cisterns that served the purpose of capturing precious rain water. An elaborate system of color-coded plastic tubing ran from the tanks down the sides of the containers to the garden rows, grapevines, and trees. Rising also from the top level of containers was a row of twelve twenty-foot poles from which hung a series of colorful banners adorned with elaborate and intriguing symbols that resembled archaic and zodiacal signs of ages past, some vaguely familiar emblems of what once may have been a thriving but now lost symbiotic language. Similar banners could be seen scattered throughout the Heap gracing the shelters of other groups, but nowhere were they in such concentration. Raoul told me that the symbols were intended to ward away evil and the spirits and demons that the children believed dwelled in a nearby abandoned archeological site.

The Newspaper Nasties lived in the most makeshift of the Heap's shelters, a simple complex constructed out of heavy canvas supported by and draped over wood and bamboo supports. The complex was plainly designed with two rows of canvas-walled rooms both fronting a single corridor that led in both directions to the outside. A few strategically placed vinyl laminate patches combined with a thin membrane roof provided enough translucent light to illuminate the corridor during the daytime. At night, several strings of Chinese lanterns were used to light the corridor. The individual rooms were lighted according to each child's choosing. The rooms were small, just large enough for a bed, small dresser, and perhaps one or two chairs, and closed off to the corridor and sight by whatever curtains each child chose. Walking through the corridor, the place had an almost bazaar-like quality due to the multi-colors and designs of the many curtains.

The Tire Boys dwelled in a large complex, commonly called the Burrow, that was built partially underground out of a huge oval of hundreds of buried, sand-filled tires. Children who had taken part in its construction told me that it had taken a team of ten Tire Boys digging round-the-clock with picks and shovels nearly a month to excavate the submerged part of the Burrow, and another month to construct its outer shell out of wood-beam supported metal and tin plates welded together and covered with about three feet of earth and sand. Were it not for its demarcated entryway, and the six four-foot ventilation pipes and fan hoods protruding from the mound, one might have easily mistaken the Burrow for a naturally formed dune.

The members of the Bottles and Cans Cabal lived in a large geodesic dome called the Canard. The dome had been painstakingly constructed out of long, thin bamboo poles and reeds bent to form a large tension-compression arche. At its center, it stood nearly forty-feet-high. Its interior was eighty-feet-wide at any point of measurement. The structure rested on a foundation made out of thirty-six disused 18-inch wooden electrical-line poles with flooring laid atop a 2x4 radial beam and joist system set about three feet above ground level. How the children fashioned such a structure given the abstract mathematics involved and that few, if any, of them had any formal schooling, I don't know. Pockets told me that the Canard had taken only a few weeks to build and that Maxi had done all the initial design work. The dome's interior comfortably housed the Cabal's members, with each having a separate room, and provided ample common space. Natural light came primarily through a ring of twenty-four octagonal-shaped windows fashioned around the dome's centermost curve. At night, with multiple candles burning inside, the dome appeared like a giant glowing gem.

The Copper and Tin Clan members lived in a loose circle of tepees and yurt-like structures made from long poles and wooden latticework lashed together with leather ties and covered with heavy canvas and sheets of colored vinyl. Each of the six yurt-like shelters comfortably held three to four children, with each of the four tepees holding two. Similar in making to the traditional tepees of the tribes of North America, the children's tents were covered with random-sized pieces of hide sewn together in large, blanket-sized panels. The hide came from a small manufacturing plant on the outskirts of the city that processed goatskin for boots, belts and other products for export, and routinely hauled its waste to the Heap. The Clan's yurt-like structures, unlike those of the nomadic groups that invented them centuries ago, had fixed, or non-folding latticework, and each structure had an open center ring at its top for light and ventilation. During the rare times a rainstorm struck, the opening was covered over with a canvas flap. Four of the yurts, sometime after their construction and before my arrival, had been redesigned by having their outer, curved walls covered stucco-like with a thick layer of concrete mixed with sand. Before the concrete had been allowed to dry, several of the children had gathered hundreds of glass bottles of many colors, which they pushed into the wet mud until each bottle's flat bottom was flush with the wall. The overall effect, especially when the sunlight struck the walls in certain ways, was stunning.

The Ragpickers lived in the Heap's most unusual shelters, eight fifteen-foot lengths of concrete cylinder piping that were about eight feet in diameter. The pipes, which had been discarded from an irrigation project because they were cracked in places, had been tightly rolled together into a single row and then were held in place by five long stakes driven six-to-seven feet into the ground on each side of the row, preventing them from shifting or rolling apart. Left open at each end for entry, each section of pipe had been divided inside at its center point by a wall made out of wood so as to fashion each tube into a duplex shelter that housed either two or more children. The outside of the eight huge cylinders had been painted with every color and design imaginable, from giant birds in flight to whirling wheels of fire, using whatever paint and dyes that were available.

The Burners lived in the Heap's most conventional living space, a two-story building that closely resembled the type of basic barn widely found throughout the English countryside and the rural parts of North America. The building, about forty-feet long by twenty-five feet wide, was made out of rough-milled planks, two-by-fours, and plywood sheathing. Its pitched roof was covered with corrugated tin. The first level of the building's interior was divided into about eight small rooms and its second level was left open, dormitory style. Surrounding the Burner's building on three sides was a very odd and immense collection of metal remnants that appeared as if they had been welded together by a madman. There were married parts of all sorts, positioned into surrealistic designs, including a varied collection of over three hundred hubcaps that had been welded to the twisted and rusted sections of old metal gates and attached at odd angles onto crisscrossed lengths of aluminum poles. Other remnants were welded atop one another and reached heights over forty feet. Particularly noticeable was a towering, disjointed piece that consisted of numerous old tire rims and axels welded tightly together in such a way that they appeared like a bizarre model of the DNA double helix. Another high-reaching work consisted wholly of lengths of rebar bent and twisted into the stick-like figures of ten acrobats standing atop one another joined by either a single hand or foot with their free appendages precariously extended for balance.

About forty meters behind the Burners' shelter, near the fence surrounding the Heap, were two long wooden sheds placed side-by-side on cinder blocks. These were the Heap's latrine and showers. The latrine, accessed by wooden steps and swinging, screen doors at both ends of the building, consisted of two long plastic, trough-like urinals and a series of eight, shuttered stalls holding toilets. Placed at each exit, was a deep-well utility sink with a large, square mirror above it. The shower shed held a row of ten open stalls, four with curtains, and two ancient, claw-legged bathtubs.

Each of the Heap's groups maintained a simple hierarchy made up of one leader, informally appointed through consensus, serving without title at the pleasure of the group, removable at any time by a simple majority. As you might have expected, most of the group leaders tended to be older children. The group leader's primary function was to direct work activities and he or she could delegate duties related only to work, but also bore complete responsibility for the group's productivity as a whole or the lack of it. Group leaders performed this role without any additional compensation. The expectation was that everyone understood that leaders were needed for the good of the Heap and that everyone was ready to serve in the role any time they were asked.

Decisions that needed to be made that concerned one group were made solely by its affected members and were not subject to review by any other group or person. Any major decision that cut across all groups was made through the formal assembly of the members of all groups who would then vote on such matters as presented to them. A simple majority decided everything. Such assemblies were called Gatherings and they were always announced at least eight hours in advance by the raising of a light blue streamer on the flagpole that stood at the Heap's center. Attendance at a Gathering was not mandatory, but rarely did anyone miss one. The reason for this may have been because inevitably after business was concluded, Gatherings quickly evolved into large parties or celebrations that lasted late into the night. I, however, believed that all the children were genuinely concerned with the well-being of the Heap and wanted to partake in any decision that related to it. Besides, the celebrations that always followed Gatherings, there was one other event that the children greeted with a high level of welcomed anticipation.

This was the Game. A unique mixture of team handball, pelota, soccer, bicycle racing, and I am sure a few other sports I've overlooked, the Game was played for what the children considered high stakes. Game times consisted of four thirty-minute quarters. Winning teams had to score at least five points within regular time, with a sudden death period of ten-minutes played for ties. Each victorious player would be awarded a handsome cash prize drawn from a pool of funds set aside by the Council. Because of its duration—never less than three hours with breaks and time-outs, often more than five—it was always played on a Sunday. The last Game I watched began about noon and lasted until almost sunset. The rules of the Game called for three teams of twelve children each. Each team was composed of four Riders, and an equal number of Blockers and Cleaners. Generally, an equal number of boys and girls were Riders and Cleaners, with mostly older boys playing as Blockers because of the severity of the position. Substitutions were allowed in any of these three categories, but only during official time-out periods, or when a player became disabled and required assistance to be taken off the playing area. That area was composed of all the Heap's common spaces that formed a loose, winding circle around its interior, covering a good half-mile of ground. The only real boundaries for the area were the Heap's encompassing fence. Teams were distinguished from each other by the wearing of solid-colored white, black, or red shirts.

Ostensibly, each of the three teams were pitted against each other, but one team, unknown to the other two as well as spectators, was secretly aligned with one of the two teams. The secretly aligned team was charged with doing everything possible, without giving away its status, to assist its assigned team. Besides competing under the regular rules of the Game, it was the task of the unaligned team to identify as quickly-as-possible which team was covertly assisting the other. This was done by the identifying team's captain making an official declaration, however, the captain had but one opportunity to do so. If he or she was wrong, the surreptitious team was then merged into its aligned team, thus doubling the number of opponents faced by the declaring team. If the captain was correct, the identified team was withdrawn from the playing area for the duration of the Game.

The Game began with all Riders mounted on their bikes— retrofitted mountain and racing bicycles equipped with special leg and face guards—and Cleaners taking up positions at a pre-selected starting point on the playing area. When a whistle sounded, the Cleaners had exactly five-minutes to proceed onto the playing area where they would do all that they could to create obstacles and hazards for the Riders. Generally, this involved dragging various objects from the Heap's refuse piles onto the area.

After this five minute period, the Riders would begin racing toward a point, generally about halfway round the playing area, where a game-ball, similar to that used in team handball, was placed on the ground. The Riders could only pick-up and handle the ball with a scoop-shaped wicker basket attached to one of their arms. After scooping up the ball, a team's Riders would attempt to advance it toward a goal-net where they would have to place the ball in order to score a point. Riders were allowed to pass the ball to one another and team Riders not in possession of the ball were allowed to intercept or steal the ball at any time it was in play. Once Riders were on the playing area, Cleaners were allowed to only reposition those objects already placed on the area. Further adding to the difficulty of the Game, was that at any point along the way toward the net, Riders would encounter the opposing team's Blockers who, through the use of only their hands and bodies, were allowed to interfere with a Riders forward progress. Blockers for the team in possession of the ball were used primarily to prevent this interference and to assist scoring. Additionally, Blockers were not allowed to touch the ball in any way and if they did, their team would forfeit a point. To add to the overall rigors and excitement of the Game, pre-game crews of children would position carefully constructed ramps and jumps along the playing track so as to provide Riders with better means for avoiding havoc and the means to gain better speed.

As you might imagine, due to the rough nature of the Game, all team members wore whatever protective gear they could glean from the Heap, and the resultant styles were sometimes surrealistic and a bit comical. Some Blockers wore aluminum cooking trays fashioned to belts as chest guards and split sections of PVC plastic piping as shin and arm protectors.

Wholly taken in by its spectators—which were never lacking in numbers—the Game was a sight to behold. Each team even maintained its own cheerleading squad, and it wasn't uncommon for small verbal and physical altercations to break out among the more rabid fans. To heighten the drama of the Game, recorded music was played at crucial moments in efforts to viscerally supplement moods and emotions.

Despite that I was there for nearly two years, it was difficult to know exactly how many children resided in the Heap. At the last Gathering, I counted a little over two hundred and thirty children, but that had not included Watchers who were on duty at the time or the full compliment of the Burners. The Heap's children were of several races, many of mixed races, and were pretty much divided down the middle by sex. The ages of the children ranged from four years old to the early teens. Many of the very young were children of those in their teens, some the result of sexual assaults that had occurred prior to their coming, a few others the offspring of Heap couples, although that was not common.

Order in the Heap was maintained through an unwritten code that, with a few exceptions, reflected the golden rules. Included among the exceptions was the prohibition of drugs, but on special occasions, such as post-Gathering parties, alcohol and marijuana were allowed. For the children who arrived in the Heap hopelessly addicted to dendrite, or glue, the substance was allowed, if approved by a group leader, and then only if the person addicted could perform regular work in the same fashion as others.

Punishment for violation of major rules was swift. Banishment, permanent expulsion from the Heap, was the most severe form of punishment. Short of banishment, punishment for breaking major rules could range from having to forfeit a prized possession or being confined to one's quarters for an extended period of time, with no contact allowed with anyone. Other minor infractions resulted in the offender being docked part of his or her pay or having to make a public apology.

Unlike those who remained on the streets in the city, very few of the Heap's children were glue users. Humbatter's younger brother, Nike, was perhaps the saddest case of dendrite addiction. Nike was a beautiful child with eyes so dark that his irises and pupils were near invisible. His glue habit left him always slack jawed and glassy-eyed with dried snot caked in layers around his nostrils and mouth. Abandoned by his mother when he was only three, he had been raised by Humbatter. Older by less than two years, Humbatter had adopted his nickname after watching a televised baseball game one day while still living on the city's streets and mistakenly concluding that the crowd's repetitive chant was the name of the glorified player who won the game. When the brothers were on the streets, Nike found that glue sniffing provided a quick escape from constant hunger and fear. Pockets said to me one day, "For Nike, glue is like Alice's magic bottle, it takes him wherever he wants to go." By the time Humbatter realized his brother had a serious problem, Nike was using about eight tubes a day and had suffered irreversible brain damage. Toluene, a primary ingredient of many glues sold commercially, as had been once explained to me, is a highly addictive, colorless, aromatic hydrocarbon that goes directly to the central nervous system producing a disoriented but apparently welcomed state.

Every morning while I lived in the Heap, I would watch the sun rouse itself from the sand's edge and effortlessly assume its prominence above where it belligerently lumbered uncaring of everything below. Artists and photographers have favorite spots where they go to capture a certain point of light, a singular confluence of nature, the elements, and the sun. Monet had his idyllic Giverny; Walter Spies, on a visit to Bali was so captivated by the magical light there that he never left; others, like Gauguin, also ventured far from home to places like Oceania to find it. Few would have ever thought to journey to the Heap's region to view anything other than its cultural or hedonistic pleasures, but there was a moment (and it really was but a fleeting moment, so sudden that I sometimes wondered if my eyes were playing a trick on me) when the morning sun nudged the night away and a shimmering shade of blue appeared that was at once so full of melancholy and promise that it pulled at the heart. Each morning I rose to witness this moment, often missing it with a mere blink of my eyes, but when I did see it, it was like a natural baptism that brought an overwhelming sense of renewal and made everything right for a while.

From a distance, in the shifting light of day, the Heap's haphazard arrangement, splashed across about thirty perfectly flat hectares, took on striking phantasmal shapes. I can only imagine the reaction of someone unknowing of its purpose upon having spotted its abstract formations. Rising above the sand as if formed by a gigantic hand, its shapes ignited timeless shared memories, summoning images of ages long past. The Heap's water system, devised originally to control dust, but then ingeniously converted by the children to greater elevations on turned I-beams and banded lengths of PVC piping to capture precious rainwater, loomed like a hallucinatory Roman aqueduct. The compound's many mounds of concrete and stone rested heavily like Cyclopean walls; its stacked metal and steel from afar appeared like a mad Mayan temple; its small mountains of compressed aluminum and plastic like some crumbling, long abandoned Albigensian fortress. In the dwindling twilight, the whole of the Heap's mass seemed like some futuristic outpost dropped into the middle of nowhere, a mirage-like image floating on a sea of sand with only a heated cobalt sky as backdrop.

Like much that happens in this part of the world, the Heap came about spontaneously. No act of planning, or official decision, created it; no apathetic bureaucrat decreed that its arid acreage be designated a rubbish ground; no forward thinking planner decided it needed to be born. Airy Bender, whose disjointed dwelling sat just meters away from the Heap's main gates, was fond of saying that the Heap came about as a result of the Big Bang theory.

"One nanosecond it wasn't," he would say, "the next, abracadabra, presto, there it was."

But Airy, as you shall soon learn, was prone to exaggeration and histrionics. Most likely, the Heap's origins were far more mundane. I envisioned that its humble genesis occurred one day long ago when a rickety, donkey-drawn cart laden with trash stopped at the spot only because it seemed as good as any for dumping its burden—not a bang, but an uneventful thump. And then eventually, along came another cart to add to the pile and then another and another, until this once vacant patch of coppery earth was transformed into something never intended by anyone. And then, as if to cement the fortuitous founding, more and more carts came along, and then larger wagons, and then rambling, overfilled pick-up trucks, and then the eight-and-twelve wheel tractor trailers and cumbersome motorized compactors that with grinding, straining groans heaved out their loads.

The absurdity of my decision to come to the Heap didn't strike me until after the taxi dropped me off at its main gates.

"Are you sure this is where you want to get out?" the driver asked, as I counted out the fare. Slowly pulling away, he shook his head, eyeing me in his rearview mirror as if at any moment I would regain my senses and wave him back.

I stood staring at the chained gates realizing I didn't have a clue as to how to gain entry. The dense-meshed fence that enclosed the Heap was six-feet high and topped with rolls of tightly wound razor wire. It was midday Sunday, horribly hot, and not a soul was in sight anywhere. I wiped my brow of perspiration, and after a moment decided to sit on my bag and wait for something to happen.

Just a few meters from where I was, inside the chained gate, stood a small wooden guardhouse with a sole window without glass. A rectangular hand-lettered sign above the window read: ALL VEHICLES MUST STOP HERE. The guardhouse was angled in such a way as to provide its occupant with a clear view of anything approaching and passing through the gates. As I squinted against the harsh sunlight, I was able to make out someone peering out the window. It appeared to be a man, but oddly his chin barely cleared the bottom sill. I looked back at him, thinking he could not have been more than four feet tall. Perhaps, I thought, he was a small child, but I knew that most likely was not the case because he was totally bald with extremely bushy red eyebrows and a knobby nose that looked to be the survivor of one too many clobberings.

I watched as the man turned from me and exited the back door of the guardhouse. Obvious now, the man was a dwarf. Despite the open window, he fetched a key from his pocket and locked the door. In the light, he looked to be at least my age, if not a good decade older.

When he began to walk away, I stood and called out to him and asked if it would be possible to come inside and speak to someone in authority.

"Someone will be along soon, be patient," he said, and then waddled off in the direction of several tall stacks of flattened cardboard, disappearing around a corner.

I didn't have to wait long. Within minutes, the voice of a child called out, "Why are you here?"

I looked about, saw nobody, and replied by introducing myself and answering, "I've come here to live."

There was a pause and then the single word, "Why?"

Confronted for the first time with having to explain aloud my decision, I must admit, was quite disconcerting. I thought for a moment with all sorts of answers coming to me. I looked about again and still saw nobody.

"Because it seems the right thing to do," I answered.

Right away my answer struck me as wholly inadequate, but what was I to say? That I had witnessed a peculiar plume of smoke that in a roundabout way told me to come?

After another long silence, a young girl, followed by an even younger boy, stepped from behind a large stack of blocks consisting of compressed plastic bottles. The two slowly approached the gate where they stopped. The girl had an oval face beautifully framed by dark hair. A vicious, jagged scar ran from her forehead, like a bolt of lightning, across one eye and her lips to her chin. From her left earlobe a large silver hoop dangled. She was wearing a soiled dark blue dress with faded azure flowers on the fabric and a pair of green rubber boots that reached to her knees.

The girl stood looking at me and then gracefully moved her left leg out about a foot from her right, set her right hand on the back of her waist and cocked her hip in an exaggerated way, moving her head forward at what appeared to be an uncomfortable angle. She stood perfectly still holding the pose.

The boy, who appeared oblivious to the girl's movements, was dressed in a pair of tattered cut-off denim pants and a torn, sleeveless t-shirt that bore the single imprinted word, *Actually*. One of his bony arms was covered with tattoos depicting a series of odd interconnected geometric designs. He could not have been any older than five or six. His companion, still holding her pose, was older by at least two years. When he saw me looking at him, he shyly moved behind the girl.

After about a minute, the girl broke her pose and motioned me forward with a wagging index finger. I moved a few steps to stand nearer the fence. The two appraised me for what seemed like a long time and then the girl nodded to the boy and he took off running back in the direction from where they had come, quickly disappearing around a large stack of thick cardboard.

I looked at the girl, who was eyeing me suspiciously, and smiled stepping closer to the fence. A look of sheer panic crossed her face and she held up her hand in a clear sign for me to stop, and furiously shook her head.

Following another ten minutes or so, with me awkwardly standing before the girl, the boy came sprinting back. Panting, he stood on his tiptoes and whispered something into the girl's ear. She nodded to him again and he looked at me and said, "Stay there." Then they both ran off, the girl casting a quick glance back at me.

I stood there until the sun began to sink from its high point and my legs began to feel weak and wobbly from the heat. My thirst was fierce and I reprimanded myself for not having thought to bring any bottled water. I moved a few steps away from the fence and sat down again on top of my bag wishing I had worn a hat to keep the top of my head from burning, as I felt it doing already.

When the sun began to tuck itself into the horizon, the girl accompanied by another boy, this one older than she by several years, returned. Walking alongside the boy was a huge black dog with mournful golden eyes. The boy held a canteen dangling from a webbed belt and, after the girl had opened the gate, he motioned for me to enter. After I did, he handed me the canteen and said, "Drink." The dog didn't make a sound when I reached for it, but drew protectively closer to both children eyeing me carefully.

I guzzled half the canteen's warm but refreshing water and thanked the boy profusely. In his other hand he held an old top hat that had an eight-inch crown with a slightly curled brim. He handed me the hat, which I accepted but hesitated to put on. He gestured that I should wear it. The hat fit quite well and I wondered if its correct sizing was a matter of design or chance.

The boy motioned to the girl and she took off running again. He picked up my bag and said, "Follow me."

With the dog trailing us, we walked past the piled cardboard and compressed blocks of plastic and across an open area with a tall, leafless olive tree at its center. A few meters beyond the tree we veered left and moved past a long line of various-sized engine blocks resting atop wooden palettes. The engine blocks were followed by more and larger palettes that served as the bases for numerous stacks of 8, 12, and 24-volt batteries. After these, there were multiple rows of neatly arranged tires sorted by size and type. Each row appeared to stretch a good hundred yards deep.

Continuing past the tire rows, we crossed another large open space crisscrossed with the tracks of heavy trucks and came to a towering stack of corrugated metal that rose about twelve meters above us and was at least fourteen meters wide. Looming at the center of this stack was a huge hydraulic crusher. Approaching the shaded area below the crusher, we ascended a set of winding metal stairs that led to a suspended catwalk. We crossed the catwalk to a welded metal platform that held an old cargo van. The van had been stripped of its wheels and chassis, and rested solidly atop a short stack of compressed colored slabs, each no more than a foot or so thick. The slabs appeared to have once been automobiles. The boy pulled the two rear doors of the van open and motioned me to go in. He followed me inside.

"You'll stay here," the boy said.

The van's interior was the size of a small bedroom and contained only a bare, but clean, single-size mattress positioned in one corner and a wooden nightstand next to it. On top of the nightstand were a small water glass and several packages of plastic eating utensils.

The perfect décor were I a Trappist monk, I thought.

"Someone will bring you sheets for the mattress," the boy said, setting my bag next to the bed.

I thanked him again and asked, "What's your name?"

"Maxi," he answered.

As he turned to leave, he uttered something unintelligible to the black dog that had remained standing just inside the van's doors. The animal watched him descend the metal stairs and then sighed heavily and slowly sank to its haunches looking at me as if to say, "What now, my friend?"

I sat on the edge of the mattress. The van's interior was surprisingly cool and I thought it was mainly due to the way it was cocooned amid the piled metal. I opened my bag, fumbling around inside for a packet of butter biscuits I had packed. I pulled out my worn Breviary book and this journal I write in now, at the time empty, purchased in the hospital's commissary, and set them on top of the nightstand. I found the packet, extracted two biscuits, and began nibbling one and tossed the other to the dog. He let it land in front of him, put his head down and cautiously sniffed it. Satisfied, he took it in his mouth, chewed it twice, swallowed it whole and then sat looking expectantly at me.

"So, you like those," I said to him, pulling another from the packet. I held the biscuit out to him but he refused to leave his spot. I tossed it over and he caught it easily in his large jaws. This time he chomped more thoughtfully before swallowing.

I slid open the nightstand's only drawer and was about to place the remaining biscuits in it when I noticed a small gray lump in a rear corner. I prodded the lump with a finger and saw that it was a long dead and desiccated field mouse. Locked into a fetal position, its eyes were gone. Its tiny skull, with pointed nose, reminded me of a miniature seventeenth century physician's mask.

About an half hour later, after the sun had near completely set and the dog had lain down and begun to softly snore, I looked up from my resting place on the mattress and saw two girls standing at the van's still opened back doors.

One of the girls, the taller of the two, had long, bright red braided hair. Each braid at its end held a short length of copper wire wound around the bundled hair. In turn, each twisted length of copper had been threaded through a series of multi-colored beads. She wore a stained, sleeveless, brown leather vest that was zipped closed with nothing visible underneath. Her bare arms were alabaster with a tint of sunburn and a splash of freckles. Below the vest was a vibrantly colored long skirt that appeared to have been made from the patchwork of several Moroccan-style cotton blankets. The long straps of the leather sandals she wore disappeared into the edge of her skirt.

The other girl had short, dark hair cut in a pixyish style, visible only from the front under a bright, lime green headscarf. She was more plainly dressed than her companion, wearing a long-sleeved, black t-shirt and a dark red sarong that reached her ankles. On her feet she wore a simple pair of rubber beach-style sandals. I noticed right away that she avoided any eye contact with me, but was careful to watch my every move. Both girls appeared to be about the same ages, which I estimated to be the early teens.

The red-haired girl nodded at me and held up two folded sheets and a pillow that had an empty brass candleholder atop it.

"Come in, please," I said, standing.

They entered somewhat timidly. I reached down and picked up the biscuit packet from the crate's top and offered each of them one. Behind me I heard the dog, now quite awake, make a sound like he was clearing his throat. I tossed him another biscuit, which he expertly snatched out of the air.

"What's the dog's name? I asked the girl with the red braids.

"He doesn't have a name," she said.

"Then how do you call him?" I asked.

"We don't," she said, "he's always here."

"I see."

"I'm Phaedra," she said, "and this is Sayu. Would you like help with the sheets?"

"I think I can manage."

"You've come from the city?" she asked, nodding towards its general direction.

"In a way," I told her. "I'm actually from London."

Her brow momentarily tightened, and I realized it was possible that she knew nothing of the part of the world I was from.

"It's a city a long way from here," I said. "A completely different world."

Phaedra set the sheets on the corner of the mattress, selected one, shook it out, and with Sayu assisting, placed it tightly to the mattress.

When they began fitting the top sheet, Phaedra said, "People always say that there are different worlds in this world, but they're wrong."

"Yes," I said, "of course. I meant it only as an expression."

"When people are young," she continued, "they say they know when they really know nothing. And when they grow old, they say, 'Oh, I just don't know anymore,' when they never knew to begin with."

She pulled her side of the top sheet tightly so that it didn't show the slightest of ripples and nodded to Sayu to do the same with the lower section.

"Where is the wisdom that people say age brings?" she asked. "Maybe that wisdom is knowing only that it's not here, in this world. It's funny, but I know that my world is the same world that we all live in, only a different part of it."

She expertly folded the top part of the sheet back and tucked it beneath the mattress. Then she turned toward me and said, "Don't you think?"

I didn't know how to respond, nor do I think I even thought about it. There was a quality in the way that Phaedra spoke that made me want to hear more. She could have been saying anything, reading instructions from an insect repellant label, and I would have been perfectly content to listen. Her singular inflections carried a mix of learned gaiety and solemn seriousness that sounded as if they were threaded directly through the core of truth itself. I must confess that throughout my years in the Heap, I often made excuses to engage Phaedra in conversation just so that I could hear the music of her voice.

Phaedra smiled at me and said, "We'll go now."

I thanked them for their help and told them they had been most kind.

Phaedra moved toward the doors with Sayu following and then stopped.

"You'll need candles for reading after dark," she said, eyeing my two books on the nightstand. "The Red Dwarf will be by later with some for you."

I thought right away of the man I had seen exit the guardhouse, and as if reading my thoughts, she added, "That's the man you saw earlier at the front gate."

As Phaedra spoke, a startling, strange sound filled the air. It was a loud sustained, hollow sounding groaning punctuated by several pinging sounds similar to those made by an underwater sonar device. Sayu drew closer to Phaedra with a look of fear.

I must have also looked frightened, because Phaedra gave a small laugh and said, "It's nothing to be alarmed about. It's only the metal below us adjusting to the night's changing temperature. It happens almost like clockwork."

She looked at Sayu and explained, "Some of us here think it is something else."

"It is an odd sound," I said.

"Some think that when the sun goes down, spirits rise up from the sand to have their ways in the night."

"I see."

"I would think that a priest wouldn't believe in such things."

"Not all of us are the same," I said.

"Is there anything else that you need," Phaedra asked.

"No, I'm fine. You've been a great help."

I watched them descend the stairs and then looked at the dog that sat looking up at me.

"No name, eh," I told him. "Well, from nothing comes something. How about I call you Nameless?" He yawned widely and set his enormous head down and closed his eyes to sleep. *Hearing no objection*, I thought, *Nameless it shall be.*

Soon I learned that Phaedra had come to the Heap with the original group three years before. She was eleven years old then, having already survived six years on her own. On the streets, after having been abandoned by her mother, she had started out selling flowers that she would steal from the marketplace and the spacious atrium of a large central city hotel. She used the meager amount of money she earned for food.

When she wasn't able to steal flowers, she sold herself. A taxi driver one night had invited her into his car to escape a torrential downpour, and that was how it began. It provided her more money than did flowers, but she hated it. Sometimes the men she was with would do things to intentionally hurt her, things to make her cry, to bring out the child in her. She understood that what they did was perverse but couldn't comprehend why they did it. When it happened, in her mind she would go someplace else, someplace safe and pure where things like that never happened.

One day on the streets, Phaedra met Sayu, her closest friend in the Heap. Sayu was a year younger than Phaedra and had been on her own for only three months. Nobody was sure what had happened to her parents. She had been in the city for only a few months, after an uncle had sold her to a vegetable merchant who also peddled the illicit services of young girls on the side. After only a few days living in a converted horse stall with three other girls, Sayu ran away. Having come from a small village deep in the countryside, she found the city to be an unfathomable din of disorder and was immensely intimidated by its corruption. Most likely she would have never survived its indignations had Phaedra not taken her under a protective wing.

For young girls, life on the streets was extremely risky, and Phaedra and Sayu decided they would be safer by living together in a large, abandoned, wooden crate near the city central marketplace. But on their third night living there, three boys drunk on alcohol and high on glue, crawled into the container and tried to rape them. Phaedra began pounding one of the boys with a glass vase, while Sayu screamed for help. At the moment two of the boys grabbed hold of Phaedra's arms, another charged into the container and struck one of the attackers with a length of two-by-four board. Bleeding from his head, the youth fled leaving his two companions behind cowering in fear at the one who confronted them with the board and a fearsome looking machete hanging from his belt. When the two scrambled out the doorway and ran off, the boy told Phaedra and Sayu his name was Maxi and that he was part of a large group that lived nearby in a disused warehouse. A boy who Maxi referred to as "the Teacher" was the group's leader. He told Phaedra and Sayu that they would never be safe alone in their container and that they should come with him to the warehouse where they could live without fear of harm. At the warehouse, Phaedra learned that the group's leader, Raoul, or "the Teacher" as some called him, tolerated no violence within the group and dealt harshly with anyone who violated the group's code of conduct. Phaedra also learned that Maxi only used his machete for cutting and carving intricate, small rain sticks, slide whistles and flutes out of bamboo shoots that he sold in the city's marketplaces. Maxi was a true artisan, a natural talent with a remarkable sense of design, but an enigma to those around him. He kept to himself, disappeared for days at a time, spoke softly and little and only when necessary, or when he offered kind words and encouragement to Phaedra whom he felt entered his life in a preordained way—a way that a power beyond all comprehension had fully intended and directed. After Phaedra came to the warehouse, she began hand painting the rain sticks and flutes for Maxi. During the region's tourist high seasons, their creations sold faster than they could make them. It had been Phaedra's idea for them to begin making finely detailed orchids out of painted balsa wood they salvaged from a small toy factory. But when the group came to the Heap, their supply of wood was gone, so they switched over to the harder task of making their flowers out of copper and metal wire and sold them to middlemen.

Even in the Heap, Maxi was a mystery to everyone except perhaps Phaedra. Before joining Raoul's warehouse group, he had briefly lived among the Tunnel Kids, an elusive band of about fifty children that dwelled in parts of the system of storm drains and sewers that catacombed beneath the city. The tunnels emptied into two narrow but deep tributaries that dead-ended into the region's only large body of water, a lake that was so darkly colored and still that it could be mistaken for a tar pit. Beyond pale, the tunnel dwellers were the most feared of all the city's street children, not because of any particular nefarious activity they carried out or level of violence they enacted, but because of the rumored dreadful bacteriological diseases and flesh-eating parasites they were said to carry in their bodies. The number of physical deformities found among their numbers seemed to bear this out. And after one report concerning a young girl giving birth to a baby with two brainless heads took flight and spread throughout the city, the group's status was elevated to mythical heights. The rumor was spurred wider by reports of sightings of dogs that ran with the Tunnel Kids that had fangs that would put a walrus to shame. By most accounts, Maxi, when he was about ten years of age had somehow found freedom from an orphanage run by one of the area's charity groups, and had only spent three or four months among the Tunnel Kids before joining Raoul's group. Beyond this, scant information was known about him, except for what he may have shared with Phaedra.

Coming to the Heap provided Phaedra with the real sanctuary she had longed for on the streets, but by then she was wise beyond her years. Like all of the Heap's children, her youth had been stripped away well before she could experience any sense of childhood wonderment. Still not an adult, she straddled a twilight state that teetered on brutal cynicism and sheer escapism. It was Phaedra who gave me the sobriquet Mr. Fantasy, after she remarked during my first week in the Heap that in my top hat I looked like a magician.

"A real Mr. Fantasy," she had quipped.

Not long after Phaedra and Sayu had left the van, the Red Dwarf arrived holding three large candles. I was sitting on the edge of the mattress reading my evening prayers from my Breviary.

Standing at the van's doors, he said, "Am I interrupting?"

"No," I said, setting the book aside. I stood. "Please, come in."

"I trust you find the accommodations to your liking."

"It's much more than I expected."

"The ambiance, I'm sure, has you in absolute wonderment," he said.

"And some have the nerve to call it a dump," I said, smiling.

"I've brought you the means of illumination," he said, handing me the candles.

"I'd offer you something," I told him, "but as you can see I'm still setting up house here."

"Then allow me," he said, withdrawing a small brown bottle from his back pocket.

I picked up the glass from the nightstand and held it out. He poured a healthy amount of a light greenish liquid into it.

I sniffed at the liquid and found the smell to be earthy with a hint of menthol. I looked over at Nameless who was now awake and closely watching our every move.

"What is it?" I asked.

"Ah, if you really need to know, it's the nectar of the gods. Trust me, try it."

I took a small sip and found it bitter. I took another and felt a pleasant sensation spread through my body.

"That's very good. Bitter, but good."

"Absinthe," he said. "With a touch of vermouth, a dash of sugar, and a few other things better left unsaid."

I took another sip. It tasted a little better now.

"Better than church wine, eh, Father."

"Please, Gabriel will do just fine."

"By the way," he said, holding out a small hand, "For want of a better name, I'm the Red Dwarf."

I told him I was pleased to meet him, shook his hand, and properly introduced myself. His grasp was rock solid and for a moment I knew that he could easily crush my hand if he ever felt so inclined.

"So, you were the one at the hospital," he said.

"My reputation precedes me," I said, taking another drink from my glass.

"Pockets spoke highly of you, but I must say your coming here is a surprise to everyone," he said.

"No more than to myself."

"Life can be just one thing after the other," he said.

"Is Pockets here?"

All at once I felt very lightheaded, but strangely at peace with the world. I sat down on the edge of the mattress and set my glass on the nightstand.

"Oh, yes. I'm sure you'll see him tomorrow," he said. "Are you alright?

"Yes, I'm fine. Just a little tired is all."

I leaned down and fumbled to untie my shoes and take them off.

"Here," the dwarf said, ceremoniously waving a hand in front of him. He held up a long kitchen match, fired it with a snap of a thumbnail, and set it to one of the candlewicks.

"Let there be light," he said, setting the lighted candle in the holder.

When I looked back up to thank him, he was gone.

The next morning, following a fitful night's sleep, I awoke to the sight of Nameless sitting next to my mattress looking at me with long globules of drool hanging from his substantial jowls. I sat up and looked at the still fresh candle in the holder and wondered who had put it out.

I slipped on my socks and shoes, and Nameless gently tapped me with one of his huge paws and looked at the few remaining biscuits on the nightstand.

"Breakfast is served," I said, holding one out to him. He carefully took it from my fingers and moved to his spot near the doors where he sat and ate it.

I didn't hear Maxi come up the metal stairs. When I looked up from reading my morning prayers, he was standing at the van's opened doors watching me with Nameless standing beside him.

I stood up, and he said, "The Council is waiting for you."

"The Council?" I asked.

"Come with me, please."

I started out of the van but Maxi stopped and motioned to my head.

"You'll need your hat," he said. "It is very hot today."

I went back and grabbed the top hat, put it on, and with Nameless leading, followed Maxi down the winding stairs. He was as tall as I was, an inch or two below six feet, and gristly thin. His hair was jet black and knotted thick and tightly to his scalp. Contrasted against his dark almond skin, his emerald eyes always appeared full of merriment despite his somber comportment. He was barefoot, as always I soon learned, and wore a pair of worn denim pants and a powder blue t-shirt. A long canvas scabbard holding his machete hung from his belt.

We crossed the same ground as the evening before. Out in the open now, the din and the glare of the sun were a sudden assault on my senses. We approached the solitary olive tree that bleakly stood in a wide, empty expanse surrounded by neatly arranged rows of dismounted engine blocks. Beneath the trees' spindly, twisting branches stood a group of seven children silently eyeing our approach. The only face I recognized was Phaedra's. She smiled as we neared, and whatever nervousness I was feeling was momentarily lost.

Maxi made my introduction to the group and a portly boy, who looked to be about thirteen or fourteen, said his name was Raoul and asked me if I was the same priest who had been in the hospital with Pockets. I said that I was and asked if Pockets was there. Raoul nodded, and another boy who said his name was Swatch and had a large lime-green parrot with a yellow and red head perched on his shoulder, asked why I had come to the Heap.

I had anticipated this question after what I felt had been my wholly inadequate response the day before at the gate. I explained, as they obviously already understood, that I had recently been ill and that the nature of my illness led me to a period of introspection. As a result, I explained, I had decided I needed more time away from my work and professional responsibilities in order to dwell upon my future.

While I spoke, Nameless lay down, angling his body to gain as much shade as possible from the scant osteoid shadows cast by the tree.

"And you came here to do that?" Raoul asked.

"Yes," I said. "I thought that a respite well away from the humdrum of ordinary life would be good."

"Are you willing to work while here?" Swatch asked.

"Absolutely," I replied.

"Everyone here works," Raoul said matter-of-factly.

Phaedra had been silent throughout all of this, but now she asked, "Did your illness make you think about your religion?"

Her question took me by surprise. There was something in the way that she asked it that seemed to request more than a simple answer.

"Yes, it did," I confessed.

"How?" she asked.

I thought about my answer while the group looked at me expectantly.

"You don't have to tell us," Phaedra said.

"No, I want to," I said. "It's just that it's something I haven't spoken to anyone about."

Nameless groaned and rolled over into a more comfortable position on his back with his bent legs pointing skywards. He looked over at me and closed his eyes to sleep, evidently bored with everything. The green parrot on Swatch's shoulder kept a close watch on Nameless, who completely ignored the bird.

"Before I came to this country," I began, "when I was in another place far from here, I read a story about a great pretender named Apsethus."

"Apsethus the pretender," Phaedra said in a dreamy, musing tone, clearly taken by the sound of it.

"Apsethus lived in ancient Libya," I told the group, "and was a skilled sorcerer who performed amazing feats. He was especially talented at making objects appear and disappear and could levitate for hours on end. Yet, despite his unusual and unique talents, he was very dissatisfied with his lot in life and aspired to be far more than what he was."

I paused and then said, "You see, Apsethus wasn't content with being a mere mortal. He wanted to be a god." I felt my dormant pedagogical proclivities rapidly coming to the surface and momentarily imagined myself a spellbinding raconteur.

"So one day, not long into his discontent," I continued, "Apsethus went about the countryside capturing countless numbers of the beautiful, multi-colored parrots that populated his area. Not at all unlike the very one perched upon your shoulder right now," I said to Swatch.

"After Apsethus had filled his shuttered home with the birds," I went on, "he spent the next several weeks laboriously teaching each and every one of them to say, 'Apsethus is a god, Apsethus is a god.' Over and over, 'Apsethus is a god.' When he finally threw the doors and windows of his home open, the parrots escaped in every direction, many so intoxicated with their freedom that they flew well beyond Libya's borders. Within days, people everywhere to which the birds traveled were astounded to hear their incessant message and Apsethus's deepest desire was realized. Soon throngs of pilgrims from far and wide flocked to his door seeking his blessings and wisdom.

"But," I explained, "not everyone was so easily taken in by Apsethus's deception. One suspecting man took great umbrage with his bold attempt at aggrandizement and thought it wrong for a man to deceive people the way Apsethus had. So this man went about gathering as many of the trained, jabbering parrots as he could and he too confined them in a closed place. There he re-schooled them to say, 'Apsethus is a god. We know this because he taught us to say it.' And when the corrected parrots were once again set free, people were outraged to hear their revised message and in the heat of their hysteria and anger they seized Apsethus and burned him alive."

Finished with my story I looked to the faces of my listeners and was surprised to see them eyeing me very dubiously. Nameless groaned again, rolled back over onto his stomach, and assumed a sphinx-like posture, alert now, with his focus solidly on me.

I looked back to the group's faces and had a moment of satori.

What in the world was I thinking, trying to use such a subtle and arcane allegory to explain my problems to a group of children? Especially these children. Did I actually believe that they could grasp the necessary nexus between Apsethus and myself?

"What I was trying to tell you," I apologetically said, "in what was, I know, a silly sort of way, is that because of my illness, I began to have some doubts about my religion."

The children continued to stare at me, and then Raoul quietly said, "You thought that you were like one of Apsethus's talking parrots."

I wasn't sure if it was a statement or a question, so I simply said, "Yes, that is exactly what I felt."

"Here there is little time for such thinking," Raoul explained. "Maybe that will be a good thing for you."

"Yes," I agreed, "it probably will be."

Raoul looked to the others and then at me.

"Your place above in the van," he said, gesturing to the piled steel, "is perfect for observation. We talked about it among ourselves and have decided that, if you are to stay, it would be good to have a daytime observer at that level to keep watch over things."

"That sounds fine to me," I said. "I would be happy to take on the task."

Raoul nodded his consent and looked to the others. Each nodded in response.

"Today is as good as any day to begin," he said.

"And if I observe anything out of the ordinary, I should do what?" I asked.

"We will work that out," Raoul answered.

And like that, I came to live and gained my place in the Heap.

I know what you are thinking, kind reader: That my job as observer was some haphazard, made-up task invented to keep me from interfering with the day-to-day business and other enterprises conducted in the Heap. Frankly, at first, I thought the same thing, but over time I came to realize that there was far more to it and that Raoul had intuitively understood the confused state of my mind when I first arrived. He understood that what I needed was the pretense of being busy while having sufficient time to think things through. But neither he, nor I, could have anticipated the events that would come to prevent any of that from happening completely.

Later that first day, after I had assumed my post atop the van's roof, I spotted Pockets standing in the opening below looking up at me. I waved to him, but when he didn't respond or move, I realized that my position was darkly shadowed by everything around it, so I called out to him. He stepped closer and raised a hand to shield his eyes from the sun overhead. When he spotted me, he waved smiling and I motioned for him to come up.

"I wasn't sure it was you," he said, as he ascended the short ladder on the van's side.

"You escaped, too?" he asked, sitting beside me.

"Well, in a sense, yes, I suppose I did."

"And the Council has given you a job."

"That they have."

"You will be happy here."

"I think you're right."

"What more could anyone want?"

"Exactly."

"Look," he said, reaching into his shirt's breast pocket.

"What is it?"

He held out an open palm. In it was a small, very small, quivering gray rat. Its eyes were barely open.

"Goodness, where did you find him?"

"In the cardboard piles. He was all alone. I don't know what happened to his mother."

He carefully stroked the rodent's tiny spine.

"I fed him some milk with an eye dropper," he said.

"What will you do with him?"

"Feed him, take care of him, until he's strong enough to be on his own."

"Who could ask for anything more?" I said.

Soon from my conversations with Pockets, Phaedra, and others, I would learn that Raoul's years before coming to the Heap differed significantly from most of the other children. He had been born in an area north of the city known for its maze of marshes and canals. The area had been settled by a group of people that long ago retreated from the corruption of the city to live an abstemious existence of rhapsodic harmony with nature. Their community was widely known for its sense of independence, ingenuity, and economic self-reliance that turned on the marsh's abundance of natural resources, fish, exotic birds, sturdy reeds and bamboo, and a coveted, hearty strain of rice.

One edge of the marsh bordered the city's airport and its longest runway used for intercontinental flights. During my stay in the Heap, I would often imagine marsh dwellers standing in their flat, pole-driven boats, used for hundreds of years, gazing up at the huge underbelly of a passenger jet roaring overhead.

The people of the marshes placed a high value on education, and their children were well schooled from an early age through to their mid-teens. Raoul was no exception, and he had been an exceptional student. It was said that his brilliance revealed itself from the moment he was born, and that by the time he was seven-years-old, he could read and comprehend books meant for adults.

Four years ago, when Raoul was nine years old, the long tranquility of life in the marshes was radically shaken after one of the region's ubiquitous rebel factions established a surreptitious camp within its bounds. The camp was to be used as a base for marauding ventures into the city, and the marsh leaders and elders were much opposed to this presence. There were constant clashes between the marsh peoples and the rebels and the conflict significantly intensified after the rebels began demanding that marsh families pay them a weekly tithe for protection. The clashes grew more heated after some families banded together and refused to pay. Raoul's family was among these, and late one night, a group of about a dozen rebels stormed into their home by smashing down its door. Raoul woke up to the sounds of his father cursing the men who were beating him and Raoul's mother.

Raoul slipped from his bed and carefully crossed the room to where his younger brother, Cerdo, was still sleeping. Cerdo came awake with a start and Raoul put his hand over the boy's mouth and a finger of caution to his own lips.

"Get dressed quickly and go out the window," Raoul told Cerdo.

His brother did as he was told, and Raoul pulled on his own clothes and boots and then moved to the room where his two sisters slept. When he opened their door, he saw that four of the rebels were already inside assaulting the girls. Raoul charged across the room to pull the men off his sisters, but he was struck hard on the back of the head and fell to the floor. Two rebels seized him tightly by the arms and dragged him from the room.

Taken outside, he was blindfolded, his hands bound behind his back, and placed in one of several trucks that transported him, and about fifty other seized men, to an abandoned factory six miles from the marshes. As the trucks pulled away from his home, Raoul heard gunfire and the screams of his mother.

In an overgrown parking lot at the factory, the captives were herded from the trucks and their blindfolds were removed. The rebels, armed with rifles and small machine guns, then manacled each captive to a long, heavy chain and marched them into the factory's cavernous interior, littered with broken and discarded machinery. The high concrete walls inside were covered with spray-painted graffiti depicting everything from crude words to impressionistic art. Centered on one wall was a huge red and black rendering of Edvard Munch's *Scream*. A cartoon-like bubble coming from the figure's mouth exclaimed, *Freedom is an illusion.*

Part of the factory, a processing plant, had been used for slaughtering goats and sheep. It was to this section that Raoul and the others were taken. The room was long and narrow with a high ceiling and metal-framed, broken windows. Suspended from steel plates fashioned to the ceiling was a system of pulleys, chains and anchor-shaped hooks. The heavy stench of animal blood and offal still clung to the room's darkened concrete floor that had a series of foot-deep drainage channels cut into it.

The captives flanking Raoul on the chain were both elderly men who had difficulty walking with the added weight. With his hands still bound behind him, Raoul could do little to help either man except to offer his own awkward weight to keep them from stumbling or falling down.

"When they begin shooting get behind me," one of the men

whispered to Raoul. "You are too young to die like this."

Raoul did his best to steel himself for what was to come. For a moment the room grew eerily silent, and he thought he could hear the sound of many beating hearts resounding off the concrete walls. Seconds later when the rebels began indiscriminately firing at their chained captives the two elderly men moved to shield Raoul between them. The sounds of gunfire and bullets ricocheting off the concrete floor and walls were deafening. Raoul felt the bodies of his two protector's jerk and shake with the force of the many rounds that struck them. He fell to the floor with both men covering his body. Beginning to panic, he thought, should he lay with his eyes open or closed to feign death? Knowing that he would be unable to prevent himself from blinking, he closed his eyes and lay still with the blood of one of the elderly men running freely into his ear and across his face. He didn't dare move, or to take a deep breath, until after it seemed hours had passed.

When he finally opened his eyes, he saw that the rebels were gone and everyone else was dead. He struggled to move the two men covering him, and standing he felt a sharp pain in his forearm. Looking at it, he saw a small, round, puckered hole between his wrist and elbow oozing blood. Chained to all the lifeless bodies it was impossible for Raoul to escape the room. He sat back down and took a leather lace from one of his boots and used it as a tourniquet.

For nearly three days he stayed there not daring to cry out for help. Occasionally, he heard the sounds of vehicles outside the building, but nobody came inside. After the second day, he grew immune to the overpowering stench all around him. By that time, flies had infested the dead and several good-sized vultures were perched on the sills of the rooms high, broken windows sizing up the prizes below. At night, the rats came to feast, scampering excitedly over the bodies looking for easy bites. There was little Raoul could do to frighten them away besides move his head and good arm wildly about, but he had become too weak to do that for long.

Finally, on the afternoon of the third day, Raoul heard the sound of the room's heavy steel door slide open and miraculously there stood his younger brother Cerdo, aghast at the sight before him. When Raoul made a feeble attempt to stand, Cerdo was so shocked he nearly fainted. Realizing that he was not seeing an apparition and this was his brother, Cerdo rushed to Raoul and helped him to his feet. They stood holding one another tightly, crying with joy. But Raoul's problems were far from over.

Cerdo was unable to find anything among the factory's discarded tools and machinery to cut the chain binding Raoul to the decomposing bodies. Raoul told Cerdo he would have to go back to the marshes to find a file or hack saw, but the younger boy was so frightened that he refused to leave his brother.

"You have to go," Raoul explained, "the rebels could come back at any time."

Raoul's wound was showing the early signs of infection, and he told Cerdo that he urgently needed medical attention. Cerdo eventually relented and reluctantly left, repeatedly promising he would return as quickly as possible. Hours later, with the sun going down, Raoul began to feel very weak with hunger, and the pain in his arm was intensifying. The swollen skin around the hole had suddenly grown grotesquely and had turned dark purple.

He fell asleep and awoke some time later to an odd sensation in his injured arm. As his eyes adjusted to the dark, he saw that several rats were greedily gnawing on his torn flesh. He sat up quickly and yanked a shoe from one of the nearby bodies and threw it at the rats that were aggressively circling him. After he threw every object he could lay his hands on, he pulled a leather belt from the body of one of the elderly men who had saved him and began swinging it every time the rats came close.

Cerdo returned the next morning after having walked and run nearly ten miles. On the road leading into the marshes he had encountered a line of families, mostly women, children, and some old men, fleeing the rebels. The group had all of their hastily gathered belongings, along with a bevy of very young children, assembled onto four mule driven carts. When he stopped to speak with the group, Cerdo saw that the sky above the marshes was a bright orange color and large black clouds were drifting up toward a perfect half moon. The families gave Cerdo everything they could to help. He carried back a burlap sack filled with matches, a canteen of water, canned food, bandages, rubbing alcohol, stale bread, and an old file and two worn hacksaw blades.

With each boy taking turns, it took the brothers nearly two hours to cut through the chain. By this time Raoul's forearm had swollen to nearly double its normal size.

Groggily, Raoul told Cerdo that there was one more thing that needed to be cut.

"No," said Cerdo. "I can't."

"You have to do it," said Raoul. "If you don't cut it off the infection will spread and kill me."

"I can't," Cerdo said. "I can't do that to you." He clung to Raoul and sobbed.

"You must," Raoul urged. "Be strong."

After it was done, with Raoul biting down hard, and eventually through, the end of the leather belt wrapped tightly his arm, and with Cerdo having to constantly stop to throw up, Raoul told his brother to light a small fire to heat the file so that his bloody stump, just above his now gone elbow, could be cauterized.

Two hours later, the two walked from the factory with Raoul leaning heavily on his brother. They went to a nearby area of tall grasses and reeds. Their movement into the grasses flushed two large white cranes from their nesting place. The birds flew up over them in a rain of small white feathers. The birds dipped their wings and glided away to find another spot. One of the feathers drifted down to where Cerdo caught it in his hand. He held it up to Raoul.

"It's a good sign, brother. We too shall soon fly from this place," he said grinning.

Having moved only a short distance, Raoul was nonetheless exhausted, and he crumpled to the soft, damp earth. Cerdo used one of the hacksaw blades to open a can of yellow corn, which Raoul ate and quickly regurgitated. He was now especially weak and hot with fever, quaking with chills. Cerdo cut one of the sleeves from his shirt, soaked it in water from the canteen and laid it across Raoul's forehead.

They stayed among the tall grasses for two days until Raoul's fever subsided and he was able to hold down some hardened bread and water. On the morning of the third day, they began the hike home to the marshes. Knowing the rebels were likely to still be in the area, the brothers stayed off the road, often moving with difficulty through the bordering brush.

A day later, when they arrived home, they found that the rebels had burned their house and many others to the ground. Raoul discovered the mutilated bodies of his mother and father among a pile of murdered villagers. He and Cerdo searched everywhere but were unable to find their two sisters. After burying their parents and the other bodies, the boys decided they would go to the city where the surviving marsh families had fled. Perhaps someone had saved their sisters from the rebels and taken the girls with them to the city, they hoped.

Neither boy expected that the city would be so large and that it held so many people. They quickly realized that finding anyone in such a place would be an arduous task. On their third night in the city, sleeping behind a shuttered food stall in the marketplace, three policemen woke the brothers by beating them with clubs. They were tossed into a van that transported them to a prison for men where they were placed in separate, crowded cells. Both boys were gang raped their first night in the prison. On the second night, when Cerdo's assailants returned for him, he fought back and was stomped to death on the concrete floor.

When Raoul learned of Cerdo's death he began keening, slamming himself against the barred door. A group of guards tried to subdue him by beating him with truncheons, but their blows only riled him into rage and despair. After he bloodied one guard and broke the arm of another, he was shot with an electric stun gun and beaten severely while lying helplessly on the floor. Unconscious, he was thrown into a windowless, unlit room in the prison's basement level. The space was so small that one person was unable to lie down in it. Raoul was kept there for nearly a week without food or water. To satiate his thirst, he drank his urine from his cupped hands.

On Raoul's third day there, Cerdo appeared to him and told him not to worry that everything would be all right. "Be strong, my brother, and don't mourn for me."

"I only want to die so that I can be with you and mama and papa," Raoul tearfully said. "There is no reason to go on."

"No," Cerdo said, handing Raoul a small white feather, "you must go on. There is still much for you to do. Be strong, my brother."

Raoul was released three days later, taken to the prison's front gates and pushed out into the street. His next eight months in the city were spent looking for his sisters and surviving on the streets by using his wits. Because of his education and skills, many street children looked up to him and soon considered him to be their tacit leader.

They referred to him as "Teacher" or "the Teacher." As you may have already guessed, following the horrors of Colonel Dreadful, Raoul was one of the prime architects of the plan to retreat from the city and to go to the Heap.

Throughout my time in the Heap, Raoul would occasionally visit me at my post. The first of these, where he would appear unannounced and we would sit and casually talk about whatever was on his mind at the time, occurred about mid-day near the end of my second week there. That afternoon at my observation post atop the van, I watched him cross the open area leading to the metal stairs. For a person his size he moved with an unexpected agility and assuredness. He was dressed in a pair of tan pants cleanly cut off at the knees and a faded forest green t-shirt. With each step the stump of his left arm wavered slightly. He wore his dark hair short, in a military-style cut, and there was always the faint trace of a smile about his mouth in contrast to the seriousness of his dark eyes. Raoul's thick girth was a mystery to all who considered it. That he was big boned was obvious, and over those sturdy bones was ample flesh. Yet rarely did anyone see him eat and when they did there was always little on his plate.

After coming up the stairs and crossing the catwalk, he paused and looked about, and then climbed the short ladder up to the van's rooftop where he sat down next to me. He gazed out at the horizon, and then slowly scanned the wide expanse toward the distant cityscape looming majestically behind layers of wavering heat.

"Things always look different when you are above them," he said.

I nodded my agreement and said, "Everyday I see something new that I didn't notice before. I am becoming an expert on the shadows cast by the sun."

"That's good," he said. "Then you like it here?"

"Very much," I told him.

He gestured with his head at the city, "Life there can be very hard."

We both sat gazing at it. Beyond the shimmering skyline, I saw the sun reflect off the faint form of a plane rising from the airport that was soon lost from sight in the haze and distance. I pointed in the direction of the airport and said, "Your home was the marshes."

"Yes," he said, "but not anymore. Now everyone is gone ... except for the rebels."

"Do you miss being there?"

He was quiet for a long time, and I wondered if maybe he hadn't heard me or if he wanted to ignore my question, but then he said, "It seems so long ago that I was there. I miss my mother, my father, my sisters, and my brother. I miss the people and families who lived alongside us. I miss the smell of the water and the sound of fish jumping. I miss the soft wind that made the grasses sway like to music."

"You'll go back someday?" I asked.

"No, this is my place now," he said. He looked down at the roof of the van and added, "You know, a long time ago my grandfather many times great, was brought here as a slave."

"I didn't know that. How did that happen?"

Raoul then told me an incredible story. It was one that made me recall many bits of history I thought I had forgotten.

Nearly eight hundred years ago, Raoul's ancestors lived in a small French village far away from the Heap. All of their names have been lost through the ages, except for that of one young boy by the name of Guillaume. He was the father of Raoul's father many times removed. In the year 1212, Guillaume journeyed to join the army of a twelve-year-old boy named Stephen. Stephen was from Cloyes, a village about sixty miles from where Guillaume worked as a shepherd. At the time, the profession was considered a lowly one and was almost solely held by young boys, many orphans whose parents had abandoned them due to poverty or who had perished from the plague. Most young shepherds led nomadic lives moving from farm to farm, never staying in any one place for long. Stephen, like Guillaume, had also been a shepherd, but he had suddenly abandoned his work after he claimed he encountered a haggard looking stranger walking through his flock's pasture. The stranger had told Stephen that he was a crusader returning from the Holy Land. He said that while he still had a great distance to travel he had no money for food or drink. Without hesitation, Stephen gave the soft-spoken traveler what little bread and water he had. When he wished the crusader well, he looked into his face and saw that the man was no longer a weary stranger, but Jesus Christ himself. Stephen soon recounted that Jesus then informed him that the crusades to take the Holy Land from the Muslims had failed because the kings and knights who led them were impure of heart, mind, and motive.

"Lord, I do not doubt your words for a moment," said Stephen, "But what can I, a poor shepherd, do to right that which you say is wrong?"

Stephen said that Jesus assured him he could do much and handed him a letter. "You have my blessing and appointment as my emissary to bring this missive to the king," he told Stephen. "Then you must go forth and summon all those innocents like yourself. Tell them to arm themselves and, with you as their leader, to do battle to free the Holy Land from the heathens who now hold it."

Stephen traveled immediately to the town of Saint-Denys, four miles north of Paris. There King Philippe II was holding court. Philippe was a veteran of the Third Crusade during which he had fought alongside Richard the Lionheart.

It is remarkable that Stephen somehow managed an audience with Philippe, but he did, as has been amply recorded in countless history books, however, the king was less than impressed with the tall, blue-eyed boy standing before him.

"You say the Lord himself handed you this letter?" inquired Philippe.

"He did, Your Majesty," said Stephen.

"And what did Christ look like?" asked the dubious monarch.

"Like nothing I have ever seen before," said Stephen.

"And what have you seen before?" asked Philippe.

The boy didn't miss a beat and replied, "Your Majesty, when the sun rises every morning I see the splendor and grandness of all that the Lord has provided and that you, with the earthly powers granted by Him, reign over."

"Go back to your sheep," said Philippe, dismissing the boy, "and tend more attentively to them before they wander far and wide like your mind."

News of Stephen's visit with the king had spread throughout Saint-Denys and when he stepped from the court meeting, a large crowd was already assembled awaiting word of the outcome of his audience. Many in the crowd, which grew rapidly as it followed the boy to the Gothic Abbey of Saint-Denys, the town square's centerpiece, called out to Stephen asking him what he would do now without the backing of the king. Stephen ignored their questions and mounted the abbey's steps where, framed by high stonewalls, he turned and faced his anxious pursuers.

Pointing to the church behind him, Stephen said, "When the cruel Roman governor Valerius cut the head from Dionysius, the good saint picked it up and walked to this spot before he fell dead so as to indicate where he wanted to be buried. It is said that Valerius was so startled at the sight that he soiled himself and sprinted back to his palace screaming. Dionysius feared no man for he knew that his mission on earth was mandated by the Lord and that the Lord would never forsake him."

The crowd that stood raptly listening to the young orator cried out its approval for his words. Never had anyone heard such erudition and eloquence come from a poor, illiterate shepherd boy. Buttressed by the response, Stephen continued his voice now more robust, resounding off the huge ornate stonewalls behind him.

"Today I stand before you and God to say that the Lord has charged me with a daunting task that I shall carry forward without pause. The Lord has instructed me to gather an army of innocents, an army of youths like myself, youths unspoiled by the taint of avarice, carnality, and pride, an army to march to Jerusalem where it will take that city from the Godless heathens that now hold it. The Lord Jesus Christ has promised me that once this army is assembled and marches to the water's edge the sea shall open up to it like it did for Moses, and victory will soon after be ours."

The crowd roared its approval for these bold declarations and a good number among them, all about Stephen's age or younger, boys and girls alike, immediately pledged their allegiance to his army. By nightfall three days later, nearly three thousand youths had joined Stephen's crusade and reports poured into Saint-Denys that the roads leading from Paris were clogged with thousands more eager children armed with makeshift spears, swords, knives, pitchforks, axes, and all manners of sharpened tools.

Here, kind reader, I should offer an aside and tell you that over the decades the story of Stephen's crusade has evolved with retelling to include that many of these children abandoned fine homes and left stunned parents and families behind, but this is far from truth. In Stephen's day, as today, the streets and alleyways of Europe were filled with children who for a variety of causes had been left to their own devices and survival. It was these children who answered Stephen's call to arms.

Guillaume, who lived many miles away from Saint-Denys in

Toulouse, then part of the independent principality of Languedoc, heard news of the fledgling crusade about ten days after Stephen's encounter with Philippe. Guillaume was only ten years of age but the boy, orphaned a year earlier, longed to leave the lonely and rocky hills of southern France to seek out adventure and to see a world he could only imagine from the words of others. Since the death of his parents, not a day had passed where, after seeing his flock bedded down for the night, Guillaume didn't lay awake thinking about all the fascinating stories he heard about life in distant and exotic lands across the seas.

Other shepherds who knew him would often say, "While many of us are bitten by the fleas that infect our flocks, Guillaume is infected with a wanderlust so strong, it frightens the pests from his flock."

Despite his stifling provincialism, Guillaume, had been well schooled by his parents who felt it important that he have a keen rounding of knowledge and the ability to converse in several languages. At the age that most boys were just beginning to grasp the basics of their mother tongue, Guillaume had become fluent in French, English, German, Spanish, and a smattering of basic Arabic. Normally, a boy of Guillaume's social ranking had no opportunity to receive an education of any sort, but his father, an enlightened man by any measure, had in his own youth been an attendant to the Court and, as such, did all that he could to reap the benefits of education, which he, in turn, passed on to his son.

Guillaume was also well acquainted with the crusades. His father, again as an attendant, had fought valiantly in the Holy Land alongside the Knights Templar and the Hospitalers. Prior to their defeat by the Saracens, he had also labored long and hard among the ruins of the Temple of Solomon. Astounded one night at bedtime, Guillaume listened to his father tell of an English knight named Robert of St. Albans who had quit the Templars to become a convert to Islam and lead an army for Sultan Saladin against the Christians.

"How could he commit such a sin?" asked Guillaume.

"It is not for us to judge," his father had replied.

Guillaume's mother and father had been executed two years earlier in the relentless campaign of Simon de Montfort to exterminate all the members of a small but growing Christian sect known as the Cathars. At the time of their deaths, Guillaume was still receiving his initial indoctrination into the sect, and he often found himself confused by the beliefs of his parents.

"Everything that exists under the sun and moon is only corruption and chaos, the creations of an imperfect God who put them here as seeds of temptation and destruction," his father had told him.

"But, papa" asked the boy, "is there more than one God?"

"Yes," replied his father. "The One good God, the God we hold high, made the invisible world that will only see and feel when the right time comes."

"Then the imperfect God is the Devil?" asked Guillaume.

"Not the Devil," replied his father. "This world is of the making of the imperfect God's angels. These angels made a hole in Heaven and fell through it to earth where the Devil awaited them with the temptations of human flesh. When the imperfect God saw the hole he put his foot over it, but it was too late."

After Simon de Montfort seized and burned Guillaume's parents, along with one-hundred-and-fifty other men and women, the boy, forced to abandon his studies and to take work as a shepherd, had little doubt about the existence of an imperfect God.

When Guillaume packed to go and join Stephen's army, the force had swollen to nearly twenty thousand ragtag children and they were camped out in mass in Vendome, south of Paris. There Stephen, who was now dubbed The Prophet, treated his soldiers to daily pontifications. Stephen's speeches were aimed at fueling their fervor for the long march to Marseille where he promised that God, in the same fashion that he had done for Moses, would part the waters of the Mediterranean Sea for them to cross.

Guillaume arrived in Marseille two days after the debacle of the Mediterranean failing to comply with Stephen's promise. Indeed, as hordes expectantly looked on, the waters did nothing but churn more wildly producing seemingly defiant and mocking curling waves and foaming white caps. As one can easily imagine, morale among the children sank to a precipitous low point after this. Many children threw down their weapons and abandoned the crusade. Stephen lost face and struggled to find ways to renew the fervor of those remaining. On his first night in the Marseille encampment, Guillaume listened to great grumbling, heretofore unheard, about Stephen's proclivity to live in a style unlike all others in his army.

"We traipse across the countryside on foot with shoes that are tattered and torn, or no shoes at all, and he rides in a chariot fit for a king, draped with veils of fine silk to shield out the sun," complained one girl, who sat gingerly massaging her calloused feet.

"Fit for a king is right," said a boy beside her. "He surrounds himself with mounted lancers like a king in fear for his life."

Added another young warrior, "He may think himself a noble, but when the time comes to bleed, his blood will flow like that of any among us."

The next day fortune smiled on Stephen. With a flourish of drum rolls and blasting trumpets, he called his army together and announced that the sea had not parted because God instead had instructed two generous local merchants, called Hugh the Iron and William the Pig in keeping with their lines of commerce, to provide seven sailing ships, free of charge, for their speedier passage to Palestine. The children's morale was instantly bolstered and a sustained cheer sounded as Stephen raised his arms triumphantly skyward. Guillaume cheered with the others, not because he had any zest for battle or blood, but because at last, he thought, he was to see those places he long dreamt about.

That evening as the young warriors made ready to embark on the last leg of their journey, Guillaume sat by a campfire with a group of other children discussing what they imagined would happen once in the Holy Land.

"I have heard that the Saracens carry swords shiny and curved like the sun, with handles filled with jewels looted from Solomon's Temple," said one child.

"Ay, I've heard they're immune to pain and fear because they devour magical plants before doing battle," said another.

"Magic plants or no magic plants," said a boy who sat sharpening a double-bladed ax, "those heathens haven't known fear until they see their turbaned heads rolling across the battlefield."

"An attendant to Stephen said that the worst of the heathens ride black steeds taller and faster than any horse known to Christendom," said a girl.

"Nonsense."

The girl continued, "He said the worst of the unbelievers, those from a bloodthirsty race of Persians, are led by an old man said to live in the mountains in a castle constructed solely out of mortar and the skulls of Christians."

"There was talk of such an old man in Vendome," said a boy, seated next to Guillaume. "People said that he claims to be the incarnation of God on earth and that he requires his disciples to murder Christian infants and drink their blood before they can enter his kingdom."

"Then that old man shall learn the hard way that the only God is our God and that no other God exists," said the girl.

Guillaume remained silent throughout. All this hatred and bloodshed over whose God is the right God, he thought, where does it all end?

The next morning, under a glorious blue sky and bright sun, Guillaume and nearly eight hundred other children boarded the seven vessels. As the ships set out to sea, thousands of people cheered and tossed flowers for good fortune into the harbor waters. Within minutes the ships caught a fortunate wind, and soon they were gone from sight. Eighteen years passed with no word, not even a murmur, about the fate of the children.

Then one day, early in the year 1230, an emaciated priest who had sailed with Stephen's army returned to Marseille. His report was a grim one for those who held out hope that the children were still alive somewhere. Four days out of Marseille, said the priest, the seven vessels had been caught in a fierce storm. Two of the ships were dashed to pieces on a craggy islet called Acciptrium, named for the rapacious sparrow hawks that populated it. All the children aboard the two ships were lost. The remaining five vessels pulled into port days later in North Africa where the exhausted and famished children were herded down the gangplanks into the hands of slave traders who sold them on the blocks of the dreaded Bujeiah market. The lauded generosity of Hugh the Iron and William the Pig had been no more than a ruse to deliver the children to slavers.

Fair haired and light skinned children, especially girls, commanded a premium price in the flesh markets of Africa's coast. Sultan Malek-el-Kamel purchased two hundred of the children, and several other wealthy Egyptians purchased about two hundred others. Nearly a hundred other children were sold to a slaver from Iraq who took them by caravan to Baghdad where reportedly at least fifty were beheaded for refusing to renounce their belief in Christ.

Guillaume was one of those sold to the Sultan, who was drawn to the boy because of his multi-lingual abilities. In Egypt, Guillaume found that he was but one of over nearly a hundred palace slaves who existed to serve every need and whimsy of the Sultan and his family, but he was treated well and frequently accompanied the Sultan on his many jaunts to other countries. Despite that he was a slave, he was rarely unhappy because his wish had been fulfilled and he was now able to see those places he had long dreamed about.

Guillaume quickly grew to love Cairo with its enchanting people, sakkas lugging water from the Nile, whirling Dervishes, plumed dromedaries, exotic foods, and myriad, teeming bazaars. He was fascinated by its many domed mosques, mysterious obelisks bearing winged lions and globes, griffons, and smiling sphinxes, and ancient temples and tombs honoring Isis, Osiris, Horus, Ra, and Thoth. From his room's window in the Sultan's palace, he could see the distant plain of Heliopolis and Mount Mokatem, where it was said the spirits of the dead dwelled and cynocephali roamed about freely. He stood in awe at the foot of the Great Pyramids of the Giza Plateau, pondered the elusive wisdom of the Sphinx, and marveled at the obelisk of Heliopolis erected over two thousand years before Christ was born.

In his seventh year in Egypt, he married a beautiful, copper-skinned Abyssinian slave whose name was Zetnaybia and they had three children whom they named Antoine, Nicole and Aclinia. When the Sultan grew old and infirm, he trusted Guillaume to travel alone and far to conduct business for him. On these journeys, Guillaume, sometimes with Antoine at his side, made many strong friendships with respected and powerful people. Before the Sultan passed away, he granted Guillaume and his family their freedom and provided them with a bestowal that allowed them to resettle in one of the regions that Guillaume had developed an affinity for during his travels.

When Raoul finished his story, I sat silently for a moment and then asked, "Your father told you all of this?"

"Many times. He would recite the story as it had been told to him when he was a boy, and he would read to us from the flaking pages of an old journal Guillaume had kept, like his father had read them to him," Raoul replied.

"And the pages?" I asked, fearing what his answer would be.

"They were lost when our home was burned."

"You should write the story down again so that it doesn't become completely lost." I said.

"I would like to do that."

"Do you know what became of the priest who came back?" I asked.

"I don't know," Raoul said. "I was hoping you could tell me."

"Why me? How would I know?"

"You have the same name as he did," Raoul replied.

"Gabriel?"

"No. Your last name," said Raoul. "Surin."

What I hadn't explained to the children under the olive tree that first morning, was that I had been drawn to the story of Apsethus through my work concerning a far more notorious sorcerer initially known only as Simon. A contemporary of Peter the Apostle, the lapsit excillis of the Church, Simon was from the small village of Gitta in Samaria. Like Apsethus he was ambitious, but his aspirations far exceeded those of the unfortunate Libyan. Simon had no interest in merely becoming a god. Instead he wanted to be regarded as the Savior of Man.

While in Samaria, where he began preaching and practicing his magic, Simon declared himself to be "the Power of God which is called Great." His bold proclamation, combined with his magic, carried enough substance that it attracted the apostle Philip who baptized Simon. The two together then worked to spread the word of God throughout Samaria. Word of their great successes soon reached apostles Peter and John and they journeyed from Jerusalem to Samaria where they intended to help baptize the many converted through the efforts of Philip and Simon. According to accounts written decades later, Simon and Peter did not get along. Peter, perhaps jealous of Simon's standing in Samaria and his amazing magical powers, questioned Simon's true intentions among his fellow apostles and said that he believed the Samaritan had duped Philip to gain access to knowledge of Jesus and the magic that he imparted to his apostles. Simon, hearing of Peter's scorn, replied that his intentions had been true to the betterment of man and God. He said that he had offered to share the Lost Word with Philip, but that the apostle had turned the offer down because he was awe struck by the power held in but one Word.

Are you scoffing, dear reader, at the claim that magic played a role in the works of Jesus and his apostles? If so, I only ask that you completely hear me out before you make any final judgment.

Peter eventually confronted Simon with his concerns and accused him of deception and practicing magic for the sole purposes of self-aggrandizement. Peter maintained that Simon's self-proclaimed possession of the Lost Word was the boast of a man deluded by his own modest talents and that no such Word existed except for the Word of God as embodied in Jesus Christ. Simon denied Peter's accusations about his motives and argued that his ability to baptize by lying hands upon a person was no less legitimate than Peter's. As to the Word, Simon said to Peter, "Would you have it that I be foolish enough to utter the Word just so that your ignorance could be tested?"

Angered by Simon's insolence, Peter countered, "There is not for thee part or lot in this Word, for thy heart is not right before God." Undeterred, Simon continued on his own to bring people to God and was, because of his amazing magic, soon seen by many as the Son of God, a mantel he welcomed and wore proudly.

According to ancient papyrus scrolls unearthed in Samaria, Simon had perfected his conjuring and necromancy skills as an initiate in Egypt, then the world's teeming center for mystery schools and esoteric training of every stripe. At the time, it was widely held that the Land of the Pharaohs was the image of heaven itself, or as others put it, the "projection below of the order of things above." By all accounts, Simon's feats of magic were astounding. Even those hostile to him and the Apostles never denied them. He was said to be able to pass through rock as if it were air, to break the strongest metal bars and chains without effort, to exist for weeks on end without food or water, to be able to animate granite and bronze statutes and have them laugh and move about dancing, to cause trees to grow suddenly, to turn himself into a sheep, goat, or serpent, to fly across the sky like an eagle, and to make gold and silver from sand. Princes and princesses, kings and queens were said to quiver in awe at his powers and to welcome him into their courts to keep him their ally.

Perhaps by now, you have recalled Simon from your readings of the New Testament and remember also that over the centuries he has become the template for even more infamous practitioners, real and imagined, of magic. Figures like Doctor Faustus and his many incarnations, Arthurian magician Merlin, Henry Cornelius Agrippa, sadist Gilles de Rais, royal astrologer John Dee, and, to a lesser extent, the controversial Aleister Crowley. Over time, beginning well after his death, Simon would also become known as an arch-heretic and eventually the Father of Heresy himself.

This, of course, was after the practice of magic had fallen to disfavor from a place of common and widespread acceptance.

Readers perhaps should be reminded that the world Simon existed in, the same shared by Jesus, was dominated by a plethora of mythological forces—gods, demons, angels, and strange beings that often, and for many different reasons, savaged mankind in the guise of sickness, from simple medical ailments to serious diseases, insanity, and various natural disasters. Gods and devils populated the heavens in great numbers. Beneath the earth, in the underworld, demons existed in enormous amounts to taunt the dead. On earth itself, both gods and demons, many difficult to distinguish from one another, ran rampant in their ways to interfere and manipulate the forces that impacted human beings. Science, as it is known today, was non-existent, and magic was much in demand as a means of remedy, explanation, cure, and atonement. Readers surely know that Jesus cured the sick, cast out demons, and raised the dead, but what they may not be fully aware of is that he was but one of many others that performed such remarkable feats. Simon, naturally, was one of these others, and he, like Jesus, was so significant that his name has survived on history's pages through the ages.

What is not so well known about Simon is that he drew his powers from the restless spirit of a murdered child, a boy whose life was mercilessly cut short when he was only about two years old. Secret accounts of Simon's interactions with this spirit cryptically read, "He delineates the boy on a statue which he keeps consecrated in the inner part of the house where he sleeps, and he says that after he has fashioned him out of the air by certain divine transmutations, and has sketched his form, he returns him to the air."

Other surreptitious, more cogent, accounts about this mysterious child reveal that he was the unearthed, eighteen-month-old grandson of Rachel who the prophet Jeremiah tells us wailed and wept through the streets after Herod the Great butchered her child and all the other children of Bethlehem who were two years old or younger. Herod was determined to destroy any child who might live to become King of the Jews, a title he believed only he and his heirs deserved. Of course, Herod's massacre of the innocents, as it has come to be infamously known and artistically documented in the works of Rubens, Dore, Poussin, Bruegel the Elder, and many others, was, of course, a fruitless act of infanticide because Jesus had been secreted to safety by Joseph and Mary who had fled first to Nazareth and then Egypt.

There, in the land of the Pharaohs, as long held secret scriptures reveal, the lives of Jesus and Simon intersected when both young boys found themselves in the same school for magic. Both were eager students, initiates in the ars magica, and frequently engaged in friendly competitions at exercising their burgeoning skills.

Eventually, after Jesus returned to Nazareth and Simon to Samaria, today an area of the West Bank, Simon furthered his studies under the tutelage of Dositheus, at the time the leader of a strange sect of breakaways from Judaism who was widely claiming to be the messiah sent by God. Dositheus possessed the science of the Astral Fire, the ability to attract and radiate tremendous electrical currents, which he imparted to Simon whose magic soon became so powerful and renowned that the Apostle John wrote that Jesus was once accused, "You are a Samaritan and have a demon like Simon."

Sometime whilst in the Holy Land, Simon took up with a mysterious woman whom hidden scriptures have never fully identified. Her name was most commonly said to be Helena, but others called her Selene and it was said further that Simon had found her "standing upon a housetop" in Tyre, a polite euphemism for living in a brothel. Simon told his followers, which were many, that Helena was the "fallen Thought of God" and that the salvation of the world depended on her redemption by him because she had once known the Lost Word but had forgotten it after her fall.

When Simon first took Helena to Samaria, she spoke to a group of women gathered there and cryptically told them, *"I am the first and the last. I am the honored one and the scorned one. I am the whore and the holy one. I am the wife and the virgin. I am the mother and the daughter. I am the knowledge of my name. I am the one who cries out, and I listen. I am the one who is called Truth and inequity.... I am the knowledge of my inquiry, and the finding of those who seek after me, and the command of those who ask of me, and the power of the powers in my knowledge of the angels, who have been sent at my word, and the gods in their seasons by my counsel, and of spirits of every man who exists with me, and of women who dwell within me."*

Following the death of Jesus, according to the conventional canon, Peter's disdain for Simon only intensified, and the favored apostle went out of his way to denigrate Simon and, on every possible occasion, declare him a charlatan. At first, Simon ignored Peter and passed his remarks off as mere jealousy, but after Peter began foraging for converts among Simon's disciples, looking the other way became impossible. Soon the two were locked into a lethal test of wills and skills that reportedly reached its pinnacle in Rome. At the instigation of the crowned fool, Emperor Nero, Simon and Peter were pitted against one another in a contest aimed at exposing the real charlatan of the two. Relishing the challenge, Simon drew on his most powerful magical talents and led things off by causing a dead man to raise his head and look about with opened eyes.

In response, Peter made the same man walk and talk. Simon reached deeper into his arsenal and allowed himself to be decapitated by the emperor's executioner. As Nero looked on in astonishment, Simon then restored the separated part to his body.

This feat gave Peter considerable pause. Unable to decipher the deception behind Simon's headless trickery, Peter resorted to a different tactic and dared Simon to ascend to heaven. Flush with the expectation of victory Simon rose so high in the air that it is written that two angels materialized at his sides. But as he drifted higher into the clouds Peter cried out summoning the will of God to reveal itself in the contest and Simon plummeted to earth where his shattered body splattered a dumbfounded Nero with blood.

The saga of Simon's contest with Peter would be a wonderful part of the canon were it not for the fact that it is untrue. Indeed, concerted study has revealed that it never happened in any form. How it wormed its way into the canonical literature is an often-repeated process that I encountered in my work more times than I care to count. Tell a story often enough, repeat it every opportunity possible, year after year, decade after decade, generation after generation, and it earns an embellished place on truth's ladder.

But, as the unfortunate Giordano Bruno said many years ago, "Truth does not change because it is, or is not, believed by a majority of people."

By now, gracious reader, you are probably thinking why is he burdening us with all this archaic nonsense? But, please bear with me, I am not losing sight of my main story. As you shall see, everything written herein relates closely to my convoluted life and to the terrible events that eventually played themselves out in the Heap.

My studies concerning Simon were conducted first in Paris, and then in Rome. There among the secret stacks of the Vatican, after intense examination of two long concealed papyri, I learned that the story of the Samaritan magician's conjuring of the dead boy's spirit was far worse than anyone could imagine. Indeed, its details would impact me in a way that I never anticipated would happen.

Simon's hidden story, as I will soon reveal, was a horrific story of mayhem, murder and a magician gone mad.

In hindsight, I suppose it was only inevitable that my work with long suppressed documents and books would lead me into a state where I began to question my religious convictions and faith. At the start, this process was a slow, unconscious one where I now imagine my mind instinctively began cataloging, perhaps even systematically cross-referencing, all of the staid accounts and teachings of the Bible and other unquestioned teachings that collided head-on with the arcane documents that I so intensively labored over.

Kind reader, you must realize that I lived with these long ignored and unknown works for years. Day and night they were with me, through thick and thin, good times and bad times, for better or for worse I shared my life with them to the extent that they became part and parcel with life. Like any attentive and affectionate spouse, I carefully touched their delicate pages and folds, gently caressed away dust from their spines and covers, ignoring their minor mars and imperfections in favor of their timeless beauty. These works were not mass produced volumes that mechanically and in great numbers slid from some mammoth machine. No, these were works that had been painstakingly produced by the sole and steady hand of but one person who set aside months, if not years, to diligently create them. Indeed, in centuries past it was not uncommon for a devoted ascetic to quite literally dedicate a good part of his adult life to producing only one text. One can only imagine the horror such a scribe would experience were that work-in-progress to suffer catastrophic danger, or be branded for burning by an outraged zealot.

I knew and understood the handiwork of the mostly nameless creators of these works so well that I could tell with ease the time of day a certain passage had been transcribed and even reveal what the weather had been that day. Fine-spun foibles and nuances in the stroke of the quill, the amount of ink applied, the girth or leanness of a specific letter or word whispered untold details in my ear. I could point out the exact place where the scribe had taken a brief break to re-cut his quill because its tip had grown too blunt from the pressure of his hand. I could show you the precise point where the monk had switched to a new source of ink, and where he had added a few fresh drops of water to dilute the mixture. A peculiar heaviness in the loop of a character would tell me it had been applied to the vellum after mid-day when the hand was growing weary and perhaps the patter of rain on the tiled roof overhead was mildly distracting. An occasional thickness in the curvature of lettering, indistinguishable to most eyes, would confide that the day it was born had been warm and humid, diluting the ink past the desired consistency causing it to meander further onto the page than intended.

But, of course, it was the collective formation of the thoughts and events transcribed that affected me. As I worked to translate, reinterpret, and piece together these divergent volumes, slowly but surely, unwittingly, small specters of doubt were slithering off their pages and worming their ways into my mind where eventually their massed entanglement would overcome me. Or perhaps it was subtler than that.

Is it not possible that my loving handling and intimate knowledge of these works evoked a supernatural response unknown to exist? I am not prone to easy belief in matters deemed superstitious, but as I have grown older and traveled more broadly I have seen things that defy simple or scientific explanation. I have learned that the world is far more mysterious then anyone can think. Could it have been that I became infected by the minute detritus, a sort of invisible chromosome left behind centuries before on these works?

Little did I realize when I began my work that for every accepted, unquestioned, dogma-rooted passage of the conventional canon I was so steadfastly moored to, there would be an opposing work that acted to undermine its hold, or to contradict it, by offering a more detailed, cabalistic, and seemingly truthful, alternative. I don't think that anyone in my position, one whereby I was so frequently exposed to the manipulations of the sacred canon and its books, could have remained unaffected by my studies, certainly not me.

Finally, after percolating for what must have been a long time, the brew began to boil over. It happened late one night, about a month before my first episode that landed me in the hospital. I awoke from a dream in which I was about to drown in a raging sea after having fallen overboard from a huge ocean liner. I had no idea where the liner was bound, but in my sleep state I had been standing on its expansive deck partaking in some sort of joyful gathering surrounded by smiling people, when suddenly I found myself tumbling toward the water below. I plunged headfirst into the dark expanse and, fully dressed, struggled to stay afloat. The waves, combined with the mountainous wake caused by the ship, pushed me further and further away from the possibility of rescue. I screamed at the passengers on deck who were mindless of my predicament and calls for help.

I woke with a start and sat up in bed sweating profusely, gasping for breath. After a moment, I inexplicably thought of the papyri I had examined months earlier in Rome that told the terrible story of Simon and the children of Gitta. I lay awake pondering the story, when all at once, there in the darkness it occurred to me that perhaps everything I held to be true was misunderstood, or worse yet, completely fallacious. There for the first time I pictured myself as one of Apsethus's trained parrots fluttering about mouthing lines I had been taught, but had no real comprehension over. These thoughts at first frightened me terribly and I forced them out of my mind, but before I could go back to sleep they began creeping back. And so it went the rest of the night, with me over and over again forcing them away only to have them saunter back all the more aggressively. By sunrise the next morning, they had taken up residence in my head like a band of poltergeists haunting me at all hours, making it near impossible to concentrate on anything else.

I had heard many accounts about other priests falling into spiritual crisis, but always thought it was something that only overcame the weak and uncommitted and that I was immune to such a condition. But there was no denying it, I was now confused and constantly questioning everything that had been the very glue of my faith. My profound confusion lasted for days before I was able to force it aside and move on in an orderly way with my work. Or so I thought.

I must be completely candid here and concede the central realization that my crisis produced: It isn't religion itself that keeps me a true believer. Religion isn't the eschatological glue that adheres me to my faith. No, it is something far more personal than that, something uniquely reserved, something, dare I say it, that goes beyond doctrine, rendering it nearly inconsequential and binding me as a person. Frankly, if it were simply doctrine, I would have lapsed and fallen away many years ago. No, the true essence of my faith is its composition of my emotional being. Religion is nothing you can put a name to or label on. It is not anything held or understood or appreciated any greater or more exclusively by one over another. For me, it is a way of transcending the limits of self and the baser pressures of the world, of moving past the trappings of the material and corporeal and rising above the human condition to reach an unknown state that is always there beckoning, slightly out of reach. But enough of what makes me what I am. When I was a child, Popeye always worked best for me when he said, "I yam what I yam."

A little past noon, Pockets came to visit. As per usual, he brought something for me. This time, knowing my weakness for sweets, it was a fancy filled pastry.

"It is fresh from the marketplace yesterday," he said proudly.

I thanked him and carefully separated the pastry with my fingers and handed him half.

"I didn't see you out working this morning," I remarked.

"No, not today," he said, not disclosing a thing.

"Something is going on," I said.

He nodded and took a large bite.

"Do you know what?" I asked.

"Tomorrow there will be a Gathering," he said, chewing. "All the groups met this morning and decided to call for one."

"That's unusual, isn't it?"

He only shrugged at this.

"There are rumors that the Tire Boys found something extremely important," I said.

He took another bite of his pastry.

"You have some custard on your nose," I told him.

He wiped it with two fingers and then licked them clean.

I motioned to the empty flagpole at the Heap's center and observed, "No blue streamer."

"Soon," he said.

I took a bite of the pastry, tasting its delectable cream filling.

"Delicious," I said.

"You will be there?" he asked, devouring the remainder of his half.

"Where?"

"At the Gathering."

"Yes," I told him. "And I have to say I'm curious."

He nodded again and bent to retie one of his shoes, a sign that he was building to ask me something.

"In the book about Alice," he said, "when the brothers First Boy and Next Boy tell her that she isn't real and that crying about it won't make her any realer because her tears aren't real tears. What do they mean?"

His question, at first, threw me with his reference to Dum and Dee as Alice had addressed them, but then even more so with its complexities about existence. What was I to say? How does one explain such a subject to a child?

"I'll have to think about that," I said after a fumbling moment, but I knew I was only buying time.

As Pockets walked away, I thought of something and called out to him. When he turned around, I pointed to my white hair and then stood on my head, and as best as I could recall recited, "I fear that standing on my head might injure my brain, but now that I'm perfectly sure I have none, why I do it again and again."

He stared at me, cracked a slow smile, and then threw his head back and, of course, stopped everyone within earshot dead in their tracks.

"You awkwardly dodged difficulty today with playfulness, mon ami," Urbain confronted me later that day.

"I know," I said. "And I'm not proud of it."

"Existence is a tricky subject, non?"

"My point exactly," I said.

"Some say that existence would be intolerable if we were not to dream."

While I was in the hospital, Urbain had begun coming to see me. His visits, which continued in the Heap after I came there, were always announced by odd occurrences—the sun in a blue sky would be obscured by a lone cloud; a dog somewhere would howl; a book would inexplicably fall from the shelf; in the still of the night trumpets would sound; the water in my glass would bubble and seethe like lava; furniture would rearrange itself. Occasionally this was disconcerting, but Urbain seemed not to be affected by any of it.

I think it is important for you, the reader, to know that despite my health problems, I had maintained sufficient enough grasp on my sanity to continually ask myself if Urbain Grandier was real or simply a delusional visitor occasionally let loose from my malfunctioning limbic system. I often seriously pondered these questions, but must say that the plain truth was it mattered very little when we were together because I enjoyed his company so much. I looked forward to his visits, but I must admit that the first time he came I was very much alarmed at his appearance and found it difficult not to be distracted by the horrible disfigurement caused by his burns. Of course, I knew that he had been burned at the stake hundreds of years earlier, but never before had I actually seen such horrific effects up close.

"This discovery that the Wheel Boys have made—" Urbain said.

"Tire Boys," I corrected.

"Oui, the Tire Boys. This talk of their discovery, I have a certain sense of foreboding about it."

"I know what you mean."

Day Three

his morning, well before the sun had moved above the distant cityscape, every quarter of the Heap was back to its normal cycle of commerce, and abuzz with talk that the Tire Boys had discovered something of incredible worth. At midday, as Pockets had predicted, Nike raised the long pale blue streamer on the flagpole, signaling that the Council was calling a Gathering that evening. I watched as Nike, well fortified with glue, followed protocol and carefully attached the streamer to the pole's pulley rope.

Once secured, he slowly raised it. When it reached the top, he stood snugly holding the rope hoping for a small breeze to animate his doing, but like always the air was still. He tied the rope off on the cleat in a neat figure eight and stood gazing up at his handiwork for several more minutes. Then he walked around the pole a few times, his shoelaces dragging behind him, before ambling off toward the spot where Humbatter stood watching. Nike grinned broadly at his brother, who smiled back approvingly and gave him a thumbs-up. Addled in his stupor, Nike flashed Humbatter the V-for-victory sign.

"He's very proud of himself," said a familiar voice behind me.

I turned to see Phaedra smiling at me. She was standing on one of the lower rungs of the van's ladder.

"Can I come up?" she asked.

"Of course," I said.

"Do you know what this is all about?" I asked her, gesturing toward the flagpole.

"I'm not supposed to say anything," she said sitting beside me and smoothing out the lap of her bright green dress.

"I see. I apologize for asking."

She was quiet for a minute and then said, "The Tire Boys found something really important."

"So I've heard," I said, thinking to two days before when I had seen Warranty and Humbatter struggling with the metallic case.

"Do you know what it is?" I asked.

"No, nobody does. There are a lot of rumors. Somebody said they found a lot of money, others say it isn't true and that they've found something far more valuable. Maxi said it's smart not to listen to anyone, and that we should wait until the Gathering."

"I guess he's right."

As Phaedra spoke, I noticed Cloudia standing midway across the catwalk looking at us. I smiled and waved her over. She looked back at me and put one of her hands on the railing and leaned back at an odd angle striking another of her poses.

"Does she ever speak?" I asked Phaedra.

"Sometimes, but very little."

"Cloudia," I called out, "please, come join us." I again waved to her to come over.

She held the pose and didn't move.

"She's afraid of you," Phaedra said.

"Why?"

She angled her head and shrugged, "You know."

I did know what Phaedra meant. It had been Cloudia who I encountered at the gate that first day. Cloudia was fearful of any adult, especially men. She had been born in one of the seven small towns that lie within a day's journey by car from the city. She was the youngest of five children. Her parents both worked to support the family; her mother by taking in sewing jobs into her home, her father by doing minor engine repairs to cars and trucks. When Cloudia was four years of age, her older brother by six years suddenly joined one of the area's ubiquitous rebel factions. Cloudia's father was extremely upset by this. He argued vehemently with his son not to sacrifice his youth to a life of violence and constantly being on the run from the state's soldiers who relentlessly hunted down dissidents. The boy wouldn't listen to his father, and one day months later, a group of soldiers came to Cloudia's home and demanded that her father tell them where he was. When he answered that he hadn't seen the boy for several months, the soldiers began beating him, ordering him to tell them where his son was. Cloudia's mother attempted to shield her three younger sons from the soldiers, but they threw her aside and bound the youngsters, taking them away in a truck with their father.

Cloudia's mother took her to live with relatives in a neighboring town, but the loss of her husband and sons was too much for the woman. She slowly went mad, sinking into a state where she did little more than sit staring at the walls, muttering to herself and refusing any sustenance. One day, soon after this, some of Cloudia's relatives took her and her mother to the city where they stopped in front of a health clinic. One of her aunts told her to take her mother inside to see if they could help her.

She did as she was told, but once inside the crowded clinic, she was informed that it was too busy and that they should return the next day. Outside, she found that her relatives were gone. For the remainder of the day, she and her mother wandered the streets of the city. That night they slept next to a foul smelling stream near a marketplace where she was able to steal two apples. In the morning, Cloudia awoke to find her mother floating facedown in the nearby water. She dragged the lifeless body to dry ground and sat next to it for several hours before someone summoned the police.

Cloudia was taken to a shelter for homeless children while authorities attempted to locate and notify her relatives. The shelter was run by an order of nuns who, unfortunately, were more dedicated to the appearance of helping children than they were to actually helping them. Children were subject to extremely strict discipline and were made to work nearly all the time. Schooling was nonexistent except for a two-hour session each Sunday where the mother superior of the order, Sister Miriam, would instruct them in basic religious and Bible studies. I had come into contact with Sister Miriam on a few occasions while at the monastery, when she and some of her sisters occasionally brought fresh vegetables to the monks that the children had grown in the convent's garden. I found her to be a peculiar woman, aloof in unfamiliar situations, hardened in her role as protector of so many women and children, and perhaps bitter that her life hadn't taken a different turn.

Sometimes Sister Miriam would bring two or three of the shelter's children along and I observed that her interactions with them were stern and lifeless, and that the children reacted to her commands with what appeared to me to be fear. Once while visiting the monastery, one of the children wandered off and was later found in the chapel gazing up in wonder at a huge mural that adorned one of its walls. The painting, completed centuries earlier, depicted a scene that easily rivaled the nightmarish visions of artists Giotto di Bondone, Pieter Breughel, and Hieronymus Bosch. It was a highly imaginative rendering of the legendary war that took place in Heaven on the second day of Creation at the beginning of the world. God had made two groups of angels, one with free wills but substantially strengthened by an act of God's grace, and the second group without grace thus with the inclination to sin. A fierce battle broke out between the two groups and the angels of good, those full of grace led by the Archangel Michael, victoriously cast out the legions of evil angels, led by Satan and said to number over one-hundred million. At the painting's center was a winged Michael, with long, flowing yellow hair, handsome face and white robe, viciously locked in combat with Satan who was depicted with horns, hairy goat-like legs, and a huge phallus marred by numerous warts. All around the two warriors were other battling angels, and beneath them reaching out of the Abyss was a huge, horrific looking beast, its mouth crammed full of broken bodies, its seven hands filled with the torn and bloody naked bodies of those who had already fallen into the depths of Hell.

When the child, a young boy, was found, Sister Miriam furiously yanked him by one of his arms and slapped him hard across the face, warning him to never again leave her company. The boy's little shoulders shook as he tried to stifle his sobs. I happened to be in the chapel at the time and I said, "Sister, he is only a child with a natural curiosity about these things." She looked at me sternly and said, "Curiosity is the devil's handmaiden." She then placed her hand on the back of the boy's neck and marched him back to the other children.

Cloudia hated living in the convent's shelter. She reacted rebelliously to its harsh discipline and forced instructions and drew the particular attention of Sister Miriam, who treated the child with an odd mixture of affection and cruelty. Cloudia ran away from the shelter and took up with a band of street children who were especially adept at stealing. Arrested one day, she was thrown into a jail overflowing with other children and adults. Her first night in jail, she tried to escape by climbing through the building's long-broken ventilation system. Caught, she was subjected to a form of torture known as "the parrot's perch." Blindfolded, she was told to squat on the floor of her cell with her knees drawn tightly to her chest and to wrap her arms around her bent legs. Like this a guard bound her arms together with long lengths of duct tape. Then a metal bar about five feet long was inserted above her bound arms and below her bent knees. Two guards raised the rod and attached it to chains about four feet apart dangling from the ceiling. When they lifted the rod, the weight of Cloudia's body spun her upside down, and she was left hanging like this for hours.

When Cloudia again attempted to escape, the guards beat her with rubber hoses and shocked her by inserting the stripped copper wires of an electrical cord into her ears. After about two weeks in the jail, one of the guards pulled her out of her cell in the middle of the night and took her to a storeroom closet where he began molesting her. When she fought back he took a knife from his pocket and slashed her face. The molestations went on for about a month before the guard grew tired of her and pushed her out into the street one morning.

By the time she came to the Heap, Cloudia had an instinctive fear of adults. Working with the Newspaper Nasties, she became obsessed with looking through fashion magazines, which were in plentiful supply from the twice-weekly paper dumps. Her room in the Canvas Dorm, separated like all the others by hanging cloth dividers, was completely papered with pages and clippings depicting fashion models. After work each day, she would spend all of her wakeful hours carefully, page by page, going through stacks of magazines studying the pictures inside. Alone in her room, she began imitating the more exaggerated poses of the models she liked best. Soon, Cloudia became notorious for her habit of impetuously striking the various poses at any given time, regardless of where she was.

"Are you still happy that you came here?" Phaedra asked.

"Yes, very much. It's been good for me."

"And your confusion about your faith… " she said hesitantly.

"Oh, I don't know," I said. "I suppose it's working itself out."

"It's hard to strongly believe in anything."

"Do you really think so?"

"Most of the time," she said.

"A wise man once spoke about what he called the 'convincingness' of things that can only be imagined. He said that feelings about what is real could be as convincing and truthful as anything that comes from mere logic."

Phaedra looked at me, smiled, but did not respond.

"Does that make sense to you?" I asked.

"It makes more sense to someone who feels that way," she said.

"Is there nothing that you believe in that you can't actually see, touch, or fully explain?"

"I believe that life is a big mystery and that each person has a role in it that's not meant to be understood."

"But do you think that precludes religious belief?" I asked.

"Religion is a way of explaining the mystery."

"And a way to apply meaning to it."

"Yes, that too. But that doesn't make it right."

"For some people, it's important to believe strongly."

"I know," she said. "And many horrible things happen in this world in the process."

"I can't argue with that."

"So, you'll come to the Gathering tonight?" Phaedra asked, changing the subject.

"Yes, " I said, "I wouldn't miss it for the world."

"There will be dancing after. The Red Dwarf made a better sound system for music."

Will you, won't you, will you join the dance? I thought.

By this time, I was amply knowledgeable that the Red Dwarf was a ready fixture in the Heap's own mythology. Everyone, perhaps even he himself, had long forgotten his actual name, assuming that he had one. He had been the Heap's sole gatekeeper and night watchman for ten years before the arrival of the children, and he knew the site's idiosyncrasies like no one else. I had spoken with him several times about the Heap and was always struck at how he referred to it as almost a living organism. It was said that the Red Dwarf possessed a proficiency in anything mechanical that bordered on pure genius, despite a lack of any formal schooling. The children maintained that he could examine any object with moving parts and within minutes master its dynamics. Airy Bender said once of him, "He is expert in matters not yet invented." Nobody knows for sure why the children allowed him to stay at the Heap. It was mostly assumed that it was due to his size and that he too was a societal outsider. But, I suspect, there may have been much more to it.

Pockets told me one evening, as we sat together atop the van and watched the Red Dwarf go through his evening routine of locking the door of the guardhouse, that dwarfs had tremendous magical powers and could foretell the future.

"I didn't know that," I told him.

"It's true. They're believed to be descendants of an ancient race that lived underground and deep inside mountains, where they dug up gold and diamonds that they piled in hiding places. Some people say they even lived under the oceans," he said.

"I didn't know that either."

"People the dwarfs like in the outside world—and there aren't very many—they share their secret knowledge with about what will happen in the future."

"Do you think the Red Dwarf has this knowledge?" I asked.

"If I said that he did, it wouldn't be a secret anymore."

"You certainly have me there."

"Do you know the story of the Fall?" he asked.

"The Fall?"

"How the angels fell to earth."

"Yes, I believe I do know that one. But go ahead and tell me what you know."

"I know that long ago, I'm not sure when but it was thousands of years ago, many of the angels in the sky were teachers to people here on earth. These angels were gigantic in size, the largest of all the thousands of angels and the most intelligent. But while they were teaching people, they came to love the women of earth and they had children with them. The children were born unlike any other children, and some people said they were very ugly. I think they were dwarfs. But because they were different from everyone else, people didn't want them around, and one day a man who played wonderful music on a flute came and gathered all the children up and led them away to an unknown place. After that they were never seen again."

"How is it that you know all of this?" I asked amazed at what he had said. What he had related to me was an odd mixture of an account about angels from the obscure Book of Enoch and the legend of the Pied Piper of Hamlin. Somehow he had confused Enoch's giants with the Hamlin children, seeing them as dwarfs.

"I read it in books," he replied.

"Tell me, Pockets, do you believe in God?" It was something I had wanted to ask him for a long time.

"I don't know," he said, "but I do believe in dwarfs."

After leaving London, and prior to traveling to the monastery, I spent six months pursuing my studies in Rome. There, each morning I would wake to the fluttering cacophony of countless pigeons making their daily pilgrimage to Saint Peter's Square, where they would solemnly take up positions around the spurting fountains, columns and obelisks, and await the arrival of generous tourists.

Each morning while there, following a fortifying jolt of thick, rich expresso, I would routinely walk from my small, one-room apartment to spend long days in the dusty, labyrinthine rows of the Vatican Library's Secret Archives. On my way across the square, the skirts of my soutane whipping in the Papal breezes, I would see the throngs of assembled visitors patiently waiting outside the Square's gates. People of all sizes, shapes, and colors, brought together, perhaps the only time in their lives, by their common desire to see what they thought was greatness and splendor.

My work was performed in a stately old stone building called the Court of Belvedere, which houses the immense collection known as the Secret Archives. When I first came to Rome, I was astounded to learn that the Archives consisted of over twenty-five miles of bookshelves most of which reach a height of eight feet or more. Once inside the Belvedere, I would pass by the stony security of the Swiss Guards who are sworn to protect the property with their lives. Then, I would make my way to my workspace, a narrow, low-ceilinged cubicle that held a single chair and marred wooden table, with the names Kadmon and Lacazze carved into it, and an ancient lamp whose innards were so unreliable that the slightest jar produced the flickering effects of an electrical storm.

My cubicle was situated in the Tower of the Winds, an adjoining structure to the Belvedere that stands some seventy-five meters above sea level. Ordered built in the mid-1500s by

Gregory XIII, the Tower was once outfitted with the day's finest looking glasses for the observation of aerial phenomena and the heavens. Many of the interior walls of the Tower feature fading frescoes depicting the four winds as god-like figures, furious Biblical scenes of the flood tossed Ark and a dark, parted Red Sea, Daniel's vision of the Four Great Beasts, and a myriad of astrological signs. The Tower's highest level, called the Room of the Meridian, had on its floor an amazing zodiacal mosaic and suspended from its ceiling an ancient anemoscope controlled by a weathervane on the exterior roof above. So impressive was the contraption, that Thomas Jefferson ordered a replica to be made and installed at Monticello two hundred years later.

When I first set up my desk in the Tower and went about arranging connections for my laptop computer (a seeming sacrilegious act given my antiquated surroundings), I was informed that the space had previously been briefly occupied by a brilliant researcher and scholar who was once regarded the successor to famed historian of religion, Mircea Eliade.

"Now, you know, of course, one can never be too careful," said the assistant to the Prefect that day. He had unlocked the door to the room, as he would do each day while I was there. When he noticed my perplexed expression, he explained that the previous occupant had met a violent end. He was found shot to death on a university campus in America, where he taught and continued his studies of the esoteric arts and Gnosticism.

The assistant turned out to be a secretive fellow who said very little, but when he did, it always sounded like he was mid-thought of his subject. When you responded to him, more often than not, he would have mentally moved on and acted as if he hadn't heard you. One evening, as I was leaving, he said, "It's very interesting. I read that no matter how far fetched anything you imagine is, it is occurring somewhere at the time you imagine it."

"Yes, I suppose that is possible," I said.

"Of course," he said, "then somewhere at this very moment, someone is having this very same conversation."

Just outside my workroom was a series of tall wooden bookshelves reportedly fashioned from split oak beams secreted out of the ruins of the Temple of Solomon. The weathered shelves held a large collection of leather-bound volumes that recorded the activities and trials of the Knights Templars, the legendary religious order that, centuries beyond its brutal extermination, still thrives in the intricacies of nearly all of today's conspiracy theories. Formed in the early years of the tenth century as an elite order named the Poor Knights of Christ and the Temple of Solomon, their ostensible mission was to protect pilgrims visiting the shrines of Palestine, after its capture and occupation by First Crusade Christians, from marauding brigands and vengeful Moslems.

Like many other youths brought up in a Christian household and schooled in sheltered sectarian classrooms, I had fantasized about being such a noble knight outfitted in white robes with boots, golden spurs and a gleaming sword with which I slew heathens out to destroy Christ's Church. It wasn't until I was in my teens that I learned how some of the Templars had been systematically tracked down, tortured and then put to death for the alleged crimes of heresy, including the denial of Christ, indecent behavior, and idol worship. In the seminary, I had nightmares about the ghoulish torture and execution of Templar Grand Master Jacques de Molay who was burned at the stake in Paris on the Ile des Javiaux in the Seine.

Perhaps coincidentally, or by design, resting on the same shelves as those holding the Templars' collection, were four bound volumes containing hundreds of detailed, infrared photographs of the delicate remains of a series of parchment scrolls entitled

Magnum Mysterium. Authored by Simon Magus himself, the scrolls, which in number were seven, had been found in the late 1940s by a Vatican team of archaeologists in a cave overlooking the plateau of Nablus, a few miles north of the Dead Sea. Meticulously reconstructed, translated, and studied for nearly two decades after their finding, the existence of these scrolls was never publicly revealed and then deemed "damned for eternity" by secret Papal decree. Every rumor about their discovery and existence had been authoritatively responded to with statements that there are no writings by Simon Magus known to have survived his times.

Nonetheless, *Magnum Mysterium* told a far different story about Simon than what is known conventionally. Written in a florid, flamboyant, and prolix style, the story also revealed that after his denouncement by Peter, Simon retreated from public life. Through frank words of his own choosing, Simon revealed that he returned to his home village of Gitta with nearly one hundred loyal followers and Helena, deeply embittered and angry about his failed attempt to gain acceptance into the ranks of Christ's apostles. Written in his final years on earth with a calamus devised from a trimmed, split reed repeatedly dipped into an inkpot of what he claimed was a lampblack mixture containing the blood of Christ, Simon's scrolls went on to tell how he and Helena plotted to act out on his anger and hinted that he was considering turning his incredible powers on the most innocent of Gitta's people, its children, but then the pages stopped abruptly.

Intrigued and eager to learn more, I scoured the shelves for additional volumes holding the balance of Simon's saga but found nothing. I went to the ancient catalogue stand and slid out the oak drawer pertaining to Simon to check for additional information and discovered a faded, handwritten note on the back of the 3x5 inch card recording the holding. It read: "Simon [Magus of Githa,

Samaria]. Parchment scrolls: seven, n.d. Thought to be AD 39. Photographed in 1973 from originals. Related and remaining (unreproduced) scrolls held in the private Dositheus and Kidron Collections, Quirinius Monastery."

As you may have already guessed, I was determined to go to the monastery the moment I examined that small card. Travel arrangements took a frustrating three weeks, but once at the monastery, I found Simon's remaining scrolls to be remarkably well preserved. Within weeks, I was able to uncover the remainder of Simon's grisly tale.

The village of Gitta was situated at the foot of a steep and rocky plateau that contained many caves. Over the years, many of the limestone caverns were used as familial final resting places; as maze-like hiding places for cultists, rebels, and kings alike; and as shelters from the face of Him, the still-to-come Lord, who was yet to appear to terrify the earth and all those who worshipped idols of silver and gold.

Simon and Helena had set up their living quarters in a large cavern on a hillside that overlooked Gitta. From their cave they could also see the twin peaks of Mounts Gerizim and Ebal, and the coast of the Mediterranean. The Samaritans, forbidden to set foot in the temple of Jerusalem, had erected their own central place of worship on Mount Gerizim. Here they carried a copy of the Pentateuch, the first five books of Moses, which they declared the only true Bible. Surrounding Gitta were fertile fields of wheat, barley, rye, and millet, and vast orchards of olive and fig trees. The husbandmen of the village also grew beans, fitches, lettuce, garlic, melons, and onions. They toiled from sunup to sundown with plow, harrow, and hoe, cutting with sickles, treading with oxen. The villagers were a quiet, peaceful people who were fiercely hated by the surrounding Jewish populations who considered

Samaritans a mongrel race corrupted by the blood of Assyrians, pagans and non-Jews. At the time, the worst term of reproach among Jews was to call a person a "Samaritan."

In his first weeks, Simon often sat at the mouth of his cave for hours silently gazing at the village of Gitta below. Nobody, except for Helena, knew that in his brooding silence he was devising a diabolical plan. Four weeks after his return, Simon walked to the village center and announced that he was opening a school for the area's children. His school, he promised, would offer its students instructions in the magical arts long reserved for only a handful of selected adepts.

Said Simon, "When I was a child returned home from Egypt, my mother, Rachel, told me to go to the fields to reap with my brothers and sisters, but I in turn told the sickle she handed me to go in my place and to reap for me. And it reaped many times over what I and my brothers and sisters could, and my mother was pleased that my skills gained in the Valley of the Sphinx could be put to such use. Now I shall impart these skills to the youth of Samaria." Naturally, the children of Gitta were much taken with Simon's words and filled with expectations that his school would provide them with such powers.

On the first day of classes, nearly all of Gitta's children between the ages of four and twelve were in attendance. As they entered the large cave Simon had selected as his classroom, he handed each child an Abrasax, a small, magical gemstone. Each smooth stone was inscribed with words they didn't understand. Simon was at the top of his form telling the children mesmerizing tales and performing amazing feats that he said were but a few examples of what they themselves would soon know how to do. Simon held his students spellbound with small tricks of the hand and stories of his travels throughout Egypt. As he spoke, some of the children noticed that there was a slight shimmering in the air about him. Soon, more, and then all, of the children saw the tremulous light about Simon, and watched as it evolved into a dark vertigo. Enveloped in it, Simon was also taking on a different shape—that of a giant winged creature with hollow eyes that appeared to have at their deepest point red-hot burning coals. Simon saw that the children were very frightened and said, "Fear not what you see in me for what is in me is in all men. I am different only in that I shed the veil when others are about."

A foul odor filled Simon's cave classroom, a smell similar to sulfur and the putrid sweetness of burning refuse, and outside, the sun slipped behind a bank of clouds and the sky grew suddenly black. Slashes of crackling lightning slammed into the ground outside, and the children drew closer to one another in fear of what was happening. Still, Simon wrote, "nary a one among the quivering innocents" had any awareness that he was summoning all of those dreadful spirits he knew from the past to be most helpful in casting spells.

While Simon worked his magic, Helena was busy in another part of the cavern summoning her own demonic assistants for the task that would soon be at hand. Swaying back and forth, she sat on a square stone block, her eyes closed, mouthing a litany of secret words that Simon had taught her. As she pronounced these words, the phosphorescent form of Naamah, the most sensuous of Satan's four wives materialized before her. Naamah, the mother of the fiend Asmodeus, was the inventor of prostitution and seduction, and constantly delighted her master Satan by descending to earth guised in the garments of women, to cuckold him. Naamah was soon followed by the luminescent shapes of Agrat-bat-Mahlaht and Eisheth Zenunim, Naamah's equals, and by Lilith, who before her arrival in Hell had been Adam's first wife who spurned both he and God to become another of Satan's spouses.

Once Helena's unearthly assistants had come, she took up a

beautiful flute, which had been carved from the hollowed tusk of a wild boar. She began playing the instrument as she walked to Simon's classroom. When she approached, the children heard her music and became distracted from their fears. When she entered the classroom, Simon wrote, "her music resounded off the craggy walls and the children sat near stunned into inactivity. At last, they were ours."

What Simon did next I hesitate to describe. To say that it was horrible acts to belittle the word and reduce the sum total of the horrors he carried out. For the next several hours, like the wild and depraved Giles de le Rais who emulated him centuries later, the magus of Gitta systematically butchered the children. Simon randomly dismembered and eventually beheaded each child as Helena continued to play her flute blowing ever more enchanting music unaffected by the grisly sights playing out before her.

In his idle days gazing down upon Gitta, Simon had devised a diabolical scheme aimed at making one last attempt at becoming the Messiah, Lord of All Things. But, of course, it was not to be. Intent on releasing and then capturing the combined spirits of each unfortunate youth that he slaughtered, Simon's intended magical finale went all wrong. Despite his best efforts, the spirits of the children eluded him and escaped the cavern. Despite his orgy of blood and gore offered up to the powers he invoked, he received nothing in return except for a sudden feeling of exhaustion and repulsion at the messy aftermath of his work. Covered in blood, standing amidst a room splattered with entrails and body parts, he realized once and for all that his deeds were all for naught.

"Agony swept over me and enveloped me, and my despair at knowing that my aims had not been met, fell on me like a mountain would a man," Simon wrote. Simon screamed out curses on Peter the Apostle whom he felt had doomed him with his denouncement. He cursed God and all his heavenly angels. Helena laid her flute aside and joined Simon in his ultimate laments.

Meanwhile outside the cavern, the storm, as if in response to Simon's shouts, had significantly worsened and several of the children's parents had decided to venture to the cavern to guide their sons and daughters back to their village homes safely. When they entered Simon's lair, they were struck by a scene they could not have experienced in their worst nightmares. Screaming out their intended vengeance, they surrounded Simon and Helena waving their field implements—determined to slay the two of them. But a cowering Simon summoned the means for escape from his magical arsenal, and he and Helena fled into the valley below and eventually into the desert where they were to spend their final years on earth as much hunted fugitives. Simon's last written words on the scroll read, "And we continue to wander, beaten but not defeated, and not the least deterred, ever vigilant in our search for yet another way to capture the souls of the innocent and to ultimately answer the brazen and false words of the alleged apostle."

My pursuit of Simon's story, which soon transcended the bounds of professional assignments and entered an intense, curiosity-driven stage, eventually led me to an even stranger and more contemporaneous tale about a man named Urbain Grandier. In the early 1600s, a time notorious for political intrigue, religious paranoia, and obsessions with demonology, Grandier was the parish priest at St. Peter's Church in Loudon, a small city in western France. By all accounts, he was more than an able cleric despite that his makings came from an eclectic recipe. Roguishly handsome, charming, charismatic, witty, arrogant, thoroughly schooled in the sciences and religion, well-read, and well-traveled, he was all these things and more. But, as was often said when I was in the seminary, you take the cake as it is baked. Nobody ever claimed that Grandier took undue advantage of his beguiling traits, at least not until one day in 1632 when, out of the blue, the sister of a shoemaker accused Father Grandier of being a sorcerer. Not just any sorcerer, but, as she put it, "in league with the Great Pretender and King of Heretics himself, Simon Magus." And, if that were not enough, she also announced that Grandier had long been a secret admirer and practitioner of Simon and his black magic, comparing him to Leutard the Heretic, a figure notorious to many in Loudon. A commoner from the French village of Chalons-sur-Marne, Leutard, hundreds of years earlier, styled himself a modern day Simon after he dreamed that a great swarm of bees entered his body through his genitals thus imparting him with amazing (albeit quite painful) magical powers. Eventually exposed by the local bishop as a charlatan, but not before he attracted a large following, Leutard threw himself into a well in the center of the village. For days after, before he died of broken bones and exposure, his plaintive cries for mercy resounded reminding listeners of his folly.

It has been speculated that the shoemaker's sister's charges against Grandier were prompted by her having possibly been offended in some way by the priest, perhaps by having her misdirected affections spurned. That Grandier posed an alluring and daunting challenge to those ladies not intimidated by his marriage to God is well rooted in the literature on the case. Indeed, it has been recorded that many women, especially a handful of rich and robust widows, considered the dashing cleric an apple most ripe for the plucking. That at times he may have stumbled on the worldly path and entertained carnal indiscretions is not out of the question, but surely not justification for his eventual fate.

Greatly compounding Grandier's situation was that he served as spiritual advisor for a fledgling convent of Ursuline nuns located on the outskirts of Loudon. Months before the shoemaker's sister accused Grandier, a series of strange and escalating events took place at the convent. At night, many of the sisters were visited by terrifying dreams in which they were attacked and brutalized by grotesque beasts that took unspeakable liberties with their bodies. Then during daylight hours they began witnessing peculiar sights around the convent. One young nun claimed that while performing her gardening chores she spotted the Monster of Ravenna, a widely reported deformed child that appeared to many throughout Europe as a hermaphrodite with the upper body of a human and the lower body of a scaled fish with hooves like those of a large goat. Instead of arms, the monster had large bat like wings and sported a single horn protruding from its child's head. After the nun screamed out in alarm and the beast ran away, cloven hoof prints were found in the soil. Another group of sisters swore that while working in the convent's kitchen they witnessed one of their order break open an egg out of which came a slithering mass of small serpents.

Soon the sisters themselves began acting oddly. Many of them would inexplicably go into trance like states where they would stand, moaning and making seductive sounds, transfixed by some invisible sight, and then they would fall to the ground and writhe and twist about for long periods of time. Others would suddenly begin stripping off their habits and underclothing while shouting out filthy, blasphemous words, much in the way a person afflicted with Tourette's syndrome would.

Understandably, the convent's mother superior was immensely concerned about what was occurring, and when some of the nuns started making lewd suggestions to male grounds keepers while undulating about in extreme contortions that would have turned any belly dancer green with envy, she knew that something had to be done. When the nuns added the extra feature of displaying parts of their bodies not intended for sight, she hastily summoned Father Grandier to come and exorcise the evil spirits who obviously now possessed her flock.

But Grandier's presence on the scene was tantamount to the tamer entering a cage full of famished lions. Quickly, he became an object of desire, and far more. Grandier had scoffed at the shoemaker sister's accusations, but now things became far more serious. Over twenty nuns, including now the mother superior, were claiming that Grandier had employed the secret arts of Simon Magus to cause them to unwittingly cavort about like whores, albeit fairly unimaginative ones given their actions as described in the official record. Others made the more serious claim that Grandier had taken advantage of their possessed state by partaking in intimacies with them that they had no control over. A Protestant pastor in Loudon observed, "They made use of expressions so indecent as to shame the most debauched of men, while their acts, both in exposing themselves and inviting lewd behavior from those present, would have astonished the inmates of the lowest brothels in the country." Unable to ignore the claims of the nuns, local authorities convened a tribunal of judges to investigate the affair. So serious were the charges that the King of France, and his close confidant Cardinal Richelieu, ordered a highly respected nobleman, Jean de Martin, Baron de Laubardemont, to go immediately to Loudon to oversee the investigation and to bring the suspected magician to trial as promptly as possible.

High on the list of charges against Father Grandier was a written pact he was alleged to have signed with the Devil himself. According to the pact, in return for swearing his lifelong allegiance to serve and obey Lucifer, Grandier was promised that he would be allowed to "never abstain from drunkenness", and to "commit fornication every three days." (Surely, I think, the Prince of Darkness could have done better than that.) Of course, Grandier vehemently denied that he had done anything improper to any of the nuns or that he had entered into any pact with anyone other than God. And, for the briefest of moments, it appeared that the entire affair would be written off as a big mistake after three of the accusing nuns recanted their statements and informed the tribunal that the good priest was innocent. But, after deliberating briefly, the judges maintained that the women "like the winged captives of Apsethus" were only parroting the words of the demons that now possessed them and sought to use them to free their earthly accomplice.

Imprisoned, Father Grandier was tortured, yet he remained resolute throughout and never, even remotely, came close to confessing to the ludicrous charges leveled against him. Finally, after days of inflicting pain upon Grandier, the authorities decided that the unrepentant priest was guilty of the crimes of sorcery, evil spells, and possession visited upon the Ursuline sisters, and that as punishment, he should suffer the ultimate degradation—public execution. The event was widely announced throughout the region by broadsides and criers that promised a "spectacle of earthly horror that would frighten the Devil himself." Grandier was to be burned alive.

On the night before he was set to die, Grandier was awakened by the sound of small stones being tossed against the bars of his window. Feebly rising, he peered outside to see a group of eight children, ragpickers all who wandered the streets and slept in alleyways, standing below dressed in tattered clothing, their faces soiled with grime and soot.

When the children spotted him at the window, one of them, a young boy with only one arm, squinted up at him and asked in a loud whisper if he were Father Grandier.

"I am," he replied, recognizing the soiled, one-armed urchin to be a boy who had come to him a year earlier pleading with the priest to rescue his only parent, his mother, from forced confinement in the local insane asylum. The woman had been taken away from her home, the boy told Grandier, after she suddenly began behaving irrationally.

"They have chained her to a wall like a bedlamite in a room so filthy that even the rodents avoid entering it," the boy had lamented. "And on Sundays after church, people parade there to torment her when she is placed in a cage in the open yard. You must do something to help her," the boy had implored Grandier.

The priest had taken pity on the boy and went straightaway to visit his mother. When he had arrived at the asylum, the woman was in the throes of a violent fit, screaming that tiny bugs were eating her from the inside out and pulling and yanking at her skin and body parts. Grandier had attempted to calm the woman and after great effort was able to speak with her. Amid her gibberish, he learned that several days before being taken away she had been scratched by a large alley cat in Loudon's marketplace. With his considerable schooling in the sciences, Grandier surmised that the woman was most likely suffering ailments related to the scratch and he convinced the asylum's director to agree to release her the next day into his custody, promising to keep her at the parish rectory where he would see to it that she would receive medical care.

But when Grandier and the boy returned the next day to fetch the woman, they found that she had accidentally burned to death after bored asylum attendants had foolishly set fire to the straw on her room's floor, finding it amusing to watch her cower from the flames in fear. When her smock caught fire, the attendants had to run for the key to her cell. By the time they returned she was dead.

When he was shown his mother's charred corpse, the boy screamed in anguish for nearly an hour and then after Father Grandier calmed him, he vowed vengeance on the asylum's director and everyone associated with it, narrowly escaping confinement by the authorities himself before Grandier was able to spirit him away to safety.

"I shall never forget what you have done for me," the boy had said to Grandier.

"I did nothing that no decent man would have done and yet I feel that I still failed you," Grandier replied.

Several weeks after the incident, Grandier began hearing sporadic reports of the boy's bold exploits to avenge his mother's death. Joined by a band of children who had fled the local orphanage and taken to the streets, the boy had lived up to his vengeful vow by murdering many of the asylum's workers, including the director.

Now, here was the same boy come to save the priest who had vainly tried to save his mother.

"Do not despair, Father," the boy told Grandier. "Watch for us on the way tomorrow."

"Don't put yourselves in harm's way for me," said Grandier, "for God will vindicate my innocence when He sees fit."

"Watch for us," repeated the boy.

The next morning, Grandier was led from his cell to a windowless, stone room where he was to be examined by a physician for the secret Marks of Moloch. According to Laubardemont, as he explained to observing magistrates, these were small areas of the body that were completely insensible to feeling or pain and were caused by the lewd touches of Satan himself. Grandier's marks, continued Laubardemont, were said to number six and were to be found on each shoulder, buttock, and testicle.

Said Laubardemont, "Only those who are high priests in the recondite and forbidden Order of Simon Magus bear such marks."

Grandier was stripped naked, blindfolded, and made to lie on a wooden table, his arms and legs strapped tightly to the wood by leather straps. The physician, Dr. Mannoury, assisted by two apothecaries, took up a long sharpened metal probe that resembled a knitting needle, and began running it into Grandier until each insertion encountered bone. There can be no doubt that the pain was excruciating and with each insertion Grandier screamed out in agony. Before long the bloody marks from the physician's deep probes covered Grandier's body yet no insensible spots had been found. Unflinching, Laubardemont brushed the failure aside with the explanation that it was highly likely that each of the spots explored were Satan's and that the priest had only feigned pain.

Laubardemont then ordered that Grandier be dragged to the prison courtyard where a tall, muscular man holding a large wood mallet stood waiting. Next to the man were two other Loudon priests, Fathers Jean Lactance and Joseph Tranquille, both of whom long and secretly despised Grandier for his innate abilities at attracting admirers at their perceived expense. The two had been summoned as mandated by procedure to bear witness to the torture to follow and to hear any final confession or admission that Grandier might make. When the muscular man ordered Grandier to kneel, the shorn priest replied that he knelt for no ordinary man. The man shoved him to the ground and brought the mallet down hard on both of his legs shattering his thighbones, and then pounded his knees and ankles to pulp.

Lactance couldn't contain his delight with the grisly sight and, casting all pretenses aside, began shouting, "Harder, hammer him harder."

Yet no matter how hard the torturer struck Grandier, Lactance continued to bellow, "Harder still, you idiot, harder."

Not to be outdone in abandoning the masquerade, Tranquille took up a less harsh tactic and began encouraging the torturer by offering such words as, "Ah, such fine skills with the tools of pain, might we see that one once more."

When Grandier, racked with pain and fading in and out of consciousness, still refused to admit to anything, and called out, "My God, whom I shall never betray, do not abandon me", Lactance began screaming, "Confess your devilish acts, Simonian, confess now and God may spare you further blows."

"I cannot admit to acts that I have not committed," cried Grandier.

After another few minutes of pounding, Grandier passed out and the torturer, drenched in perspiration, crumpled to the floor in exhaustion.

"Bring a bucket of water to revive him," Lactance ordered the torturer's assistant.

Conscious again, Grandier's tattered, bloodied tunic was torn from him and he was forced into a shirt soaked in sulfur and a knotted noose was hung around his neck. The priest was then carried outside and tossed into an open cart drawn by six mules.

The cart, led by a contingent of mounted archers and lancers, with thirteen dignified magistrates tucked safely between them, rumbled slowly through Loudon's main streets to the steps of Father Grandier's church, St. Peter's, where it stopped. One of the magistrates commanded Grandier to disembark and kneel before the church so that his sentence for execution could be read. Vainly Grandier tried to comply, but with his smashed and broken joints he only tumbled from the cart onto the cobblestones. Another magistrate ordered two lancers to dismount and to hold the crumpled priest upright so that the sentence could be properly administered. As they lifted him, another priest, a good friend, stepped from the church's front doors and, with eyes full of tears, rushed to embrace Grandier. Weeping now himself, Grandier told his friend not to be sad because soon he would be one with God who knew better than anyone that he was innocent of any crimes.

Hearing this, and confronted with what by any measure was a very moving tableau, the crowd gathered at St. Peter's, many of them parishioners of Grandier's, began calling out for mercy for the condemned priest. Outraged at this reaction, Laubardemont ordered the two lancers to remove Grandier's friend from the scene and rebuked the crowd by telling them that the crafty and unrepentant magician Grandier had once again duped them with his Simonian magic.

With the swelling crowd in tow, the cart's next stop was at the gates of the Ursuline convent. Here yet another magistrate ordered Grandier to beg the forgiveness of all its good sisters. But Grandier responded that the more proper command would be for the magistrate to tell the nuns to ask God to forgive them.

"Insolent, unrepentant cur," shouted Laubardemont. "Confess now before the stench of your burning flesh signals your end to all."

When Grandier again refused to admit to anything other than his loyalty to God, Laubardemont began crying out the names of the demons claimed to possess Grandier.

"Achas, Zabulon, Isacaaron, Amand, Cedon, Behemot, Asmodeus, Easa, Achas, Leviaton, Cham, Ureil, Isacaaron, Rahab, Moloch, Mammon, in the name of God and His only begotten Son, Jesus Christ, we call on you to let loose your hold on this man and to return to the wretched confines of hell where you belong."

Grandier, ignoring Laubardemont, made the sign of the cross on himself and closed his eyes to pray. At that moment, the front doors to the convent flew open and four naked novitiates came running outside crying out Grandier's name. Quickly following them was the Mother Superior and three other sisters, who in hot pursuit were attempting to throw blankets over the nuns, and take them back inside. But four nuns eluded capture and threw themselves on the ground and began writhing about assuming all sorts of livacious positions calling out for Grandier to come and join them. Many people in the crowd of onlookers called out encouraging words to the seemingly possessed nuns, clearly welcoming and finding entertaining the completely unexpected scene. But, as outrageous and scandalous the scene may have been, Loudon and its morbidly curious citizens were soon to be treated to a far more compelling, and completely unexpected, spectacle that infamous day.

It seems that prior to their visit to the prison, the band of street urchins had appropriated from the local arsenal a large trebuchet, a sophisticated catapult, which long before had been placed in dusty storage after being rendered obsolete by the advent of canons and mortar. The children had disassembled the device and, with the able assistance of two mules, hauled it to a high, wooded bluff overlooking Loudon. The trebuchet, constructed out of heavy red oak, forged metal, and thick marine cord, had decades before been a feared weapon commonly used for propelling menacing payloads of rocks, chunks of spiked metal, flaming balls of tar, and diseased corpses into enemy encampments. But the children had no intention of using their catapult as a weapon. Instead they were going to use its tremendous throwing power to rapidly transport themselves into the midst of Grandier's procession so as to better enact the element of surprise in their objective to free and spirit the condemned priest away.

After situating the device on the bluff and aligning it to the best of their limited abilities at calculating, they were disappointed to discover that the trebuchet's cup, the hollowed out portion at the end of its eight foot throwing arm, was too small to accommodate more than two of the smallest among them, a girl and a boy whose names are never mentioned in any of the few surviving narratives devoted to the incident. There was no opportunity to practice their planned feat, and it took nearly the remainder of the night, and all of the combined strength of the children, to wind the oak arm down into its throwing position and to lock its hinged catch into place.

Now with Grandier just a few cart rolls away from the calculated spot, the appointed time had arrived. With the larger group of the divided children positioned in the crowd of onlookers, one of them gave the signal, the opening of a brightly colored parasol, to the two boys left behind to man the trebuchet. One of the boys motioned to the two children positioned in the cup and the other took a deep breath and yanked the cord releasing the hinged catch. Everything at the start went perfectly according to plan and the two small children rocketed a good seventy meters high, smoothly arcing, like two giant birds, and extending their arms perpendicular to their bodies, their fingers barely touching. The airborne boy whooped with glee and banked slightly when he spotted Grandier's cart below almost striking one of two white doves that were flying in his path. The startled doves pulled up sharply in flight, with a flurry of fluttering wings that shook feathers loose. As if performing a finely choreographed act, the girl banked in unison with her companion and the two, with their hair whipping behind them, began their rapid descent.

With the sound of the boy's whoop, heads in the crowd along the street collectively turned upwards. One contemporaneous record documenting the incident states, "Onlookers stood awe struck at witnessing two aerial borne urchins."

One woman standing on the sidewalk near Grandier's cart pointed at the two and cried, "My God, it's the hounds of hell come to fetch the priest."

At this point, the flying children had become more like two screaming dive-bombers headed directly for the procession. A startled lancer among the group sat astride his steed transfixed by the sight of the two plummeting children. When it became apparent to every onlooker that the flying boy was headed straight for the lancer, a hushed silence fell over the crowd. Moments later, the boy's head impacted that of the lancer with such tremendous force that surgeons who received the two corpses said that their faces were so completely melded together that all of their features had disappeared.

A split second after the boy collided with the lancer, the girl struck the cobblestone street a few meters away splattering everyone nearby with blood. The crowd stood aghast as the girl's body shuddered in the throes of death, and a small white dove's feather drifted down to land on her stilled chest. Because of his awkward position flat on his back in the cart, Grandier had clearly seen the descending children, but was not able to witness their grisly fate, however, the aggregate gasps that resounded from the onlookers surely told him that it was not good.

It was at this point that the remaining children, undaunted by the deaths of their two colleagues, made their move to save Grandier. The children, all told about a dozen in number, charged out of the crowd screaming and yelling wielding an array of weapons. The cart was flanked by a troop of archers and led by a dozen royal lancers and at first they hesitated at the sight of the children, but after an archer was disabled by a small girl armed with a blacksmith's hammer, they sprung into action and fiercely fought off the attackers.

Realizing what was happening, Grandier cried out to the children, telling them, "No, no, please. Do not sacrifice yourselves for this humble priest. Let God have his way with this affair."

But it was too late. Within minutes the cart was surrounded with the lifeless bodies of the children. The crowd that lined the street stood stunned in silence. This was not what they had come out to witness; this was not like any public execution they had ever seen.

Thinking quickly, Laubardemont jumped down from his mount

and went to stand next to the body of the older boy who had led the group.

"Do you see what the Devil has wrought with this so-called priest, his earthly and dedicated servant," he said pointing to Grandier. "Such is his demonic inspired power that he commands our innocent youth to his evil ways."

A murmur went through the crowd and someone yelled, "If this be the work of friar Grandier in alliance with Satan then I say burn him not once but twice." Other voices echoed those harsh sentiments, and soon the hysteria that had bound everyone moments before had regained even stronger its hold over the onlookers, and the procession reassembled itself and moved on.

When the group arrived at the prearranged funeral pyre, the executioner, a huge man wearing a black hood with round cutouts for his eyes and mouth, carefully lifted Grandier from the cart and carried him to the center of the pyre, where he tied the priest to a tall post. As he tightened the last knot, the executioner begged the priest's forgiveness for what he was about to do.

"Father, if I could have it any other way we would not be here," he said.

"You do me no intentional harm," replied Grandier. "It is only what your duty demands."

"You are most kind," the executioner said.

"There is one last kindness on this earth I request from you," Grandier whispered.

"What is it?" asked the executioner.

"Before the flames reach my flesh, strangle me with this rope," said Grandier, nodding to the noose around his neck.

"You shall have your last kindness," said the executioner to Grandier's great relief.

Again, as was customary in the day, a magistrate read Grandier's sentence to the hundreds of people encircling the pyre.

One can only imagine Grandier's agony with the prolonging of the process, but when the magistrate asked the priest if he was ready to finally admit his guilt, Grandier replied that he had already said all that he could about his innocence.

As the bound friar answered, a snow-colored dove, perhaps one of those so disturbed by the flying children, fluttered over the pyre, circled it once, and then landed on top of the post Grandier was tied to. The dove sat stoically while a flock of white doves slowly glided from above to land at various spots encircling the pyre. A ripple of amazement went through the crowd, which collectively thought this was surely some sort of sign. Fearing that the crowd would conclude that the ill-timed birds were a divine rendering of Grandier's innocence, Laubardemont leaped forward and pointed to the doves and proclaimed that they were winged demons come to carry Grandier's doomed spirit back to Hell. The crowd was mostly unresponsive to this, and while Laubardemont urged the executioner to his duty, Grandier informed the crowd that Laubardemont was wrong and that the doves were the souls of the children slaughtered minutes before who had come to join him in his journey to God's gates.

Outraged at this perceived insolence, Laubardemont seized the burning torch held by the executioner and thrust it into Grandier's face and, with spittle flying from his lips, screamed, "Wretched sorcerer of Simon, I command you to renounce Satan."

"I renounce nothing but the injustice done here today," Grandier defiantly said. "God, who is my witness, knows that I have told the truth."

Growing ever more angry, Laubardemont began setting fire to the bundles of straw stacked around the pyre. Alarmed at all the sudden activity and flames, the dove perched atop the post fluttered upwards, signaling the others still resting on the ground to join it. The executioner protested Laubardemont's actions and, now out of control, Laubardemont struck the man with the torch and continued firing the straw. With hot flames now licking his legs, Grandier implored the executioner to quickly grant his promised kindness, but it was too late. The fire spread quickly, and Grandier's sulfur soaked shirt burst into a ball of flame. The crowd stood motionless and silent as the priest struggled against his burning ropes. With one last frantic twist of his burning body, Grandier broke the ropes, staggered forward, and fell face first into the blazing inferno.

You might expect, dear reader, that this was the end of Grandier's story, but it wasn't. Three weeks after his blackened, flaking remains were buried, Father Jean Lactance, the priest who took delight in Grandier's torture, returned to his rectory house one evening to find the horribly disfigured Grandier, his charcoal, blistered face still oozing fresh fluids and blood, sitting in the kitchen calmly slurping from a bowl of porridge he had helped himself to from the stove. When Lactance entered the room, Grandier looked up from his dripping spoon and said, "Ah, Father, I hope you don't mind that I started without you. Twenty days in the ground and one becomes a bit ravenous, to say the least." Running screaming into the streets of Loudon, Lactasse had to be subdued by strapping him to a chair with heavy horse harnesses. Still he screamed in terror and foamed at the mouth like a mad dog until days later his heart ceased beating.

Father Joseph Tranquille was no less fortunate than his cohort Lactance. A few weeks past Lactance's passing, Tranquille began convulsing so violently while saying Mass one morning that two altar boys were forced to escort the priest into the vestibule. Here Tranquille began throwing off his vestments, crying out that devils had entered his body and were consuming his soul. "Can't you see how I am suffering," he yelled, as he ran nude from those who attempted to restrain him. Two days later, after the odd spell was thought to have completely passed, Tranquille, once again completely unclothed, appeared at the gates of the Ursuline convent demanding to be allowed inside. With many of the sisters peeping out the convent's drawn windows, Tranquille inexplicably cried out, "Tell that harlot Helena I am here to make the whole of her hide blush with passion." Carted off by perplexed authorities to the local jail, Tranquille died hours later while suffering terrible convulsions.

Fate was no less kind to the physician, Dr. Mannoury who claimed he discovered "Devil's marks" on Grandier's body. Late one night, Mannoury ran terrified into the local grenadiers station claiming he was being pursued by a pack of children who were threatening to eat him. When one of the authorities attempted to calm him by saying there was nobody outside, the panicked doctor berated him, shouting that any fool could see that demonic urchins had surrounded the place. When the doctor refused to leave, clinging to anything he could latch onto, he was carted off to an asylum where he died screaming within days. Surgeons who attended to his body were baffled by numerous small bite marks on it, but wrote it off to the odd manifestations of irrational hysteria.

Laubardemont eventually followed his fellow inquisitors to a grim end, but not before his wife and children first passed away, all under peculiar circumstances. Laubardemont, following the death of his youngest son, the last of his children to die, fell into a sustained state of despair and depression that often found him wandering about the streets of Paris at all hours of the day and night, muttering to himself, or standing perfectly still for hours on end gazing at sights only he could see. So deep into his state did he sink, that he was often found sleeping in alleyways and, when awake and hungry, foraging in garbage heaps for food. After months of such existence, he went completely mad, and, the once highly respected confidant of the King who would shudder at having one hair on his head out of place, began approaching strangers on the streets reeking of foul odors, his skin covered in open sores and puss-filled boils, telling them he was Balaam, loyal servant to the Devil. One night, while mucking about in a pigsty, he seized a large scythe and cut the head and tail off a huge sow. He then hollowed out the head and fashioned a partial mask of sorts from it, which he jammed onto his own head. Then, throwing off all his clothes, he thrust the husk of the stiff tail into his rectum where it stayed. When he was spotted the next morning wearing only the sow's head and tail standing outside a Sunday school replete with women and children, his body covered in excrement from the sty, a group of outraged men chased him down and beat him so badly that his heart gave way and he died.

Airy Bender fancies himself an alchemist. Like many of those that preceded him in his precarious profession, chemical burns and the sting marks of solvents mar his hands. His house is the nearest, by at least three miles, of any structure standing outside the boundaries of the Heap, situated only about five thousand meters from its western end.

As if to match its sole occupant, Airy's house is an architectural oddity that appears to have evolved solely through the impetus of impulsiveness and spur-of-the-moment necessity. The low-lying, single-level structure was composed of about six or seven box-like additions to an original one-room shack that once served as a maintenance shed for the Heap's mechanics, prior to their banishment by the children. Airy lived alone, discounting his several cats that freely roamed his house, and only added on so as to accommodate his on-going experiments and ever-expanding collection of books.

Before coming to this region, Airy had been a well-known microbiologist and medical researcher. When he came, it was only for rest and relaxation and with every intention of returning to his prestigious work at a world-renowned university. However, he looked about and listened and apparently saw and heard something that caused him to completely abandon his stellar career and to instead pursue a long secret passion for alchemy. Rumor has it that he sent a postcard as notice to the research institution where he worked that read: "To identify microbes never intended for sight or to discover the very elixir of life; the choice is remarkably simple. See you."

Airy was a peculiar man in appearance. Tall and fairly muscular, he was handsome in a delicate sort of way. His androgynous-like features, which were all the more striking when one considered his sparkling blue eyes, were only betrayed by his primary physical contradictions: an ever retreating hairline and an ever advancing waistline. When I first came to the Heap, he had a thick, straggly beard that nearly touched his waistline, but one night an experiment he was working on went awry, blowing up in his face and setting his beard afire. When, in a panic, he ran ablaze outside, two children on night watch next door at the Heap reacted quickly and smothered the flames.

On this day, Airy welcomed me into his house after I knocked at his door—which was adorned with a most unusual array of chemical, mathematical, and arcane symbols – with a broad smile and the greeting, "Ah, Father Surin, I have been expecting you."

It had been so long since anyone had referred to me as such that I almost looked behind myself for someone else.

"Please, come in," Airy said, "It's very warm outside."

It seemed even warmer inside, and I wondered why he didn't notice. A cornucopia of odoriferous emissions filled his home and were accentuated by the slow fumes rising from the ever-present cannabis reefer that dangled from his lower lip. I found myself unconsciously attempting to breathe only through my mouth.

"Tea?" he asked, moving toward a small hotplate that rested atop a long worktable covered with Bunsen burners and glass canisters of all sizes, shapes, and colors.

I shook my head no, still trying to adjust to the assault on my nostrils, and he countered, "Water then?"

I nodded in agreement.

"You're here about the discovery," he said, taking a deep drag from the reefer. The *discovery*. There was no mistaking what he meant.

"You've heard?" I said.

"Well, who hasn't in these parts, pilgrim" he said, mimicking a languid, American western-style drawl. He grinned impishly at me and moved to one of several deep-well porcelain sinks.

One wall of the room was filled, floor-to-ceiling, with handsomely bound books. I moved closer to the stacks and began examining titles. Many had to do with chemistry and rare metals with unfathomable titles like *Opusculum Chymico-Physico-Medicum* and *On Phlogiston and the Constitution of Acids*. There were copies of Franciscan friar Roger Bacon's *Breviloquium Alkimiae* and *Tractatus Expositorius Enigmatum Alchemia*. Others organized by rows, concerned alchemy, mysticism, and metaphysics. Beneath those was a thick volume that bore the incredibly long and gold inscribed title, *The Sacred Book of Abraham the Jew, Prince, Priest, Levite, Astrologer and Philosopher, to that Tribe of Jews, who by the Wrath of God were Dispersed Amongst the Gauls*. These were followed by a good many titles that dealt with the Knights Templars. Some I recognized as books I had read when I was a boy. Several were in their original editions, like Michelet's two volumes of collected trial documents, William of Tyre's extremely rare and privately published tract, *Historia Reformo*, that expresses doubts about the alleged sins of the Knights, and

Hodgson's masterpiece on the Order of the Assassins.

I was surprised to see these on Airy's shelf as I knew of no link between the Templars and alchemy. I was even more surprised to see stuck in the midst of the Templar books two works by Gerard de Nerval, the French writer the doctor had alluded to when I was in the hospital.

"You're familiar with de Nerval?" Airy asked when I slid one of the Frenchman's books from its place.

"Only slightly. I was recently told about his antic with the lobster."

"Ah, yes. And the hippopotamus!" Airy exclaimed, handing me a tall glass of water.

"Hippopotamus?"

"One day at the Jardin des Plantes, Gerard took off his hat and tossed it to a hippo because it didn't have one of its own," he explained.

"Generous," I remarked.

"Yes, but not long after he hung himself with an old apron string he always carried about believing it was the Queen of Sheba's garter."

"Oh."

"He was a Templar, you know," Airy said in a hushed tone, as if there were someone else in the room that should not hear.

"I thought they were all long dead before his time."

"The originals were, of course, but there were many revised pedigrees well after their burnings."

"I see," I said thumbing through the pages of the book, which appeared to be an account of de Nerval's travels throughout the Middle East.

"Nerval was a very crafty writer, but the passage of time has revealed his secrets."

"How so?"

"Are you familiar with the Templars, Father?"

"In a general sort of way, yes."

"And their history while in the Holy Land?"

"I know it's the subject of a fair amount of speculation. Some of it thought to be quite silly."

"That it surely is," Airy said, "but not all of it."

"It sounds very intriguing."

"It is. In closed circles it's said that de Nerval actually killed himself because he had become overwhelmed with temptations to utter the Word."

"The word?

"The Word," Airy said, arching his eyebrows. "With a capital W."

"The Lost Word?"

"Exactly."

"But how did de Nerval learn what it was?" I asked skeptically.

"Sometime, somewhere during his travels, it's assumed."

Airy pointed to the book I still held. "It's all possibly related to his chapter that tells the story of Hiram Abiff's murder like no other book published before or after."

I was familiar with the story of Hiram Abiff. In the conventional version he had been an eminent artificer brought to Jerusalem from Tyre by King Solomon to design and oversee the building of a temple initiated earlier by Solomon's father, King David. The temple was to be not only a place of worship, but also a secret repository for ancient esoteric texts said to contain great wisdom and knowledge about powerful magical practices. Hiram, a widow's son, was appointed by Solomon to be the chief architect and master mason for his temple and was given the coveted title Master of the Builders. To carry out his daunting task, Hiram organized his workman into three groups, Apprentices, Companions, and Masters. To each of these divisions he gave secret passwords and signs. Through these, the various workers could be identified, gain access to the site, and receive remuneration by their respective levels of excellence of craftsmanship. Hiram more than measured up to Solomon's expectations and completed his task in seven or eleven years, depending on which version of his story you go by. His name and accomplishment might have been long ago lost in history's glut had he not been murdered just as the finishing touches were being made on the temple.

One day around noon, when Hiram was expected to visit to see how final work was going, three disgruntled Companions, who felt they should have been designated Masters, set an ambush for him. At the appointed time when the Master Builder appeared, each of the three Companions individually assaulted him and demanded to be given the secret Word of the Masters. Hiram refused to comply with all three demands, and was respectively struck on his throat, chest and head with an iron rule, square, and maul. Bleeding profusely from his wounds, Hiram quickly died. According to the classic account of occultism and magic by rebel priest Alphonse Louis Constant, a book I relished as a youth, the three panicked Companions "concealed the corpse under a heap of rubbish" and "planted on the improvised grave a branch of acacia" before fleeing.

When I told Airy what I knew of Hiram's story, he agreed that it was correct, and then cryptically added, "However, there's a bit more to the story that's far from widely known."

"And what is that?" I asked.

"Do you know who Simon Magus was?" he replied.

For a moment I thought I had misunderstood what he asked. I'm sure in retrospect it was only wishful thinking on my part, but when I responded, "Who?" he said once again, "Simon Magus."

"Yes, I'm quite aware of him," I replied.

"Ah, it's kismet." Airy took a huge draw from his reefer and inhaled deeply.

I was beginning to feel very dizzy. I worried I was about to have another episode and thought, here again my life was moving in a singular circle, looping back to a haunted place, whose seeming momentous meaning kept eluding me.

"But I don't understand the connection between him, de Nerval, and the Templars," I said, watching his cheeks bulge. Finally, he let out his breath with a gasp.

"It seems that somewhere during de Nerval's travels, he came across an ancient Syriac manuscript that the Templars had secreted out of the Holy Land," he explained. "It told of a horrific incident, most likely a made up fable of sorts, about how Simon had murdered a group of children in his quest to learn what the Word was. In reading the manuscript and combining what it said with his version of the Hiram story, he somehow deciphered on his own what the actual Word was. Or so it's said."

When Airy finished, I didn't know what to say, and I felt dizzier, like I was about to faint. I gulped down the remaining water in my glass, and waited for him to say more, but fortunately, given his short attention span, he changed the subject.

"So, about this *discovery*," he said.

"What about it?"

"Do you know?"

"What it is?"

"Yes," he said, his eyes widening in anticipation.

"No, I don't."

"Oh." Disappointment apparent. Then, "I hear it's something big."

"I'm sure we'll know soon," I said. "But I have an uncomfortable feeling about it."

"How so?"

"I don't know, it's not something easily explained, but I think it would be a good idea if you came to the Gathering tonight."

"For my *technical* expertise?" he asked, studying my face closely.

"Perhaps."

"I see," he said. "Dare I venture that it sounds as if you know a bit more than what you're saying?"

By dusk everyone had assembled for the Gathering. Children have little tolerance for preliminaries, or pomp and circumstance, and in the Heap it was no different. Gatherings were known for getting right to the point. Tajo, an albino boy who was a member of the Copper and Tin Clan and about eleven years old, had been selected by the Council to act as the event's master of ceremony. He stood on a platform elevated about two feet off the ground with the Council seated behind him. The platform had been set in front of the olive tree and all of the Heap's children sat on the ground before it. Under the rules for a Gathering, the Council was empowered only to decide when it would be held and the appropriateness of the subject to be considered. No substantive discussion regarding the subject could be engaged by the Council prior to a Gathering, and no formal or informal recommendations from the Council were expected by the Heap's residents.

Tajo led the Gathering off by explaining succinctly, in the event that anyone had not yet heard, that the Tire Boys while going about their daily routine had discovered a weapon. He continued by saying it was thought that the weapon had what he termed "awesome destructive powers," and the Gathering had been called to decide what to do with it. When he finished, a sustained hush fell over the children.

After a full minute passed, Tajo asked, "Does anyone have anything to say or ask about this?"

Sayu, her dark hair pulled back into a tight bun, stood from among the children, indicating that she wanted to be heard. I was surprised because in my two years in the Heap I hadn't ever heard her voice. Tajo nodded in recognition to her.

"What do the Tire Boys plan on doing with this weapon?" she asked.

Tajo looked at Raoul seated behind him and asked, "Do you want to answer that?"

Raoul stood and said, "Like everything we find and collect, it is for the use of all. It is in a safe place known to all the members of the Council. It will stay there until it is decided here what we should do with it."

"Has there been any consideration that it will be used?" Sayu asked.

"No. No consideration has been given to anything," Tajo said. "As with all matters that affect everyone, it is up to all of us here to decide what should be done."

Maxi stood from his place among the Council and said, "The men that make the decisions in the city, and in other cities beyond that, will want this weapon back."

"It isn't theirs to begin with," Raoul said.

"Anything that threatens them or that can make them stronger, they take as their own," said Maxi.

A boy stood and asked, "Who does this weapon belong to?"

"We're not sure," Raoul said. "We found it hidden among some debris with no signs of who had placed it there."

"Whoever it belongs to will surely come back for it," said a member of the Burners.

"That's a good point," Tajo said.

Bianca, a girl with the Ragpickers, stood and said, "I came here to be safe, because here there are no police or men to do things to me. I am safe here, but what about now? Am I safe now? I say give it back to them."

"That's crazy," a boy jumped up and said. "Give it back and nobody is safe. Then when anyone comes to hurt us, we'll have nothing to protect ourselves with."

"We had nothing before this," Bianca said.

"But now it is different," said the boy, "things have changed now."

A girl called Iseult stood and asked, "If we decide to keep this weapon, what good will it bring us?"

But before anyone could answer, the boy named Fly stood and said, "It was wrong for the Tire Boys to take this weapon. Weapons are made to cause destruction, and I'm afraid that is all that will happen here."

Firestone, one of the Tire Boys, jumped up and responded. "That is foolish," he said. "The world is full of weapons just like the one we have. We should use it to help ourselves. We should demand that improvements be made to this place, things like hot water and better electricity."

At that, another boy stood and said, "Water and electricity are nothing compared to the value of the weapon. We should ask for much more than that."

A girl with hair that nearly touched the ground said, "We could ask for better homes for ourselves to be built here."

Another small boy said, "We should ask for all those things that we don't have. Like televisions."

"And better plumbing," sang out another girl.

"And air conditioning," called out another.

Then a boy called Nardo stood and said, "We don't need any of those things. We live fine without them now. We shouldn't try to become like the people in the city. The more they have, the more they want. They are slaves to the things they own. We should tell them we have this weapon and that we aren't afraid to use it. I say we tell them that we will use it to destroy the city, or any other place, that threatens us."

"Why wait?" shouted another boy. "We should kill them all now."

"Does that make us any different from them?" asked a girl. "Good people don't kill one another."

"Maybe you had too easy a time of it in the city," said a boy to the girl. A snicker went through a small group around him.

"We shouldn't fight among ourselves over this," said another girl. "But I say it is only right that we do something to defend ourselves."

"And take what we need for ourselves," shouted another girl.

"She is right," shouted another voice. "We've earned those things by going without for so long."

A small girl, no older than six, stood and shouted, "It is our turn to be rich. With the weapon, our turn has come."

Quickly, a chorus of agreement sounded from many children.

Raoul stood again, and held up his hands calling for silence. "If we use the weapon," he said, "we have no other in its place. Then others will come and hurt or kill us. If we decide to keep the weapon, our strength is in having it, not using it. But it is up to everyone here to make that decision."

"They'll come and kill us anyway now," a boy shot back.

"Not if we kill them first," shouted another boy.

"We can use the weapon to get more weapons," shouted another boy.

"With more weapons we could take the city," came another cry.

"And force all of them to take our places here," another child shouted with a chorus of agreement following his words.

"I say we use this weapon now and not wait for anything."

I sat watching Tajo, seeing a look of concern come over his face, thinking he was losing control of the Gathering. He noticed me looking at him, and raised his hand for silence.

"Mr. Fantasy, do you have anything to add to this?" he asked.

I stood hesitantly, removed my top hat, and thought about what best to say. A familiar voice in my head said, "*Truth we learn in pain and sighs.*"

"Our situation is a confusing one, without doubt," I said, immediately dissatisfied with that.

"Begin again," said the voice. "*What you hear me whisper in your ear, shout out to all.*"

I took a deep breath and started again. "I think everyone knows that I am a man of the cloth, a priest. Many years ago, I made a decision to give my life over to God. I came here nearly two years ago because I stumbled on my chosen path. I became confused and had doubts about my faith. My soul was sick. I was questioning many of the things I had believed strongly in—things that I held dearly and that were very important in my life. I didn't come here to tell anyone what to do with his or her life or how to live. I came to discover those things for myself. And since coming, I have learned what is important in life, and I believe I've learned this through the good graces and the presence of everyone here. Because of this, I trust that all of you will make the correct decision about what to do with this weapon."

When I finished speaking, I looked about and saw that the eyes of every child were on me. I felt transparent standing there, as though everyone could see right into and through me. Suddenly I was very nervous, and I thanked everyone for listening and sat back down.

The Gathering continued for about another half-hour after I spoke. Debate about what to do with the weapon went on, and more and more it appeared that the children were evenly divided on the issue. From my place among the children, I could see the mostly placid faces of the Council, but Raoul looked troubled by the debate. Phaedra and Maxi did little to conceal their agreement with those that spoke in favor of giving up the weapon, occasionally nodding in agreement. It was amply clear to me that each and every child fully understood and felt the gravity of what they were discussing. Eventually, after nearly everyone had had their say on the matter, and the solidarity of the opposing sides was more than evident, Tajo called to halt to the discussion, and briefly huddled with the Council. He then announced that a vote on the issue would be postponed for a day or two so as to allow everyone more time to think about their positions.

Following the finish of the Gathering's formal part, a group of about twenty-five children began gently drumming on oilcans and pipe sections retrofitted with goat hides. Their sound was syncopated and slowly infectious. A dozen other children sat randomly about the platform playing other percussion instruments like wooden shakers, pebble filled rainsticks, and claves; still others played reed-like instruments made from thin bamboo lengths and metal tubing. The sound was similar to the mesmerizing drone of the jajouka pipers of Morocco and added to the drumming, made for eerie but pleasing music. Within minutes, the music produced a hypnotic effect that had many children swaying together or dancing with each other, or alone, with many chanting what seemed to sound like nonsensical words or phrases. The scene would have been a sheer joy to watch had it not been for the gravity of the matter preceding it. I was concerned about the indecisive way in which the Gathering had been concluded. My better instincts told me that if indeed the Tire Boys had discovered a weapon of the magnitude Tajo had hinted at, things wouldn't stay static for long. The weapon had to have come from somewhere, and it only seemed logical that someone had an interest in retrieving it, if they knew it was now in the possession of others.

"Amazing, aren't they," someone near me said.

I turned to see Airy Bender standing there, a fat reefer dangling from his lower lip, his head bobbing up and down in time to the music.

I nodded my agreement.

"I love these damn kids," Airy said, "It's times like this that I know I don't want to be anywhere else in the world."

"What are your thoughts on the weapon?" I asked.

"Well, I'd like to see it before I draw any conclusions, but I don't think that's going to happen."

"Are you at all concerned about it?" I asked him.

"Look at it this way, Father, today nearly everyone has weapons of mass destruction, why not them?" he said.

He saw my expression and added, "Of course, I'm being facetious. What can I say about it? It's a real conundrum, no? But, at the same time, I can think of a number of other groups I'm a lot more concerned about."

He shrugged, and moved away to help the Red Dwarf and Humbatter string wire across a section of the Heap to the platform. On the spot where the Council had been assembled only minutes before, several girls from the Ragpickers were connecting wires to several microphones and four huge speaker cones that had materialized from the Red Dwarf's genius. Behind the platform, I saw Nike squat and take a piece of cloth from his pocket and hold it tightly under his nose. His eyes were closed, and when he lowered the cloth and tried to stand up he swayed, lost his balance and fell onto his side grinning foolishly. Maxi brought a chair from the platform over to him and helped guide him into it, tousling Nike's hair as he walked away. When Maxi saw me watching, he changed course and came over to stand by me.

"You spoke well tonight," he said.

"Thank you, but I'm afraid I didn't say anything to really help matters."

"Why do you say that?"

"I didn't suggest anything specific."

"It's better that a decision isn't rushed," Maxi said. "If things had been forced tonight, the majority would have voted to keep and use the weapon."

"And you agree that would be wrong?"

"I don't think it's a question of right or wrong. Why is our survival any less important than any other group?"

"But nobody is threatening you now. You're not in any danger here."

"Mr. Fantasy, you know better than what you say. Every day we are in danger. It's only a matter of time before someone will want to force us to leave here."

"So what do you think should be done?"

Maxi gestured toward the platform and assembled children. "I think we should forget ourselves for a little while and try to have some fun," he said moving away.

As we spoke, the music had intensified and more of the children were dancing. Most now danced alone but in close proximity to one another, as if connected by an unseen force of kinetic energy, their eyes closed, swaying back and forth in time to the music.

Within minutes, many of the children brought out giant masks they had made. They wore the masks by either strapping them to their heads and midsections or actually slipping into them, like one would a t-shirt, with the mask covering nearly their entire bodies. Other children brought out huge stick-puppets, some of which were two and three times the size of the child controlling it. The masks and puppets, made out of thick cardboard and paper mache, were of exaggerated animal faces like cats, frogs, birds, goats, and bulls with huge horns, lions and tigers. There were also frightful death masks and those of grotesque, imagined beasts and monsters. Several of the masked children strapped long stilts to their legs draping the portions of their bodies below with black cloth so that the effect created in the semi-darkness was of a strange floating being. The sun by this time had fully set and a group of three Burners were moving about setting fire to torches anchored onto posts stuck in the ground. In the light thrown off by the flames and the colored electrical lights strung around the platform, the entire scene, underscored by the music, took on a mesmerizing, phantasmagoric quality.

Standing entranced by it all, I felt a tug on my sleeve and looked to see Phaedra at my side smiling beautifully.

"Come," she said, taking my arm, "dance with us."

It wasn't the first time Phaedra had attempted to induce me to dance. At least twice before it had happened, but I had always found an excuse to not do it.

"Oh, no. I can't, really."

Will you, won't you...

"You must, Mr. Fantasy, it will be good for you," she insisted, drawing me into the mass of moving bodies.

Will you, won't you... will you join the dance?

"Really, I can't."

But I did. At first it felt awkward and I was self-conscious, finding it difficult to allow myself to slip into the rhythm of the music. But after I noticed that nobody had any interest in my presence, or even seemed aware of it, I began imitating Phaedra's movements until they seemed to meld into my own. It felt good to move so freely, and I realized that I was grinning broadly. Everything was rhythm. I thought of the Paleolithic man depicted on a cave drawing dancing about in a buffalo skin. I thought about of the grotesque dancers of the Middle Ages and the dancing manias of Saint Vitus's chapel. Everything was rhythm. My body felt vividly alive and a previously unknown sense of abandonment swept through me. I felt wonderful beyond any measure. Nothing else in the world mattered except for the moment at hand.

My dancing went on until I was near the point of exhaustion. I stopped moving and went over to a table set up next to the platform where I filled a glass with water from one of several portable containers. I stood breathing heavily. My clothes were drenched in perspiration, my hair matted to my scalp. The day had been a long one for everyone in the Heap, and a little past midnight things began to wind down and the children headed off to their respective shelters to go to sleep. I said goodnight to the few still around and walked back to the van. The moment I lay down I was fast asleep.

I was startled awake by the sound of urgent pounding on the back doors of the van. I sat up on the mattress and fumbled for my watch, which rested in the same spot where I had set it when I first established quarters in the disabled vehicle. I held the dial close to my face squinting. It was half past four. Moving to peer out the back windows, as the pounding increased in intensity, I saw Phaedra's anxious face on the other side of the glass.

"Quick, get dressed," she said excitedly when I pushed the doors open. "You have to come now, we need help."

"What is it? What's wrong?" I asked, hopping on one foot to pull my pants on.

"Hurry," she said tugging my arm, moving us down the stairs and across the open area toward the center of the Heap where in the darkness I could barely make out what appeared to be a large group of figures.

Why was anyone up at this hour? I wondered.

I slowed my gait as we moved closer and I saw what appeared to be a huddled group of children with strange silhouettes circling them.

"What's going on?" I asked Phaedra.

"It's them," she whispered, urging me forward.

Them? I wasn't sure what she meant until we were within a few meters from the group and I was able to see nearly all of the Bottles and Cans Cabal kneeling close together on the ground. Five masked men holding rifles and handguns stood over them. The tallest of the five stepped away from the others when he saw us approaching and held up his hand.

"That's close enough," he instructed.

We stopped and Phaedra who was holding my arm in both hands now drew closer to me. Through her tightening hands I could feel that she was trembling.

"What do you want?" I asked the man who was now standing close to us. The mask he wore was a simple bandana drawn loosely across the bridge of his nose and veiling his lower face. His skin was dark from the sun, his hair shaved short on the sides with three long, oiled ringlets dangling over his forehead. His eyes were intense, darting about nervously. He wore a dark t-shirt and fatigue-style pants loosely bloused over a pair of laced black boots. In his right hand he held a large, nickel-colored revolver and on his belt hung a large knife held in a flat black metal sheath.

"You are the priest?" he asked, ignoring my question.

"I am," I said.

He reached out and yanked Phaedra from my arm and pulled her close to him. She began to cry and he cupped her chin in his large hand and jerked her head up forcing her to look at him.

"You did a good job fetching the priest, little one," he said to her. "For that maybe we will take you with us when we are finished here."

Phaedra tried to twist away from him, but he grabbed her hair and yanked her closer.

"Please," I said stepping towards him. "Don't hurt her."

He looked at me like I had violated a sacred rule, then he violently pushed Phaedra away toward the other children. She stumbled and fell. Maxi who was kneeling nearby, stood up and helped her to her feet, telling her it was okay, that everything was going to be all right. One of the other men guarding the kneeling group moved to Maxi and smashed him in the head with the butt of his rifle. Maxi's head jerked back sharply with the blow and he lost his balance. Phaedra tried to keep him from falling but his weight was too much for her and he crumpled at her feet. She knelt down and lifted his head onto her lap, but another of the men pulled her to her feet and shoved her towards the other kneeling children.

"Please," I said again, "don't hurt anyone. There are only children here."

The tall man looked at me with a changed expression as if he were seriously considering my plea. Then he struck me hard on the side of my face with his revolver. I fell to the ground with the force of his blow and immediately tasted blood on my lips.

"And you, priest," the man said, spitting on me, "you are only a child, also?"

I struggled to stand up, but he kicked me back down where I thought it better to stay for the time being. He kicked me again hard in the ribs, and reached down and pulled me up by my hair.

"Where is it?" he demanded.

My ribs felt as if they were broken and I had a difficult time trying to regain my breath so I could answer. He jerked my head up by my hair again and demanded, "Where is it?"

"Where is what?" I asked wiping blood from my mouth and chin with my hand. I knew for sure then, of course, why they were there, what it was that they wanted.

The weapon was theirs. It had been them, or someone with their group, who had hidden it where the Tire Boys had found it.

But what could I say? I had no idea what had been said or had happened before I arrived on the scene with Phaedra. And where were all the other children? Surely by now the Watchers that always patrolled at night had sounded some sort of alarm, unless of course they had been subdued, or worse, by our unwelcomed visitors.

"Don't play games with us," the tall man said, setting the heel of one of his boots on the side of my face. "I don't think you'll like the outcome."

"I'm not playing games," I said, gasping. "I don't know what you're talking about."

He looked at the man who had struck Maxi, who was still lying unconscious on the ground. Something silent was communicated and when the tall man nodded the man put the barrel of his rifle on Maxi's temple and pulled the trigger. Maxi's body jerked upwards and blood and brain matter splattered the man's boots and pants. Phaedra and several other children began screaming.

"You see, priest," said the tall man, grinding his boot on my face, "we are quite serious about matters here."

What happened next still plays out in my mind in a sort of slow motion, surrealistic fashion. The sight of Maxi's senseless murder acted to alter time for me and things seemed to grind down to half speed. I began screaming like Phaedra, not in fear but in sheer anger and rage. I twisted away from the boot and jumped to my feet. Startled by my sudden movement, the tall man took a step backwards and then stopped and grinned widely at me.

I charged forward, lowering my head, striking the man, before he could react, solidly in his stomach with the top of my head. He fell backwards and to the ground, with me on top of him. When I began beating his face with my fists, still screaming all the while, he started cursing and shoved his revolver in my face. I slapped the gun away just as it went off, the sound painful and deafening to my ears. The man twisted his body hard, forcing me off him, and he jumped to his feet. Now screaming curses himself, he pointed the revolver at me.

"Tell your God you are about to knock on his door," he said, wiping blood and dirt from his mouth with his free hand.

As I readied myself for the bullet that I knew was sure to come, I saw him suddenly stiffen. His eyes grew wide with surprise and confusion. His arm holding the gun wavered slightly, and then began wobbling back and forth. He staggered one or two steps toward me, a low gurgling sound coming from his throat. The revolver fell from his hand, and he raised both his hands to the glistening steel rod that protruded a good foot or two from his chest. A stark spectre of realization crossed his astonished face, and blood bubbled from his mouth as he sank slowly to his knees staring down at the rod that his hands now clutched.

I stood in partial shock and watched him slowly topple over to the ground. His body began jerking and when he tried to stand back up I ran to him and yanked the rod from his body. He rolled over on to his back and I saw one of his hands pulling the knife from its sheath.

"Don't," I said. "Don't."

But he continued to slide the knife out, and I raised the rod and then drove it down into the place where I knew his heart was. His body arched high off the ground and then slowly slumped back down. His eyes were wide and fixed on me, and I watched as the life went out in them. I stared down at what I had done and crumpled to my knees. My stomach revolted at my actions and I vomited twice.

When I had stopped retching, I looked toward Phaedra and the other children and saw that they were all now standing, and a large number of the other children had joined them. A grinning Warranty, holding a steel spear like the one that pinned the tall man to the ground, reached down and helped me to my feet. Someone handed me a torn white towel to wipe my bleeding face with. Standing now, I saw Sayu across the yard comforting Phaedra. Both girls were crying and holding one another as Pockets and Raoul draped a blanket over Maxi's body.

I gazed about for the other four men and saw three of them lying bloody in a row not far from where they had stood moments earlier. Their lifeless eyes were directed at the dark sky above. Nameless was cautiously sniffing at one of the corpses. Several of the children were systematically stripping their bodies of clothing and going through their pockets, removing any personal items, which they tossed into a neat pile. The fourth man, his mask now gone, lay writhing in pain several meters away from the children. Nobody paid him any mind. A small hatchet was stuck in the center of his back and he was desperately trying to reach behind himself with his hands to remove it. He saw that I was looking at him and he looked back at me, his eyes filled with pleading.

Help me, priest. Help me.

I stood without moving, and watched as Raoul and Pockets approached the man.

Father, forgive them, for they know not what they do.

I turned away and began retching again, but nothing came up except for thick globs of bile. When I looked back at the man through watery eyes, he was lying motionless with the hatchet now gone. Phaedra appeared at my side with Sayu and Raoul standing nearby.

"They made me come to get you," she said. "They said they'd kill everyone if I didn't." Her small shoulders shook and she began crying again. "I'm so sorry," she sobbed.

She was breaking my heart with her selfless concern for me, and I drew her close to me and told her, "No, no, you did what was right. There is nothing to be sorry for."

Over Phaedra's back, I saw Pockets approach holding the hatchet. Its dark blade was dripping thin ropes of blood. When Phaedra moved away, he came up to me and took my hand in his, smiling up at me.

"You okay?" he asked.

"Yes," I said. "I'm okay."

He looked at me like he wasn't so sure.

"You did good," he said.

That night I had a difficult time getting back to sleep. Just before dawn, when I knew I'd have to get up soon, I thought of an incident that had occurred when I first came to the Heap. I was returning early one morning to my post from breakfast when I heard the sounds of loud and angry voices, followed by some sort of physical fight. The sounds were coming from the other side of one of the Kitchen Krewe tents and I ran to the spot. There I found Pockets and two other boys on the ground wrestling, taking every possible opportunity to hit one another with their closed fists. By the looks of things, it was two against one with Pockets on the short and losing end. His nose was bloody and one eye was already partially swollen closed.

"Hey, come on," I shouted pulling one of the boys off Pockets. The other boy looked up at me, rolled away and quickly stood up.

"What's going on? Why are you fighting?"

Pockets wiped the blood from his nose off on his sleeve, sat up slowly, and pointed toward a dark lump on the ground. A few feet away from it, turned on its side, was a can of lighter fluid.

"What is it?" I asked him. He looked like he was about to cry.

I bent down and saw that the lump was the remains of a burned rat. Then the thought struck me, Pockets' rat. The one he had shown me months earlier.

"How did this happen?" I asked.

"They did it," Pockets said pointing at the two boys.

"You burned his pet?"

"It was only a rat," said one of the boys defiantly.

"They're dirty animals," said the other boy. "They carry diseases."

"But why would you kill it?"

The boys looked away and ignored my question.

"It didn't matter to you that he cared about it?"

Still, they refused to respond. I thought of other things to say to them, the "what if" and "how would" questions that most people would ask, but I knew it would do no good. The damage was done.

"Go on, get out of here," I told them.

They walked away, and Pockets picked up his burned pet and carefully wrapped it in a piece of tissue he took from his pocket. I could see that he was now softly crying.

"I'm sorry," I said. "People do stupid, thoughtless things."

"I shouldn't have taken him from the pile," he said. "Whenever you care about something, it only ends up hurting you."

Day Four

he line of sleek, black limousines arrived around half past noon, just after the mid-day break had begun. As the three gleaming vehicles glided to a halt at the Heap's front gates, two dark colored helicopters swooped in to hover above them. The whomp-whomp of their blurred blades whirled large amounts of sand and paper off the ground. A uniformed military officer stepped out of one of the limousines and, clutching his gold-leafed hat in one hand, he motioned to the helicopters to move further away. As they did, a door on another of the limousines swung open and a woman dressed in a dark pants suit stepped out and ran to the closest vehicle to her, opened one of its doors, and stepped inside. A short man dressed in a white suit quickly followed into the same vehicle and pulled the door closed.

The doors of the third limousine opened and six men emerged. It was a peculiar sight to see so many well-dressed individuals near the Heap. Three of the men wore dark suits and ties and each was flanked by a burly man wearing a blue flak vest and camouflaged pants bloused into desert boots. All three clutched sleek, lethal looking machine guns. Held by Velcro straps on their thighs were black holsters holding large handled revolvers. One of the dark suited men held a bullhorn and the others formed a tight circle around them. About three hundred yards away, both helicopters lowered themselves to the ground. Their struts briefly kissed the earth, lifted a few feet, and then gently landed, their rotors whining down.

Beyond the limousines, down the road from which they came, I could see a huge cloud of dust moving steadily toward the Heap, and beneath me I felt a low tremor moving through the metal. I left my spot atop the van and moved higher on the piled steel beams. After a moment, I was able to make out a slow moving convoy of about ten canvas-covered trucks. I had seen the same type of trucks often pass by the monastery filled with troops. They were following three lumbering tanks, two outfitted with octagonal turrets and long cannon barrels, and the third with what appeared to be a long battering ram.

I scrambled down from the pile and ran across the catwalk. Nameless, who had been lying in the shade of the van, sensed my alarm and followed me from a distance down the stairs and across the Heap as I sprinted to the entryway of the Tire Boys' Burrow. I had never before entered the place, as there had always existed an unspoken maxim that only those who resided there were permitted to enter. But, alarmed as I was and without giving it a second thought, I scrambled down the long plank leading into the darkness only to be seized immediately by a set of strong hands.

Someone spun me around and demanded, "Whoa, Mr. Fantasy, where are you going?"

It was Firestone flanked by Astro, both Tire Boys.

Panting, I pointed behind me and said, "They're coming, they're coming now."

"Who's coming?" Firestone asked.

"Soldiers," I said. "Truck loads of them. And tanks," I blurted out. "There are several cars already here. We have to warn the others." Firestone threw an alarmed look at Astro who by then had released me.

"Follow us," Firestone said.

We moved further down the long plank into the main part of the Burrow. Inside, I was astounded to see the living quarters there. I had always imagined the interior to be little more than a dark, cramped, earthen hole where the Tire Boys slept and whiled away their idle hours, but that vision could not have been further from what I saw before me. After passing through a series of heavy curtains and down more winding planks, we entered a large, perfectly round cavern with a high ceiling from which hundreds of small, stringed, multi-colored lights were suspended. Four precisely placed passageways, running north, south, east and west, were cut into the cavern's walls. It appeared that each passage led deeper into the Burrow and may have had additional corridors or rooms leading off from them. The floor of the round room was completely covered with small pieces of colored ceramic tile, granite and marble—thousands of neatly fitted pieces that formed a startling mosaic of a huge many branched tree surrounded by abstract stars, whirling planets, and multi-phased moons. Beneath the tree were several strange symbols and what appeared to be some odd lettering, none of which I recognized.

On the curved walls of the cavern was a section of multiple shelves holding countless books, and dominating the remainder of the wall were floor-to-ceiling shelves that held all sorts of objects, from the mundane to the bizarre, a virtual menagerie of modern society—there were old radios of all sorts, televisions of all shapes and sizes; computers; computer printers; typewriters; cameras; pots and pans; lamp shades; telescopes; binoculars; tools; farm implements; clocks (some working); framed pictures; painted portraits of obscure, unknown individuals; flat irons; coffee pots; and much, much more. The room's illumination from the myriad of overhead lights had the effect of casting an eerie glow over everything.

Near the center of the room, standing next to a rickety, striped lounge chair, Raoul and Pockets stood listening intently to two children who were talking very animatedly, their arms and hands gesturing wildly. When Raoul saw me, he said something to Pockets and motioned me to come over. As I went to join him, Pockets darted down one of the passageways.

"The Watchers say that soldiers are coming," Raoul said. "You've seen them, too?"

"Yes, they're in trucks. It looks like there may be a lot. There are tanks coming with them."

"And the cars at the gate?"

"I'm sure they're here as part of the same thing. They'll want to talk with someone."

Outside, as if on cue, an amplified voice suddenly sounded, *"Hello, you there, inside… can you hear me? We'd like a word with you, please… It's very important that we speak to someone now."* Everyone in the room looked to Raoul for a response, but he said nothing.

"Can you hear me in there?" the voice sounded again.

After another long silence, Raoul asked, "What do you think we should do?"

"Talk to them. See what they want," I said.

"I think we all know what they want," he said.

"Are you willing to give it to them?"

"Please, if you can hear me, send someone out to talk to us."

Raoul looked about the room and said, "No decision has been made yet."

"You're going to have to tell them something," I said.

Raoul held up his hand indicating me to hold on. He moved a few feet away and called to Humbatter and several of the other boys to join him. They huddled for a few minutes, discussing intensively something I was unable to hear. As they spoke, Pockets came back down the same plank I had entered followed by all the other group leaders, except for Phaedra. They joined Raoul's group in conversation and the discussion soon grew heated. Several of the children furiously shook their heads and said something to Raoul. Nodding, Raoul stepped away from the group and came over to me.

"It's the consensus of the Council that you go out to hear what they have to say," Raoul said.

"Me? Why me?" I asked.

"You're their age; you understand them better than we do," he said.

I couldn't argue with his logic, but I still didn't want to meet with whoever was out there.

"Go ahead," Raoul said, seeing my reluctance, "We won't let anything happen to you." He looked to Firestone and Astro conveying a silent directive.

"What do you want me to say to them?" I asked.

"Nothing," he replied. "Just hear them out, listen."

"We know what they want ...you said so yourself. How do you want me to answer to that?"

"Yes, the weapon," he said. "Hear them out and we will meet with the Council after that."

I went out of the Burrow with Firestone and Astro at my sides. Phaedra and Sayu were standing at the front gates. As we approached, Sayu unlocked the heavy chains holding them closed and partially pushed them open. Phaedra smiled at me as we passed through the gates and handed me one of her metal flowers.

"It will bring you good luck," she said. For a moment, my nervousness vanished in her smile.

As we neared the limousines, the group of armed men around one of the vehicles carefully eyed us, and Firestone and Astro instinctively dropped away from me and stopped.

"We'll stay here and wait for you," Firestone told me. "If you need us, just holler."

After another few steps, a muscular man wearing sunglasses and a thick, matted vest ordered me to stop about ten yards from the vehicle. He approached me cautiously and ordered me to raise my arms and stand still. I complied and he carefully frisked me, turning out all of my pockets and running his fingers through my hair several times. Once satisfied with his effort, he gestured me toward the limousine with the barrel of his machine gun. As I neared the vehicle, one of its tinted rear windows noiselessly slid down.

"Please, come inside where it is cooler," said a man's voice from inside. The vehicle's rear door swung open.

I slipped the top hat from my head, leaned down, and stepped into the vehicle where someone guided me onto a thick leather-cushioned seat. The air was uncomfortably cool and dry, and I looked across the vehicle's interior at three stony faces silently appraising me.

I recognized one of the faces from newspaper photos I had seen while in the hospital. I couldn't recall the man's name but remembered he was a prominent foreign diplomat. Today, he was dressed in a tan silk suit with a white shirt, tie-less and open at the collar. Long-legged and lean, he had short-cropped, graying hair. His face was sharply chiseled, a strong jaw showing just the faintest signs of advancing age, an aquiline nose, but he had the pallor of someone who spends far too much time indoors. His dark blue eyes were intense, penetrating. He had a disconcerting way of holding your gaze that made you feel like he was staring well beyond your face and into your mind, where he could see every thought. Around his lips, he maintained the hint of a smile, but instead of happiness or warmth, it conveyed subtle mockery.

The woman seated next to him had a regal demeanor and the habit of looking not at you but to the side of you as if the act of locking eyes was inconsequential, unnecessary. She was small bodied but broad backed and thick in the shoulders. Her short, black hair hung satiny to her neck, cut squarely at the edges, parted severely at the middle. Her nose had a slight upturn to it and beneath her lip revealed the obvious signs of multiple plucking producing an almost mannish shadow across it. Her hands were small, fingers short and stubby, nails painted a garish red. Oblivious to the heat, it seemed, she was dressed in a black pants suit with red silk blouse and a gold chain tight to her throat.

The man seated to her right was small and near completely bald with one willowy wisp of hair drawn across his bare dome from the side of his scalp. The look was almost comical had it not been for the elusive criminal aspect to the remainder of his appearance. To compensate for his baldness, he sported a thick mustache that draped his lower lip. A scowl, enunciated by an oddly clenched right cheek, seemed to have taken up permanent residence on his face. He sat fidgeting, repeatedly reaching up with his right hand to brush his chin as if something invisible were attempting to crawl across it. His eyes were small, close together, and so dark that their color was indistinguishable. They were constantly moving, darting about nervously and rodent-like, never lighting anywhere for long. He wore a wrinkled white cotton suit turned yellow in places from wear and frequent cleaning. On his feet was a pair of combat desert boots that matched those of the security men outside. Despite the coolness of the limo, he was sweating heavily, the underarms of his suit coat soaked dark, the perspiration on his brow an oily sheen.

"Allow me to introduce everyone," said the man I had

recognized. "My name is Simon Driver."

He extended his hand and I offered mine, telling him my name but leaving the clerical title out of it. His grasp was limp, the gesture merely perfunctory.

"And this is Helen Gray." He said indicating the woman next to him. "She is here to assist. As is this gentleman," he said, indicating the small man. "His name is Schneider. Dr. Victor Schneider."

I offered my hand to the woman and the doctor. The woman's grasp was strong, and the doctor's firm, but oily with sweat.

"I trust you know why we are here," Simon said.

"The weapon the children have found," I answered.

"Precisely."

"They're attempting to make a decision as to what to do with it."

Simon didn't seem pleased with this response. I saw Helen purse her lips tightly and squirm on the leather seat as if she weren't accustomed to sitting so close to others for long. She cast an expectant look at Simon.

"Is this attempt on their part anticipated to take very long?" he asked.

"I really don't know. In a sense, I'm only an observer here. Despite that I live here, I'm little more than that."

"Meaning?"

"Meaning I don't meddle in their affairs when not invited."

"So you're an observer," Simon said. He looked out the window for a moment toward the Heap's front gates.

"I think you were a tad more than an observer last night," he said turning back towards me.

"What does that mean?"

"Oh, come now, we're not schoolboys here." He leaned forward and handed me four thick sheets of white paper.

I turned the top sheet over and gazed down at a grainy, black and white photograph of myself. It was clear that the picture had been taken the night before. It had captured the moment when the tall, masked man had struck me with his revolver. My face in the photo registered both alarm and pain, and on my cheek was the first dark spot of blood. The second sheet revealed me moments later standing over the rebel gripping the metal rod, just seconds away from thrusting it downwards. A look of absolute rage was on my face and my eyes appeared full of hate. It was shocking for me to see myself like this and an odd sensation passed through me. The third photograph was a blurry, tight shot of Maxi's bloodied, lifeless face. The fourth photograph was a close-up of Phaedra, her eyes wide with alarm, mouth caught mid-scream.

"You had someone here last night taking these?" I asked, confused at the existence of the photographs.

He nodded, never taking his eyes from mine.

I looked back down at the photos.

"I don't understand," I told him. "There was someone here watching the whole time, and they didn't do anything to help?"

"There has been a small observation team in the area for the last couple days," he said.

"Where?" I asked.

"I don't think that matters now, does it?"

"But they could have stopped things last night," I said, growing angry. "They could have sounded the alarm, they could have warned the children—"

"They were specifically instructed not to engage anyone," Simon flatly replied.

"What does that mean?" I asked.

"Precisely what it says," he explained.

"Would you care for a drink of water," Helen asked, extending an unopened plastic bottle. I thanked her, but waved the offering off and looked down at the photographs again.

I handed the pictures back to Simon.

"What is it you want?" I asked him.

"We want the same thing that they wanted," he said, gesturing with the photographs. "Only, of course, we are going about it in a much more civilized fashion."

"Well, that's debatable," I argued.

"I'm not here to debate with anyone about anything," Simon said. "I want to be perfectly clear on that point."

"Then we have something in common."

"Lets get right to the point," Simon said. "We want the weapon."

"What exactly is it that they have?" I asked.

Simon looked at me most perplexed.

"You actually don't know?"

"Other than that they have some sort of bomb," I said, "no, I don't."

"I find that difficult to accept, but yes what they have is a bomb," he said. "But it's not just any sort of bomb, it's a very powerful bomb."

"How powerful?" I asked.

"If it were to be detonated, nobody would survive within a hundred mile radius. The fallout after that could spread over hundreds of more miles, perhaps further."

"There are millions of people in this general area," Helen said.

I shook my head slowly digesting what they were saying.

"And that's not the half of it." Helen said.

"Not the half of it?"

"What she means," Simon said, "is that some of our local sources tell us the bomb may be outfitted with an aerial biological device."

"What does that mean?" I asked.

Simon looked at the bald man, nodded and said, "Would you like to tell him, Dr. Schneider?"

"In simple terms," Schneider said, "if it's detonated, not only does it create a nuclear explosion, but it also releases millions of lethal micro-organisms into the atmosphere."

"What sort of micro-organisms?"

"Without going into the actual science, the kind that could cause thousands more people to suffer unimaginably painful deaths."

"But doesn't it take some knowledge to detonate this bomb?"

"Little more than it does to turn on a light switch."

"I sense you have a grasp on the situation now," Helen said, with a not too subtle note of sarcasm.

"As awful as all this seems," I said, "I'm sure everything can be worked out. I know these children. I know them quite well and, given time, I'm sure they will reason things out."

"Yes, perhaps that is so," said Simon. "As to the reason part, we see that as your task."

"My task?"

"As a matter of policy, we don't negotiate with terrorists," he said.

"Under no circumstances can we engage face-to-face with them," Helen added.

"Terrorists?" I said. "You're not serious, are you?"

"Please be assured that we are quite serious," Helen said.

"For God's sake, these are children, not terrorists," I said, growing exasperated with the tone of the conversation.

"Age is of little consideration in these situations," she said.

"Indeed, if it were, it wouldn't weigh well in their favor."

"Any group with the capability of wiping out innocent people without provocation or reason are terrorists," Simon said absently, gazing out his window at the Heap.

The words "without provocation or reason" struck me in a profound way and I shook my head sadly.

"Are you refusing to help us?" Simon asked.

There was no sense of impatience in his question, and it hung there as if he had a universe of time to await a reply.

"I'm not sure what I'm doing," I said, feeling the first pangs of one of my headaches coming on.

"This is no time for procrastination."

"Exactly what is it you want me to do?" I asked.

"Let me make it very easy for you," Simon said. "The only message you have to carry back to them is that they must turn the bomb over to us within the next twelve hours."

"What if it takes longer than that?"

"I'm sorry. Twelve hours is all the time that you have."

While time, the endless idiot runs screaming 'round the world. Inexplicably, the line I had read somewhere years ago popped into my head.

"And if they don't turn it over?" I asked.

"Then we will do anything we feel appropriate to secure the site and to remove the bomb."

I didn't reply and thought about what "to secure the site" meant.

"If they turn the weapon over to you, what then?" I asked.

Simon hesitated, then said, "We'd like to resettle them elsewhere."

"Resettle them? Resettle them where?"

"Somewhere away from here, someplace where it matters little if they talk about what's happened here."

"Like where?"

"We're not sure."

"It's not going to happen," I said.

"Why is that?"

"They'll never agree to it."

"That would be very unfortunate."

"I won't agree to it," I said challengingly. My anger was growing again and I had to contain myself not to let it get the best of me.

"And why is that?"

"There's no need to move them anywhere. This is where they live; this is their home."

"This, Mr. Surin, in case you haven't noticed, is a refuse dump," Simon said smugly. Next to him both Helen and Schneider snorted their amusement.

"Perhaps to you it is."

"And?"

"And they're not going anywhere unless they want to, and I can assure you they won't leave here."

"This from a mere observer," Simon said beginning to lose his cool demeanor. "How can you be so sure of that?"

"Simply put," I said, leaning forward closer to him, "they wouldn't trust you."

"What about you?"

"Does it matter?"

"It could."

"I don't trust you at all. But it's not my decision to make."

Simon now glared at me. His eyes betrayed boiling anger.

"I know who and what you are," I told him. "Both of you," I added looking at Helen.

"I fear that you are dancing dangerously close to the edge," Simon said. "But that aside, the question remains, will you help us?"

"What if I don't?"

"Then there's no need to wait twelve hours, and we'll do whatever necessary to take the weapon."

I would be lying if I didn't admit I resented the position I was in. My disdain for Simon and his assistants was mounting by the minute. I didn't want to have anything to do with them. But at the same time I was well aware of what was at stake. In retrospect, I think it was the feeling of utter helplessness that most affected me. For the first time in my life I was impacted by the sensation a defenseless child must feel in the face of insurmountable odds.

"You have to give me your word that nobody else will be harmed," I said.

"I can give you that specific to the next twelve hours provided nothing untoward happens."

"And that means what?"

"It means the sooner they turn it over, the better for everyone," Simon said. "I don't think that I need to point out that we are wasting time right now."

"I'll do what I can, but nobody else can be harmed." I slid across the seat, opened the door, and stepped from the limousine.

"Wait," I heard Simon say behind me. He followed me out into the sunshine, his eyes blinking. He raised one hand to shield them from the harsh light and reached into his suit jacket pocket and took out a small cell phone, which he handed to me.

"Take this. You need only to push the 'on' button and you're instantly connected to us." I accepted the phone and put it in my pants pocket.

"Please, don't fail us," he said. As I walked away from him, he added, "I can't emphasize how very important it is."

Astro and Firestone were where I had left them. Behind them, still standing by the gate, were Phaedra and Sayu, with Nameless sitting beside them. When I entered the gates, I saw that Sayu was staring at the departing line of limousines. Something about the look on her face concerned me.

"What's wrong?" I asked her.

Still staring at the limos, she softly said, "I know that man."

"What?"

"I know that man," she repeated.

"How"" I asked. "How do you know him?"

She turned and ran back into the Heap. As I watched her run

away, I realized the meaning of what she had said to me.

I found Raoul and the other group leaders waiting for me under the olive tree. The Red Dwarf was also there, squatting several yards away with a group of about ten children intently watching as he sketched something with a stick on the ground. Phaedra had gone in search of Sayu and said she would soon join the group. I explained to the Council what Simon had said, emphasizing that he had given only twelve hours to turn over the weapon.

"What if we don't?" came the inevitable question from Alsirat, head of the Ragpickers.

"I'm not sure," I answered. "My guess is they'll send the soldiers in to take it."

"What more did he say?" asked Raoul.

I took a deep breath. "They want to resettle all of you elsewhere," I said bluntly.

"What does that mean, resettle?" asked Jazz from the Burners.

"That they want to move everyone away from here. He didn't say to where."

He reacted to my explanation with an indignant look.

"Over our dead bodies," he scowled. The other group leaders voiced their agreement. I watched as the confusion on their faces turned to anger.

"Jazz is right," Raoul said. "We won't leave here. My family and home were taken once, but never again."

"I told him everyone would feel this way, but it made no difference."

I held up the cell phone Simon had given me and handed it to Raoul.

"He gave me this to contact them directly."

Raoul looked closely at the phone, and then called out for the Red Dwarf. When he came over to us, Raoul handed him the phone and asked that he examine it. Within seconds, the Dwarf had it apart into two sections. He handed one back to Raoul and closely examined the other. After a moment, he carefully reached into the section he held and extracted a small cone shaped object, which he dropped to the ground and smashed with one of his feet, grinding it into the dirt.

"Listening device," he said, handing the section back to Raoul, and returning to the group of children waiting for him. Nameless ambled over and carefully sniffed at the spot where the Dwarf had destroyed the device. After a moment, he circled the spot twice, lifted his leg, and urinated on it.

As you may have already thought, kind reader, after the dust settled from the departing limousines, the soldiers and their tanks and trucks stayed behind. When the sun began to set, about twenty look-alike soldiers clad in tan camouflage began unpacking and laying out several large tents, which they soon began erecting about ten meters from the Heap's main gates. In the heat, the soldiers worked slowly while some of their comrades perched on the tank turrets and jeeps watched and occasionally called out oft-handed remarks. With the sun poised perfectly on the horizon's distant edge, seeming to threaten to sink no further, the children began drifting out of their shelters to stand by the fence and watch the soldiers. Within minutes, the entire population of the Heap was lined along the wire silently observing them. When the men noticed, they stopped working for a moment and stood looking back at the children. The soldiers seemed unsure of themselves before so many young faces.

After the sun had set, Phaedra and Pockets came to the van. Pockets brought a bag holding about a dozen clementines that he handed to me.

"Is Sayu all right?" I asked Phaedra.

"Yes, she's fine," she said.

"She's told you about him?"

Phaedra shook her head. "She didn't have to. A lot of us knew him from the streets," she said staring down at the floor.

"I'm sorry," I said, wishing that I had thought of something better to say. I selected three clementines from the bag, handed each of my guests one, and began peeling the third.

"No," she said. "You don't have to be sorry."

Pockets grinned and said, "People from your part of the world, they are always sorry for things that stay the same and never change."

"I know; I understand," I told him.

"That is better than sorry," said Pockets, stuffing half a clementine into his mouth.

"Why weren't you with the other group leaders today?" I asked Phaedra.

She shrugged and looked down at her hands folded in her lap.

"I'm not sure," she said. "It didn't seem right without Maxi." For a moment she was lost in her thoughts, and then she looked up and smiled. "Besides, I wanted to make sure that you would be all right."

"I appreciate that. I really do."

"What is going to happen now? Phaedra asked.

"I don't know," I said. "I wish I did."

"I wish it had never happened," she said, her mood shifting again. "I wish they had never found that thing. Now it will never be the same here."

"I think things may turn out alright," I said, with a twinge of guilt.

"That things are never the same is what I like best about here," Pockets said.

"You don't know what I mean," Phaedra said sharply.

"She means that she's worried about what may happen," I explained to Pockets.

Pockets moved closer to Phaedra and put his arm around her shoulders. She leaned her head on him and mumbled she was sorry for having snapped at him. I sat leaning against the wall of the van looking at the two of them, marveling at their strength.

After a short while Phaedra sat up and brushed her braids away from her face.

"Do you think the soldiers will come soon?" she asked.

It was a question I didn't want to answer, but I said, "Yes, I do. They don't know any other way of doing things."

"It's always the same," she said. She leaned over and kissed Pockets lightly on his cheek.

"I should get back and be with Sayu," she said standing.

We watched her cross the catwalk and go down the stairs.

"You like her, don't you?" Pockets said, watching Phaedra disappear into the darkness.

"I like everyone here," I said.

"Not like that. I didn't mean that way."

"She's just a child," I said, perhaps a bit too defensively.

"But in time, she will be a woman...."

He was right, of course, but to me she would always be a child and, more to the point, she would always be the personification of innocence and beauty. To do anything to alter that would strip those things away from me forever. But there was no denying that I was physically attracted to her.

"And you will still be a man."

He cocked his head and grinned knowingly at me. Then he leaned over to retie one of his shoes.

I wished he hadn't said it. It was true. And his saying it acted to ordain the thought in me.

"Do you talk to the burned man about her?" he asked.

"What?"

"Do you talk to him about Phaedra?"

"Who?"

"The burned man that comes to see you."

"You've seen him?" I asked, not knowing quite what to think.

"He's your friend, isn't he?"

Now I was completely lost. I didn't know how to answer him. All I could do was nod.

"Yes, he's my friend. An old and dear friend."

He bent down and began retying one of his shoes.

"In the Alice book, the King says to her, 'Why it's as much as I can do to see real people, by this light!'" he said.

I waited for him to say something more, but he didn't. After a few more minutes, he said that he was tired and bid me good night.

Later that evening, I went up on top of the van and sat thinking about what Phaedra had said, recalling her exact words.

It's always the same.

What had she meant? What was always the same? I knew she didn't mean life. Over the past two years, I had observed her almost daily, and I knew, despite her difficult years before coming to the Heap, she possessed a transcendent zest for life. Indeed, one of the things most attractive about her was that she radiated life and all that was good about it. Maxi's death had surely drained her of a good portion of her vibrancy, but I had no doubt that it would restore itself with time. If, of course, there was time.

It's always the same.

No, she had meant something else other than life. Most likely that age old something else that amounted to the tired adage: no matter how much things change they always stay the same—that the weak would always stay weak, the poor always poor, the powerless always powerless. Jesus Christ had once said. "The meek shall inherit the earth," and I suppose the question was, when?

Despite Phaedra's never having traveled anywhere beyond the region and having had no exposure to different cultures, she intrinsically understood the social order of the world. And, more to the point and to the immediate situation, she understood that the threat hanging over the Heap was very real, and that it was most likely destined to doom everything that was good and right about it. My realization of this admittedly was a simple one given its stark obviousness, but it made me want to cry out at the heavens, to shake my fist at God and shout that some things were too much to take, that sometimes the old way was the wrong way and that goodness had a right to prevail more than just once in a while.

I looked up at the night sky dotted with millions of stars. A near full moon bathed the Heap in a peaceful light. I thought back to my first episode that had landed me in the hospital, thinking about that fading moment of consciousness when I held the absolute secret to life's mystery. That moment had carried such an odd mix of amazement, relief, and peacefulness. It was suddenly all so simple, so obvious, so perfect—yet when I woke up and found myself strapped to a hospital bed, it was gone, and all awareness of what it was or might have been, had vanished. I was left only with the knowledge that I had known what it was, that there was an answer, but with time, even that awareness became less than comforting. With time I came to understand it amounted to little more than what I had known or felt, prior to the episode. It was as if someone had played a cruel joke on me at my expense, and I was back to relying on my faith, the very thing that had initially provoked everything.

Near the front gates, I saw a fleeting shadow that could have been one of the soldiers or one of the few animals indigenous to the area. Occasionally at night, wolves, with their wily instinct and sharp sense of smell, would venture close to the fence and try to dig under it. But between vigilant Watchers and Nameless, who usually roamed about after dark, none were ever successful. Some of the children said the wolves came from a nearby place called the Field of Heads, which lies about a kilometer away, on the side of the highway that cuts from the city into the heated expanse like a long dried bone. The area is covered with huge, intricately carved stone heads, some of which have been damaged by vandals or constant exposure to the elements. Nobody knows for sure how old the heads are, their purpose, or what civilization made them. That they are priceless artifacts is without question. Archeologists speculate that the heads, which are taller than those found on Easter Island and less rotund than those thought to have been carved by the mysterious Olmecs, were assembled centuries ago by an unknown people to appease their gods and to reflect their order in the heavens. The wolves, the children claimed, lived in a series of labyrinthine tunnels that networked beneath the heads and mysteriously connected to the area beneath the Heap. Once, when discussing the Field with Pockets, he remarked that some in the Bottles and Cans Cabal claimed that Maxi had explored one of the tunnels, barely escaping with his life after he entered a large chamber containing a limestone sarcophagus. When he peered into the coffin he came face-to-face with a huge she wolf who was nursing her cubs. Others among the children maintained that they had seen a minotaur-like creature by the fence after nightfall. Whether or not what they saw was real or imagined I don't know. These were not children easily given to exaggeration or flights of fancy, so I tend to believe them, at least in part. After nearly two years in the Heap, I knew the area surrounding it was far more than a blank canvas and that it held many mysteries.

One evening during my first year in the Heap, about an hour before dusk, I sat observing the formation of one of the very rare thunderstorms that passed through the area. It was, as usual, a day replete with boiling sunlight and a robin's egg blue sky. I watched as a dark opaque mass rapidly materialized to the city's east. Beneath the mass, the wind began blowing wildly, whipping the sand in its random path into surreal sculptures and winding shapes that looked like strange creatures concealed beneath, inhuman rough beasts. Above the mass, which draped the lower atmosphere like a gauzy shroud, the sky turned gray and then blackened, and as if in announcement, a faint roll of thunder sounded. This was followed by a stretch of silence long enough to cause one to think that the storm had already exhausted its resources, but then the thunder sounded again, this time more loudly, as the winds picked up speed and moved quickly over the city.

The darkness opened its floodgates and drenched everything beneath it and then continued moving before it appeared to pause and hover over the Field of Heads. As it moved, the sweet smell of rainwater and wet earth swept the air around me. The billions of heavy droplets rebounding from the ground formed an eerie smoke-like layer low to the earth. There was a great crackling sound and a single bolt of lightning flashed and drove itself into the ground near the densest cluster of heads, throwing up a rain of sand and clumps of earth. Another bolt followed, striking the same spot like an electric dagger, throwing up more sand; and then, a third bolt struck one of the largest heads at what appeared to be the center of its forehead. The dark, granite colored head seemed to come alive with the blue and gold electricity encircling it, first like a nimbus, and then a swirling infinity-like pattern that made the head's stone eyes seem filled with anger and vengeance. After that, anytime my gaze fell on the field, the frightful image would return, and those unmoving eyes seemed wider and filled with vindictive fury.

"You look tired, mon ami."

I looked up from my thoughts to see Urbain sitting across from me.

"I am," I told him.

"You should not become so distracted by reality," he said. "It isn't healthy."

"But, I'm concerned about what may happen here," I said.

He sighed. "Gabriel, what happens will happen. What you must do is what you must do, and that, my dear friend, will make everything right."

"Here," I said, handing him a clementine from my pocket.

"Merci beaucoup."

I thought about what he had said. Grandier often said things that sounded so simple yet upon reflection were quite complex. His words seemed completely removed from the conversation at hand, but had a way of sneaking back later on. This was no exception when he said, "I was thinking about history the other day."

"History?" I asked.

"Oui, I've come to the conclusion that it is never to be trusted. Who better to understand that than you and I?"

He came and sat beside me and began peeling the clementine.

"History is a great sanitizer," he said. "It picks the gray lint from the fabric of things and scrubs them clean. Ambiguity is dyed over with conviction. Lucky men are recast as heroes; men with noble intentions are presented as fools. The innocent become a well-rehearsed Greek chorus in matters that escaped them. History reshapes things into more attractive forms; it edits out the pesky little details until all that is left is a fable fetched from fact."

I understood what he was saying. Nearly my whole life had been lived in the role of someone doing precisely what he described. *But now things were different, I thought.*

As though he was reading my thoughts, he said, "Look at my own history, Gabriel. For centuries now people have marveled at my story—a well-intentioned parish priest brought down by a shoemaker's sister and a bunch of disenchanted noviciates whose names are inconsequential to the history they sparked."

He put a hand on my shoulder and gestured toward the Heap with his other. "What happens here will soon be history," he said. "Our business is to bear witness in good spirits."

Day Five

hey came minutes before dawn, a few hours past Simon's twelve-hour deadline. As the first line of light slipped beneath the dark horizon, the shapes of about fifty soldiers clad in sand brown and camouflage uniforms slowly rose from the sand like ghosts, and advanced toward the Heap's main gates.

Things went wrong for them at the start. The children, at some point unknown to me, most likely with the able assistance of the Red Dwarf, had electrified the front gates by jerry-rigging them to one of the heavy electrical lines that fed the Heap. Two soldiers who attempted to use bolt cutters to sever the chains on the gate were tossed into the air, their bodies framed in eerie, dancing blue lines. After the power line was disabled and cut, another group leaned telescoping ladders against the fence and quickly scrambled over, only to stumble and fall into one of the many concealed pits dug along the fences' inside perimeter. Each pit had been filled with waste from the latrines, and I could hear the soldiers muttering curses and calling out warnings to their comrades coming over the fence. The soldiers pulled back and regrouped.

There followed a long silence and then a small explosion blew the front gates apart. When the smoke cleared, a group of about thirty heavily outfitted soldiers began moving in coordinated lines over the downed gates, across the rubble and piles of trash and in the general direction of the Tire Boys' Burrow. Behind them, two tanks slowly rumbled forward to take up positions just inside the Heap. One of the tanks circled the Red Dwarf's guardhouse and drove over it, crushing and grinding the wood into the dirt.

I had been watching from my place atop the van and, as prearranged, when I spotted the soldiers approaching, had sent a signal to the Watchers below waiting outside the Burrow. After the gates had been downed and the soldiers began advancing again, I knew that my time would be better served below, and I descended the metal stairs.

I was crossing the open space, moving toward the Burrow, when I saw Pockets, Warranty, and Humbatter, all carrying towels, coming from the direction of the latrines. I was about to call out and warn them of the advancing men, when a group of six soldiers came around a corner of the Canard. I slipped behind a pile of crushed plastic bottles, but was still in the sight line of the boys. I frantically waved my arms to get their attention, but they were preoccupied with talk among themselves, unknowingly moving toward the soldiers.

Both groups spotted each other at the same time, stopped moving, and silently stood considering one another. After a moment, Humbatter said something to Pockets and Warranty and the boys began slowly backing away. One of the soldiers took a few steps forward and ordered them to stop, drop whatever they were holding, and to put their hands in the air.

The three boys looked at one another, as if trying to decide what to do, but continued to move slowly backwards. The soldier called out the order again and told them it was their last warning.

"Stop right where you are, drop everything, and put your hands up now," he yelled.

"After you," Humbatter called out defiantly, and the boys stopped moving and stood their ground.

One of the soldiers raised a long tubular device to his shoulder and aimed it at the three. There followed a whooshing sound, and a plume of smoke came from the rear of the weapon. I looked toward Pockets and the other two boys, just as something deafening loud burst in the air over them, spewing dark smoke and a nauseous odor. Warranty was doubled over and he took a few erratic steps and then fell to the ground. Pockets and Humbatter, dazed by the blast, began staggering about. Humbatter groped the air in front of him as if he were now sightless. Pockets outwardly shook off the effects and grabbed Warranty, who had stumbled into a pile of cardboard, and helped him to his feet. As he put his arm around Warranty's waist to support him, another soldier raised his tubular device to his shoulder and aimed at the boys.

I stood up quickly, heedless of revealing my hiding place, waving my arms, yelling at the soldier for him not to fire.

"They can't harm you," I hollered. "They aren't armed. Please, don't shoot them."

Next to the soldier with the tubular device, another camouflaged figure dropped to one knee and fired his rifle at me. I froze in fear, the rounds breathing hotly past me, slamming into a pile of chrome bumpers with a hard metallic, slapping sound; others ricocheting, producing whining sounds. Another soldier appeared fifty yards to the right of me, and fired a burst from his gun. The bullets whizzed by, chipping the side of the latrine building, sending bits and slivers of wood flying everywhere.

I dove forward and lay on the ground with my hands covering my head. When the firing stopped, I cautiously lifted my head and looked about. Pockets was still struggling with Warranty's weight, trying to help him toward the Burrow. The soldier with the tubular weapon had moved several yards closer and was taking aim once more. I yelled for Pockets to get down, and again a cloud of smoke blurted out the back of the tube. This time, whatever was fired from the weapon exploded several meters above the boys, and something struck Pockets, knocking him high off the ground and backwards. The concussion from the explosion pushed me harder onto the dirt. Thick smoke swirled around, and the air reeked of powder and an unfamiliar acrid odor.

When I looked again, I saw that Pockets had landed several meters away from where he had been struck. He lay motionless while Warranty, who had fallen again, crawled about, screaming out for Pockets and Humbatter. I cursed the soldiers and ran toward the injured boys.

As I sprinted across the open space, something exploded over me, the repercussion almost knocking me off my feet. I ducked down and swept Warranty, who was closest to me, up in my arms, and carried him to the spot where Pockets lay unmoving on his back. The front of his shirt had been singed away, and I smelled burnt flesh. Near the center of his chest was a large surface wound oozing blood and a clear fluid. With one arm firmly gripping Warranty, I leaned down to lift Pockets with my other, when Raoul suddenly appeared and scooped Pockets up in his arm, shouting at me to follow him. We ran toward the Burrow. I stumbled again, fell, picked Warranty back up, and ran the last few yards to the Burrow's entryway.

A short way inside, Raoul sat panting heavily, Pockets, still unconscious, in his arms. The weight of Warranty made me stumble toward him, and when I regained my balance, I leaned against the wall, also trying to catch my breath.

"You okay?" I asked.

He nodded and took several deep breaths. He carefully set

Pockets on the planks and stood.

"I need to go back out for Humbatter," he said. I looked at Pockets and saw that his eyes were closed, but his chest was moving up and down.

"I don't think he's hurt bad," Raoul said. "Get some of the others to help you take them inside." He moved back up the ramp.

"Be careful," I called to him.

When he finally came back inside, carrying Humbatter's limp body, I had managed to get Pockets and Warranty into the round room, and onto two makeshift gurneys set up by Airy Bender, who Raoul had summoned to the scene. Phaedra, Sayu, and Cloudia were assisting him.

Several of the other children inside the Burrow quickly dragged out a mattress from one of the corridors for Humbatter. When Raoul laid him on it, I saw blood spurt from a large wound in the injured boy's thigh. Airy saw it too and yanked off his belt, looped it above the wound, and pulled it tight before fastening it. Humbatter, whose shirt had been blown to tatters, had another more serious looking wound on his left side. Several inches of thick flesh hung from a ragged, bloody hole. Airy squatted down and fumbled around inside an old black leather satchel that bore his initials. When he came up with a pair of surgical succors and several other implements, he said something to Phaedra and she went running down one of the corridors. She swiftly returned with a large first-aid kit.

I went over to the gurney where Pockets lay. Phaedra and Sayu were carefully cutting away the remainder of his shirt so as to fully expose the wounds on his upper torso. His eyes were still closed and, visible injuries aside, looked like he was only asleep. When Sayu lifted his shoulders slightly for Phaedra to slip his shirt out from under him, his eyes fluttered and he let out a short moan. Sayu took a wet washcloth from a bucket of water beside the gurney, folded it over twice, and placed it across his forehead. Phaedra untied his worn running shoes and slipped them from his feet.

When they were finished, they moved to the gurney where Warranty lay. Next to it, Airy was still working on Humbatter. At some point, Nike had come into the Burrow, and he was standing silently next to Airy, staring down at his brother. He stood stiffly with his hands bunched into tight fists.

I leaned over Pockets, readjusted the washcloth and pressed it gently to his head so that he might absorb more of its coolness. The air in the Burrow was hot with strong traces of powder in it from the earlier explosions.

Pockets' eyes fluttered again and came open. He slowly focused on me, squinting in confusion.

"I'm alive?" he asked, his eyes now wide.

"Oh, yes, very much so," I replied, fighting back tears.

"I'm alive," he whispered, and his eyes closed as he drifted off again.

"How's he looking?" Airy asked from behind me.

"Good," I said. Adding, "I guess. I mean, what do I know."

"Here, let me take a look at him."

When I stepped aside, Airy said, "Father, you look exhausted. Why don't you go and sit down for a bit."

I was exhausted. I felt more tired than I had ever been, like I could sleep for days. But my mind was full of cascading thoughts. I felt it was my responsibility to bring things to a satisfactory end for all concerned; but at the same time, part of me felt the situation was hopeless. Neither side was going to relent in their positions. It was clear that the Council would turn the weapon over if the demand for resettlement was dropped. It was equally clear that Simon and Helen had no intention of allowing the children to remain in the Heap. Just thinking about everything made me exhausted. I sat down and leaned against the wall of the round room, and closed my eyes in an attempt to clear my head. Within seconds I was asleep. Sometime later, Phaedra and Raoul helped me to my feet and guided me down one of the corridors and into a room that had several beds. Again, I fell into a deep sleep, and I dreamed.

I dreamed I was in the middle of the ocean on a grand sailing ship. Under a red sun high in the blue sky, I was standing with Pockets watching Raoul man the vessel's wooden wheel, which inexplicably, was not round but square. Phaedra was standing beside me with her arm linked through mine.

Raoul was saying, "Each edge of the wheel represents a direction in which we can go. This edge is north, this one south, the others east and west."

"Where are we going now?" Pockets asked, his hair whipping in the steady sea breeze.

"To the Land of Dust," Raoul said. "Soon we shall see it on the horizon."

"What will we find there?" Pockets asked.

"It's not what we will find there that we should be concerned with," Raoul said. "It's what we will not find there."

"And what is that?" asked Pockets.

"The world and all its splendor," said Phaedra.

The four of us stood peering ahead, waiting for any shape to take form, when a large multi-colored parrot landed on the wheel.

"Simon is a god," the parrot cawed over and over, and then, "we know this because Helen told us so."

I went to shoo the bird away, and it rose up in a flutter with one of its wings striking my shoulder before it flew off. I watched it fly high and disappear into the blue sky.

Phaedra reached for my shoulder and picked a small feather from it. She held it up to me.

"Here, Gabriel," she said. "It will bring us good luck."

"Look," cried Pockets then. "What is that?"

Ahead, a large cloud of gray smoke loomed on the horizon.

"Is it the Land of Dust?" asked Pockets.

The cloud grew ever larger, rising ever higher, blotting out the sun, slowly spreading until it took on the shape of a mushroom. The sky grew ominously black and a fierce, biblical wind began to blow. The waters around the ship quickly turned tumultuous with huge, foamy waves reaching up towards the ship's deck.

I opened my eyes with a start to see Urbain standing over me, his hand gently shaking me awake.

"You were having a bad dream, mon copain," he said.

"I'll say," I said, slowly sitting up. "I was dreaming I was on a large sailing ship."

"Dreams about ships on the ocean portend great decisions to be made," said Urbain solemnly.

"I didn't know that."

"The mushroom cloud, of course, is self evident."

"You know what my dreams are?" I asked.

"Where do you think I reside when I am not here?" he replied.

When I didn't answer, he said, "The parrot part, I am not so sure of."

I had never heard of the priest who had returned to Europe with knowledge of the fate of Stephen's army of children. That part of Raoul's story had been new to me, but I did know of another Father Surin who appeared centuries later. Shortly after the public burning of Urbain Grandier, Father Jean-Joseph Surin came to Loudon. Father Surin had been discretely summoned by Baron de Laubardemont who informed him, that despite Grandier's execution, the demonic possession of the nuns had gone on unabated and, indeed, had intensified.

Surin had come to Loudon to perform a superhuman task in

finishing the exorcism begun by Grandier, but unknown to everyone, he was a sick man. Plagued by what was in his time called "melancholy," Surin had been suffering for months from a multitude of ills, or what he thought of as "agonies and pressures so extreme that I did not know what would happen to me." He often felt unduly confused, disoriented to the point that he lost his bearings, exhausted for no apparent reason. His limbs ached and were sometimes unmovable, and he experienced painful, debilitating headaches that forced him to seek refuge in darkened rooms, because he couldn't tolerate even the weakest light.

As a young boy, Jean-Joseph Surin had been obsessed with history. Well before entering the Jesuit seminary at Bordeaux, he had become notorious for spending days and nights on end in libraries surrounded by stacks of archaic historical volumes, which he devoured without break or time to eat and sleep. His voracious appetite for tomes of the past came from his having been quarantined from the plague when he was eight years old. Sent by his parents to stay in a countryside cottage with only an elderly governess, his only real companions were the twenty volumes of Josephus' Jewish Antiquities written in the decades following the death of Jesus Christ. It was said that after a period of some months away, young Surin had memorized huge sections of the books and had by then decided to give his life over to the much admired, and sometimes feared, Society of Jesus.

In Loudon, despite his mounting ills, Father Surin, then thirty-four years of age, stoically devoted himself to chasing out the devils that possessed the nuns of the unfortunate Ursuline convent. Held hostage by the most powerful of these creatures of the underworld, was the mother superior, Sister Jeanne. To Surin, she presented his most daunting challenge. Rid Soeur Jeanne of the demons that possessed her, and the rest were sure to follow, he thought. So it came to be that he focused all of his energies and attentions on her.

Soeur Jeanne was, to say the least, an intelligent and crafty woman. Today, given the proclivity to explain away any anomaly through the use of science, there is some speculation that she may have invented and orchestrated the demons that invaded her convent. But Father Surin, ever committed to doing combat with anything that interfered with God's way, never for a moment doubted that the Loudon demons were not the minions of Satan. Indeed, doubt found no quarter in Surin's mind. He was fond of saying, "The man who does not have excessive ideas in regard to God will never come near Him."

Surin was excessive in his time spent exorcising Soeur Jeanne, and after considerable effort, was able to get the demon that commanded Jeanne's body to speak to him.

"Who are you?" demanded the priest.

Said the devil, "I am that I am, you fool, and I can easily match wits with you any day even with my mind and limbs occupied elsewhere."

Surin sprinkled holy water on Sister Jeanne's sweaty brow and responded, "Leave now and return to the depths of depravity where you belong."

"Not until I have finished taking full advantage of these juicy depths," mocked the demon.

"Identify yourself," ordered Surin.

"I have many names," replied the demon, "more than there are leaves on the trees of your pathetic world."

"Which name do you go by?" persisted Surin.

"Some call me Moloch, others still Mammon," came the reply, "but my true name is Simon."

"Simon, I command you to depart this good woman's body," Surin shouted, and the demon laughed in response.

As devil and man conversed, Soeur Jeanne writhed about on the cot on which she lay, sometimes lewdly thrusting herself at Surin, other times twisting in pain and screaming out.

"Leave now," Surin again commanded.

"And go where?" replied Simon. "Do you not know that I am always here and that it is only through my choosing that you sense and hear me." Simon let out another peal of laughter, followed by a sensual and sustained groan.

Soeur Jeanne screamed out, and Surin shouted, "Take me, beast, instead of this poor woman. Take me a more fair match for your skills."

"But, you come so ill equipped, if you know what I mean," said Simon.

Soeur Jeanne looked seductively at the priest. "Don't you recognize me, Jean-Joseph?" she asked. "Can't you see that it is me?"

Father Surin puzzled, had no idea what she meant.

She reached out to him and ran her hand across his cheek, down his neck, his chest. "It is I, Helen, the whore of Tyre, the temptress of Samaria."

With this the mother superior's wagging tongue appeared at her parted lips. Her mouth opened wider and her tongue snaked its way toward Surin. It lapped at his face, worked its way into his ears, and began winding round his neck.

"Take me, coward," shouted Surin, tugging the tongue from his neck and forcing it away from himself.

"In good time," replied Simon, "in good time."

That evening Surin woke up in the middle of the night with the oddest of sensations sweeping through his body, and he realized that Simon was now inside his body, gnawing away at his soul. The next morning he told Soeur Jeanne, who appeared and acted remarkably well and normal, "Good sister, your trials and tortures are over. I am now engaged in a struggle with hell's most malignant servant."

And like that, it ended for Sister Jeanne. But Father Surin's battle was just beginning, and it would go on for months and months, until the combination of his illness and possession drove him to the brink of utter despair.

One evening, he stood at the window of his room, in the seminary to which he had returned. He was gazing down at the churning waters of the sea below, waves crashing on the rocks; and Simon said, "Inviting, no?"

"No," resisted Surin.

"Ah, come now, what more pain can you endure? End it now."

"Only God decides when the end comes."

"Do it and I'll tell you the *Word*," whispered Simon enticingly.

"What?"

"The *Word*. I'll tell you what it is, and when I say it aloud, the choice will be gone, as will everything else on this sad earth of yours. And your misery shall cease forever."

"No," said Surin, "you don't know it, and your kind never has."

"Do you really want to try me, priest? Are you so sure of yourself that you would wager the world and all its wretched creatures?"

Surin contemplated Simon's bold taunt, and for the first time in his life he felt the germ of doubt creep into his being. By everything he knew to be right, Simon Magus, despite his best efforts, was never able to learn the Word, but did he dare risk the entire world to test his beliefs? What if he was wrong? So overcome by this sudden rush of confusion, Surin stepped closer to the window, thinking he had to do whatever necessary to prevent putting Simon's challenge to the test.

"If I were to die this very second," he told Simon, "then so too would you." And with this, he threw himself through the closed window, shattering glass and wood, and falling many feet to the jagged rocks below.

But he did not die. Miraculously, he suffered only a broken leg and many, but superficial, cuts and bruises to his head and body. Also, inexplicably, Surin lost his ability to speak and to read and write. Frequently, at the start of this strange malady, he would desperately try to communicate, and failing would fly into a fury of frustration.

And the devil Simon, you ask? Yes, he too was dead. Or at least Surin thought that he was.

Father Surin was sent to the seminary's infirmary to recover from his injuries, which everyone believed had been caused by an attempt at suicide based on his inability to cope with the devil. Because he was unable to explain what had happened, those around him concluded that he had lost faith in God and gone stark raving mad. His peers shunned him, and the lay brothers, who ran the infirmary and tended to him, were cruel, doing all they could to increase his pain. The few priests who visited him, came to berate him and one even struck him in anger.

Not everyone, however, treated Surin so poorly. One young boy, who worked at the infirmary as an orderly to change linens and empty bedpans, was most kind to the mute priest. The boy, whose name was Arnaud, was ten years old. Two years earlier, he had lost his parents to disease and was left homeless, wandering the streets and begging for food. Discovered one day foraging through the seminary's garbage, he had been taken in by the Jesuits, who gave him a roof over his head and work to keep him occupied.

Arnaud did all that he could to see that Father Surin properly recovered from his injuries. When the priest was able to gingerly walk again, the boy would often take him for strolls around the seminary's campus. Sometimes the two would sit in the gardens there, and Arnaud would tell him entertaining stories he had heard from other Jesuits at the seminary.

One glorious spring afternoon, while sitting in the garden,

Arnaud told Father Surin a story about Simon Magus, the ancient magician, who, he explained, had once been close to Christ and his apostles. Arnaud's story centered on Simon's obsession to learn the lost and secret Word, and the boy told Surin, as wise and powerful as Simon had been he had nonetheless been fooled into believing that the Word was composed of simple letters, which formed a single, uttered sound. No, explained Arnaud, this mysterious Word, which had been with us since the beginning, was more than that, but Simon in his relentless greed for power failed to see it.

Surin listened politely, as Arnaud explained what Simon had failed to see was that the Word was actually language. "Even a blind man can hear and understand words," Arnaud said. "Even a man deaf and dumb can know and understand them." Arnaud went on, "Because God made language in the beginning, calling it the Word, and gave it to us so that we might devise ways to love one another and always have hope in the future."

When Arnaud completed his story, Father Surin sat silently for a long while and then looked up at the boy and said, "Hope."

"Yes," said Arnaud, visibly pleased with himself. "Hope."

Surin again sat without speaking. He knew from his own studies concerning Simon Magus and the Word that the story the boy had told him was essentially nonsense. Indeed, the tale was a tired old anecdote he had heard many times himself as a young boy; a tale he knew some of his fellow priests were prone to tell to common folk, peasants, if you will, to promote hope over despair in those who basically had little to look forward to, but who always accepted the flimsiest of reasons to look optimistically, hopefully, toward the future. Yes, Simon had obsessed after the Word; that part, Surin knew, was quite true, but the rest was manufactured, mawkish drivel.

Nonetheless, as Father Surin sat quietly with Arnaud, he clearly understood that the child had made a valiant effort to console him and to boost his spirits, and on that account Surin did find himself feeling much better. And, of course, there was the not so small matter of Surin having uttered his first word in a period of many months. That the word happened to be "hope" would surely be interpreted as having far more significance than it actually had. So, Father Surin went along with Arnaud's effort, and to everyone's amazement, he soon returned to the state of normalcy that had once elevated him in so many hearts and minds.

Day Six

*J*ust after sunrise, Cloudia woke me. When I heard her soft voice say, "Mr. Fantasy," I thought I was dreaming again, but when I opened my eyes and saw her standing by my bedside, I knew that something was wrong.

"Pockets," she said, when she saw my opened eyes.

"Pockets what?" I asked, sitting up and quickly pulling on my shoes.

"Pockets," she said again, and disappeared out of the room and down the corridor.

I rushed to follow her into the round room, where she led me to Airy. He was wearing a stethoscope and leaning over Pockets, listening to his heartbeat. Phaedra and Raoul, stood nearby and I saw that Phaedra looked as if she had been crying. When she saw me looking at her she smiled, but it was strained.

"What's wrong?" I asked Airy.

He motioned for me to be quiet, and continued listening, moving the chestpiece to different places on Pockets' exposed abdomen.

After a moment he moved away from the gurney, motioning for me to follow.

"He took a turn for the worse in the middle of the night," he told me, after we were standing well away.

"And?"

"It's not good, Father."

"How bad is he?"

"Bad," he said.

"Then shouldn't we take him to the hospital?"

"There's nothing they would be able to do for him there," Airy said. "Besides, assuming we could get past the front gates, we'd never make it in time."

I felt my knees begin to buckle. "You've got to help him," I pleaded. "You've got to save him."

"I've done everything I can."

"Do more, damn it," I shouted.

"Gabriel—" he started and then stopped. He put his hand on my shoulder. "Short of a miracle, he's not going to make it. It's amazing he's lasted this long."

"What the hell happened?" I asked. "How did he get this way so quickly?"

"Whatever struck him, hit him with such force that it broke three or four of his larger ribs. Actually, it shattered them…puncturing one of his lungs, as well as one of the vessels to his—"

Airy stopped as if catching himself in the midst of saying something inappropriate. "Look, I know what you're feeling," he said.

"Has anyone told him how bad it is?" I asked.

"Raoul spoke with him earlier, but I don't know what he said."

I looked over his shoulder at the other two makeshift gurneys. Both held sheet-draped bodies. Warranty's two feet sticking out from the sheet were shoeless, one with a bloody sock still on.

Needlessly, I asked, "Warranty and Humbatter?" Something in me had to hear it.

"They're dead," he said. "I don't think they suffered much at all."
Oh, Christ, I thought. *Oh, Christ, where are you? Where were you
when all of this happened? Why did all of this have to happen? Grant
me strength, please.*

"Can I speak with Pockets?" I asked.

"Of course you can. He's already asked for you."

"Look, I'm sorry that I was upset with you," I told Airy.

"It's all right. I understand."

I beckoned to Cloudia, and asked her to go the van and get my
Breviary on the nightstand. As she went, I called out to her to also
bring my stole, which had sat unpacked in my bag for nearly two
years. It was the first time I had given the Last Rites to anyone,
and I wasn't sure of the words or proper prayers. It was then it
struck me; amid my revulsion at having taken a life, I hadn't
thought to administer the rites to Maxi's lifeless body.

I thanked Airy for all that he had done, apologized again, and
walked back to where Pockets lay. It was then for the first time
that I noticed the room was near full of other children who sat
silently watching me. Later, I would learn, sometime during the
middle of the night, the soldiers inside the Heap had withdrawn,
and when word of the injured boys went out, all of the children
had flocked to the Burrow, many of them electing to stay.

"I think he's sleeping," Raoul told me when I approached.

I placed my hand on Pockets' forehead, silently praying for a
miracle. His head was hot and wet with perspiration. His eyes
opened slowly and he looked up at me. He smiled and reached out
and took my hand in his, squeezing it tightly. His eyes had dark
circles around them, and a small trickle of blood came from one of
his ears. Squeezing my hand, he said, "Will you, won't you, will
you, won't you, will you join the dance?"

Smoothing the damp hair back from his forehead, I said, "Hey,
little man. It' okay. Just rest for now."

"I had a dream last night," he said.

"What was it? " I asked.

"It was wonderful," he said. "I dreamed that the Heap was surrounded by the ocean. There was water everywhere, as far as I could see, and you were there, and Raoul, and Phaedra, and we all—"

I closed my eyes and fought back tears. I didn't want to cry in front of him. I waited for him to say more, but he didn't. I opened my eyes and looked down at him for what seemed like a long while before I realized that his hand had gone limp in mine and his eyes were blankly staring at me. My shoulders shook and my chest felt as if I'd been struck with a tremendous force. I stood rigidly for a moment trying to gather my emotions, then I leaned down, kissed his forehead, and drew his eyes closed with my fingers.

Cloudia just then returned with my items. When she came close to where Pockets lay, she sensed right away that he was dead and froze in her tracks, her eyes wide with confusion. Phaedra came over to her and held her tight and then whispered something in her ear. Cloudia, who was now crying, nodded slowly and handed Phaedra my Breviary and stole and went to stand beside Nike, who was sitting on the floor a few feet away from where his brother's body lay.

I slipped the stole on and thumbed through the book, after Phaedra handed them to me. By this time I felt as if I was moving about in a twilight state. Nothing seemed quite real; everything appeared as if from a distance, through a haze. I asked Raoul to have the bodies of Warranty and Humbatter moved closer to Pockets, and began reading from my Breviary.

"May God shine on your heart and grant you salvation, and lead you to eternal life."

It was a struggle to say the words, to force them from my throat, which had no interest in cooperating with the effort. Tears burned my cheeks and my hands would not stop shaking.

Whenever you care about something, it only ends up hurting you.

Cloudia moved away from Nike and came and stood beside me. After a moment she leaned against me and reached up and held onto one of my arms.

"What we suffer in this life can never be compared to the glory, as yet unrevealed, which lies in wait for us—"

I looked over at Raoul. A tear appeared in the corner of one of his eyes. Defying gravity, it stayed there for several seconds, and then gave up the fight and moved down the length of his face. Soon, others followed it. Raoul stood stiffly, staring at Pockets, and did nothing to conceal his tears or to wipe them away.

I tried again to continue, but the words now caught in my throat like small pebbles. Nameless, who had been stoically sitting besides the gurney, let out a low whine and pawed at the ground.

When it was obvious that I could say no more, Raoul told everyone except for Firestone, Astro, and Nike to go outside. He stepped closer to me, put his hand on my shoulder, and said, "Thank you, Father." And then, "Go with them. We'll be out soon."

Outside, near the olive tree, some of the children had already constructed three bamboo platforms, each about two meters high. The wrapped bodies of Humbatter and Warranty were placed atop two of them. Beneath the platforms, several children, at the direction of an older girl named Alida, were piling pieces of wood and bunches of crumpled newspaper. When the pile reached to within inches below each platform's bed they stopped and moved away. Alida took a large can of lighter fluid and squirted it onto the wood and paper.

A few minutes later, Raoul and the three boys stepped outside carrying Pockets' body now tightly wrapped from head to toe in white sheets, which they placed at the center of the empty platform's bed. When Raoul and the boys moved away, Alida stepped forward again and struck a large wooden match with her thumbnail, watched it burn for a moment, and then tossed it onto the pile beneath Pockets' platform. The match burned slowly for a few seconds looking as if it might go out and then there was a loud whooshing sound as the fire came alive. She went on and repeated the process twice more. When the combined flames began to roar and lick the bottom of the platform beds, each child stepped nearer and took something from his or her pocket— small toys, pencils, crayons, pieces of paper, candy, bits of ribbon—and tossed them into the fire. A thick black smoke poured from the platform and a strong acrid odor filled the air. Small burning pieces of paper were swirling upwards toward the sky.

Raoul stood next to me watching the flames. "It's better this way," he said, looking toward the Heap's front gates. He took a small book from his pocket and handed it to me. It was a coverless, tattered copy of *Through the Looking Glass*, what Pockets had called "the Alice book."

"It was in his pocket," he said. "I thought you might like to have it."

"It was his favorite," I said. "Thank you."

As I spoke, Astro stepped next to Raoul and whispered something in his ear. Raoul looked at me. "The people in the limousines are back. They're asking to speak with you again."

"No," I said, "I'm finished with them. I have nothing else to say to them."

"Please, go ahead and hear what they want," Raoul said. "It will help. We need a little more time to do some things here."

"Only if it will help you," I reluctantly agreed.

"It will."

As before, Astro and Firestone accompanied me outside the gates and stood nearby waiting for my return. This time, Phaedra and Sayu were nowhere to be seen. I went through the same frisking procedure as before and when I stepped into the limousine, besides Simon and Helen, there was a new face to greet me in place of Dr. Schneider.

The man, seated to Helen's left, closest to the window, was a middle-aged military officer dressed to the nines in a green dress uniform complete with several rows of ribbons and medallions. An officer's hat, with a thick gold braid and buttons placed above its polished black visor, rested on his lap. Simon introduced the man as Lieutenant Colonel Boynton, the commander of the soldiers.

Boynton nodded curtly at me. He was a big man; big even for the expansive rear seat he sat on. He looked to be in his mid-forties, had thick, curly brown hair, cut short, and the kind of blunt, hard features one would expect on a professional soldier. His eyes were steel gray, his thin lips set in a determined jaw.

Simon looked out the vehicle's closed window and absently ran a long, thin finger across the leather upholstery at its bottom. He said nothing for a long time, and I shifted uneasily on the seat across from him.

"I'm hoping that you have good news for us today," he said after a while.

Helen sat next to him glaring at a spot somewhere next to my head, a small smirk on her face. She seemed to have only one look reserved for me in her repertoire, disdain.

"Your soldiers killed three children yesterday," I said to no one in particular.

"Well, I regret hearing that," Simon said. "But it is not like I didn't warn you there might be dire consequences."

"That's all you have to say?" I asked.

"What more would you have me say?"

"Nothing," I replied. "Not a damned thing."

Helen's head jerked sharply towards me, reacting as if I had reached out and slapped her colleague. Her tongue darted out to wet her lips.

"I can appreciate your concern for the children," Simon said, "but I find it best not to become too emotional at times like these."

The conversation froze into silence. Somewhere behind me, in the vehicle's front section, came the steady sound of emitting air. Outside I saw Astro and Firestone standing near the gates, eyeballing the soldiers surrounding the limousine. The men appeared nervous around the two children, and stood fidgeting with their weapons.

"I would imagine that any type of true emotion would come hard for you," I told Simon.

Helen threw Simon a look that seemed to say that he was wasting his time with me.

When I didn't say anything more for a long while, Simon again said, "I am hoping that you have good news for us today."

The radio on Boynton's belt broke out with a burst of static, crackled, and then a voice on it said, "*Colonel, we have movement in the northern quadrant.*" There was another burst of static, then, "*Six of the little bastards with the big, one-armed gimp.*" More static. "*Clear targets. We could take them out.*"

Boynton slipped the radio from his belt and lifted it to his mouth.

"Negative. Hold fast. Report mode only, for now. Out."

I watched Boynton place the radio back on his belt and shook my head in disgust. *Little bastards. One-armed gimp.*

"I have nothing to tell you," I told Simon.

For an instant his face lost some of its firm countenance, and he blew out an exasperation of air. He leaned back, the leather cushion faintly crackling in the vehicles cooled air.

"I find that very difficult to believe," he said.

"It's the truth," I said.

"Just what is it these little shits want?" Helen said, through clenched teeth.

Simon put a cautionary hand on her shoulder but, of course, it was too late. Her words, her demeanor, coupled with everything else that had happened were too much for me.

"They want you," I said, ignoring Simon's look at me. "They want you in exchange for the bomb. I tried to talk them out of it, knowing the unspeakable and disgusting things they would do to you, but they wouldn't listen to me. They wouldn't have any part of my reasoning. It's either you or nothing."

"You're just like they told us you would be," she said glaring at me, her face red with anger. "You're insane, completely insane."

"Whatever I am, I am not someone who murders innocent children."

"Well, we all have our faults now, don't we?" Simon said, leaning forward to look at me.

I felt an odd but familiar sensation in my head and my ears filled with a buzzing sound. Simon's question sounded as if it were coming from a long distance away, and the air around him seemed to quantify itself through a strange shimmering that forced him into its shadows. His silhouette moved and formed a dark cloudy mass that took the shape of a bearded, robed man. When I strained to see the man more clearly, I saw a look of pure rage and hatred on his face. I shook my head and squinted my eyes to clear away what I thought was a hallucination, a manifestation of my malfunctioning limbic system. Slowly, Simon assumed his regular appearance and I saw the glint of a sly smile work his lips. My temples were throbbing and I felt the first pangs of a crushing headache coming.

"Do you really believe that you are free of any guilt here?" Simon asked.

"What I believe is of no concern to you."

"Or perhaps more appropriately what you don't believe, *Father*

Surin," Simon said, mockingly emphasizing his last two words.

"That I'm a priest has nothing to do with anything here."

While we talked, the look on Boynton's face was oscillating between disinterest and impatience.

"Have it any way you want it here," Simon said, "but it's time they surrender the bomb."

"I don't know if that's going to happen now or not."

"You're not saying that they intend to use it, are you," Simon asked.

"After yesterday, anything is possible."

"That's sheer insanity and you know it," Helen said, glaring coldly at me.

Simon took a more tactful approach. "Time and patience are no longer options in this situation," he said. "You have to convince them to turn it over to us now. There is no more time to wait."

"I can't do that," I said.

"You can," he said, "and you must. They trust you."

"Do you honestly believe that they'll listen to me, even if I wanted to convince them now" I asked. "Do you really think they listen to anything I have to say?"

"You live among them," Simon said.

"Yes, I do. I live with them" I said. "And they trust me because I'm not a threat to them... because they know I care about them... because they know I have no desire to hurt them, or to use them like some others would. "

"Reason with them," Simon said, ignoring my words. "You have to tell them what's at stake."

"What's at stake?"

"You know exactly what I'm saying."

"Don't you see what's at stake for *them?*" I said. "For once in their lives they have something that they've never had, something they've never experienced. Good God, man, can't you see it? For once in their lives, they have a sense of worth, a sense that they actually mean something in a world that is near meaningless to them."

Colonel Boynton muttered, "Well, let me tell you, if it's power they're concerned with, then we can teach them—"

"Teach them what?" I interrupted, turning to him. "What are you going to do? Do you really think they're frightened of death?"

"What they're afraid of is of no concern to me," Boynton said. "I have my orders and I follow them, and I have no doubt that God knows what we are doing here is right. You of all people should realize that."

"Yes, we've heard your battle cry in the past," I said. 'Kill them all and let God sort them out.' Is that how it works, Colonel? Is that how you justify slaughtering innocents?"

Helen smirked at my last remark. "This is all psycho-babble," she said. Then turning to Simon, she added, "We're wasting our time here. It's time to put an end to this."

"At last," I said, "we have something we can agree on." I knew it was a foolish thing to say but I couldn't resist.

When I slid across the seat to exit the vehicle, Simon glared contempt at me. "You're making a serious mistake," he said. Pushing the door opened, he added, "A very serious mistake."

"It won't be my first," I told him.

I stepped out into the sunshine and took a deep breath. I felt as if I had just stepped out of a dank and dark cave and had been near the point of suffocation. I breathed deeply again, and walked back to where Astro and Firestone waited for me. For a moment, I felt dizzy and nauseous. I thought I was going to throw up, but then realized I hadn't eaten for a long time. I was also suddenly extremely thirsty.

I returned to the Burrow with the two boys, and we found Raoul and Nike waiting for us outside. Nike's eyes were glassy and he wore a backpack and old baseball cap I had often seen on Humbatter.

I gave Raoul the gist of the meeting, but he appeared to be only half listening, distracted by other thoughts.

"Is it true there are others like us in the world?" Raoul asked.

"Others?" I said, not sure what he meant.

"Like us. Other young people without parents and families that live in places like this," he motioned about the Heap.

"Yes," I answered, sad to have to say it.

"Where?"

"Nearly everywhere, near and far."

"Many?"

"More than anyone cares to count."

Raul looked at Nike and said, "See, like I said, we aren't the only ones." Then to me, "It's the same everywhere, isn't it?"

"I fear it is," I said, watching for Nike's reaction. He half nodded at Raoul, and I could plainly see he was still trying to grasp the reality of his brother's death.

"Nothing to fear," Raoul said.

And then after a moment, he asked, "So, if we were to use the weapon others like us would die?"

I nodded. "Many, yes. Perhaps thousands."

"Do you think they would then be better off?"

The logic of the question threw me. I thought for a moment, and then said, "With life there is always hope." Right away I wished I had never said it. What was hope to Raoul, or to any of the children in the Heap? Did hope, as you and I, dear reader, understand it, find any place in their thoughts or lives? I didn't know. I had lived in the Heap for many months and felt embarrassed that I couldn't answer these questions.

"What will the Council do now?" I asked.

He didn't answer my question, and instead said, "I never thought things would turn out this way."

"I understand. I didn't either."

"There's been enough death here," he said.

"Yes. What do you want me to do?"

"You've done enough. You've been a good friend to all of us."

"I don't feel that I've done a thing."

"You should leave before this gets worse."

"What?"

"There's no reason for you to stay and risk being harmed here."

"Raoul, I'm here no matter what happens."

"You're sure you want to stay?"

"I've never been surer of anything."

"Fine," he said looking closely at me.

"But, you don't look so well," he said. "Are you sick?"

"It's nothing. What are you going to do? What about the weapon?"

"Don't worry, Father, everything is being taken care of."

"Are you all right?" I asked. He nodded and began to walk away, but then turned and motioned me to follow him. I fell in beside him.

"Where are we going?"

"There is one more thing to do," he said.

We went to a side of the Burrow where Firestone and Astro stood. Raoul gestured to them and pointed at something. The two boys pulled back the corner of a dirt covered canvas sheet revealing a metallic case. The case was about two-feet wide and five-feet long. On both ends were fastened carry-handles. It was the same case I had seen days earlier.

Raoul told Astro, "Get the others," and then bent down and flipped open three metal buckles and lifted the case's lid. Inside, set into a thick, gray-foam mold, was an ominous looking device. Oddly, someone had painted it pink.

"So, that's it?" I asked.

"That's it."

"Was it that color when you found it?"

"No, that... that was Pockets' idea," he said. "He did it thinking of the surprised looks on their faces after we gave it back. He called it the 'Pink Bomb.'"

Raoul held out a small instamatic camera he had fished out of Nike's pack.

"Here," he said. "Take our picture for remembrance."

It was only then that I noticed I was still wearing my stole and holding my Breviary. I set them aside and took the camera.

Remembrance?

When Astro returned, he had Phaedra, Sayu, and Cloudia with him. Nameless followed them by a few yards, his tail uncharacteristically wagging. Raoul closed the metallic case and set it on the ground, and the children assembled behind it. Everyone smiled, as if it were simply any other day in the Heap. Even Nameless looked directly into the lens without moving. I took several pictures, and slipped one into my pocket and gave the others to Raoul.

Later that day, I returned to the van and, after stowing away my Breviary and stole, I went to go up on its roof. Coming up the ladder, I was surprised to see Phaedra sitting in my usual spot.

"I wanted to see things one more time from up here," she told me.

"That sounds a little too fatalistic."

I sat beside her, and looked across the Heap to the place where the main gates had once stood. The tanks were now positioned facing us and in the descending darkness I could make out the forms of several soldiers standing near them. Beyond the tanks and the erected tents, bright lights had been turned on around the helicopters and more figures were moving about them.

"If you had it to do all over again, would you still come here?" she asked.

"Nothing in the world could keep me away."

"You're not just saying that?"

"I'm saying it because I mean it."

Phaedra smiled at this. She leaned back and stared up at the sky. Stars were just beginning to appear.

"I don't know if you remember, but when I first came here," I said, "you told me about how people become older and come to realize what little they know of life. That's true, but in my time here, just the opposite has occurred. Here, I've come to again know the imminence of those wonderful things that make life complete. I can feel those things alive inside of myself, things that I thought completely lost."

I looked up at the sky to see that it was now replete with countless, sparkling stars.

"No matter how bad things become, no matter what happens here, nothing can ever take those things away from me."

She was quiet for a long time and then said, "I think I know what you mean. As bad as things seem sometimes, there's something in me that always makes me feel that it will be all right. No matter what, I feel something is with me, or near me, or part of me, and that it will always take care of me and make things right."

She looked at me and asked, "That sounds silly, doesn't it?"

"No, not at all," I said. "Some would say what you sense is God's presence."

"God?"

"Yes."

Phaedra was quiet for a moment. Then she shook her head. "No, it's much more than that."

Day Seven

hey came again with force just before dawn. The soldiers swept into the compound after one of the helicopters swooped in and hovered overhead, flooding the area below with two intensely bright beams of light. This time, double the number of armed men came over the downed front gates. They appeared prepared for anything.

I had fallen asleep atop the van and woke to find myself alone. When I stiffly sat up, I saw the main force entering the compound like a tan wave. Behind them, at the edge of the horizon, there was a brief, shimmering shade of blue that on this new morning seemed horribly out of place and full of false promise.

Three small groups of soldiers broke away from the line, and I watched one as it went about setting a number of explosive charges near the unguarded entryway to the Burrow. I scanned the Heap and saw no children anywhere. I looked down into the Kitchen Krewe's tent and saw no one. On top of one of the stoves sat a large pot with wisps of steam rising from it. Not a single tray or utensil was set on any of the tables. I climbed to a higher point on the pile of steel so that I could see the area that held the latrine and showers. There was no one there.

The charges placed near the Burrow went off simultaneously, and when the smoke and dust cleared, there was a large, gaping hole where the entryway had been. Within seconds, several soldiers cautiously entered the opening. I watched for what seemed like a long time hoping that I wouldn't hear the sounds of gunfire issue from the Burrow. A soldier finally emerged holding a lit flashlight. He shook his head to the group standing apprehensively outside. His comrades soon followed him, also signaling that they had found nobody.

Moments later, the two other groups, one on the northern side, the other on the southern, blew large openings in the fence for two tanks that rumbled through. The soldiers then huddled behind the heavy vehicles, and moved with them toward the Heap's center. Each time they passed a shelter, they broke away from the protection of the tanks to check inside. But the effort was in vain. The soldiers moved from shelter to shelter, appearing to grow ever more anxious and frustrated, but they found nobody.

I climbed back down to the van, crossed the catwalk, and descended the stairs to the ground. Looking about, I saw no soldiers, and I cautiously began moving toward the Burrow, hugging the stacks of cardboard and crushed plastic that lined the way. At about a quarter the way from my destination, the ground began to shake and I heard a low rumbling. The tank with the long battering ram came into full view as it swiveled around a corner, moved across the open space flattening the olive tree in its path, and stopped before the Burners' two-story building. Hanging limply from an antennae attached to its turret was a small white flag bearing a red X. After a moment, four soldiers holding rifles and wearing gas masks stepped from the entryway of the building. One of them gave a signal to the smoke spewing metal behemoth, and the tank spurted backwards for about twenty yards, and then surged forward. The long battering ram struck the building full force causing its front wall to issue a sharp cracking sound and splinter in several places. The tank backed up again and repeated its assault. With the fourth try, the wall gave way from its moorings, teetered some, and then collapsed, narrowly missing the withdrawing tank. With its interior now in full view like an opened doll's house, I could see that nobody was inside.

The tank surged backwards again and stopped. A small port on its forward side slid open and an object projected from the opening landed with a thud on the first level of the exposed building. It appeared to be a canister about the size of a large soup can. Within seconds there was a loud popping sound, followed by a hissing, and thick, black smoke poured from the canister. Immediately, even at the distance where I stood, my eyes began stinging. I ripped the sleeve from my shirt and holding it over my mouth and nose, moved further away. In the distance, off toward the rear section of the Heap, I heard more popping sounds and the shouts of soldiers. I moved even further away from the Burners' building, finding it increasingly difficult to breathe.

Someone nearby yelled, "Fire in the hole," and there was a small explosion, quickly followed by several more. A fireball shot up into the sky above the spot where the Kitchen Krewe's tents stood. The burning orb arched, dripping bits of flame, and fell back to earth somewhere beyond my sight. My eyes were stinging more and watering fiercely from the smoke. Amid more shouts and small explosions, I began coughing, finding it harder and harder to breathe. In the billowing, spreading smoke, I collided with something hard and fell down.

"Over here," someone yelled. "Over here."

I rolled onto my back and tried to take a deep breath, but my lungs felt like they were on fire. I sat up and leaned over gagging. My throat was coated with a foul tasting bile that I couldn't purge. Overhead now, a helicopter hovered, its rotor blades stinging me with bits of dirt and gravel, creating a sound fit for an inferno. Trying to stand again, someone grabbed me around my neck from behind and I was struck hard on the head. I remember turning as I fell and seeing a soldier wearing a gas mask. On the ground, the last thing I heard was what sounded like someone calling out to me, "Mr. Fantasy."

After I lost consciousness, I was visited by a dream. But it wasn't at all like the ominous dreams I had been having. In this dream, I found myself in a remarkably beautiful place that was composed entirely of light and color, absent of all matter. I remember thinking in the dream that this had to be a place of pure divine, ecstatic wonder, but I felt, without doubt, it was real, and I never wanted to leave. From somewhere came the words "deep as the respiration of the ocean, serene and limitless as the blue firmament."

Everyone was there in this wonderful place: Pockets, holding his pet rat, Raoul, Phaedra, Maxi, Warranty, Humbatter, all alive and smiling, Nike, Sayu, Cloudia, Astro, Firestone, and all the Heap's other children. I moved to join the children my heart filled with an oceanic happiness. Then, suddenly, I was a distance away from everyone, but still walking toward them through a narrow corridor of clouds, but no matter how far I walked I never moved any closer to everyone. Soon it appeared that they couldn't see me any longer and the children turned away to leave. "Wait," I called out. "Wait for me. Don't leave me. Wait for me."

My dream went on, and its setting changed to a large, green playing field where all of the Heap's children stood once again. Surrounding the field was a huge, many-tiered, oval-shaped amphitheatre, filled with thousands more children. They sat raptly as Pockets walked across a wide green playing field to stand at its center before a microphone stand.

Behind Pockets, suspended high in the sky from invisible means, was a mammoth projection screen that, in rapid secession, revealed still shots of Cloudia as she struck fashion pose after fashion pose. These shots were interspersed with still life photographs of automobile tires and various bottles and cans. Each time a new projected image would appear the assembled children would roar out their approval louder and louder.

Also standing in the middle of the field was Raoul, who now inexplicably had both his arms and was dressed in a dark suit with a doorman's hat on his head. Next to Raoul was Phaedra who held a single copper flower in her hand. She was dressed in a brilliant, white Crusader's robe with a large red cross on its front. Next to Phaedra sat Nameless, who appeared to be grinning at all the children.

Pockets at the microphone, said, "Will you, won't you, will you, won't you, will you, won't you…." And the children in the amphitheatre roared back, "Join the dance." The crowd them burst into cheers and thousands of multi-colored parrots were released from somewhere and flew up in the sky

Witnessing this great spectacle in my dream, it dawned on me why Simon Driver wanted to resettle the children, why he hadn't wanted to run the risk of having any public attention. When I thought of Simon, a limousine appeared on the field and inside were Simon and Helen. I could see their faces pressed against the window, both of them staring in abject fear at all the children.

Raoul approached the limousine, with Nameless following close behind. He opened one of its doors and gestured for Simon and Helen to step outside. Both had looks of utter terror when they followed Raoul's direction, and Helen began crying, imploring Raoul to let her go back inside the limousine. Raoul shook his head and pointed out the assembled children, as if he thought they hadn't yet seen them.

Pockets, still at the microphone, took up a new line saying, "You may cry all the tears you want, but they won't make you any more real." The assembled children took up the same line, and soon they began moving in single file onto the field. From the far right end of the field, the Red Dwarf, dressed as a drum major, holding a marching baton as tall as himself, came high stepping, leading a group of children. The children pouring out of the stands moved to join this group and soon they surrounded Simon and Helen and still they pressed forward. When they stopped, they all turned toward the now empty stands where I sat alone observing everything. Nike stepped from the assembly and gave me a V-for victory sign. I stood and gave him a thumbs up, and looked at the children on the field. They all smiled back at me, and then began joyfully crying out my name. Over and over it went, until I was filled with an emotion that was overwhelming in its magnitude. Over and over and over and over and over, "Mr. Fantasy, Mr. Fantasy, Mr. Fantasy, Mr. Fantasy, Mr. Fantasy."

I awoke from my dream. I was lying on the ground, my head inches away from the downed trunk of the olive tree. Sitting up, I looked about, and saw nobody. Not a single person or child. The Heap appeared empty of all life except me. I shakily stood and walked to the Burrow's gaping opening and peered inside. I carefully walked down the shattered ramp and called out for Raoul, but he didn't answer. I went back outside and looked about.

Nobody. Not a soul. Where had they gone?

There was something wet on my neck and when I reached up to see what it was, my hand came away covered with blood. I gingerly felt around my neck, found nothing, and then ran my hand over my right ear and the side of my head above it. About an inch above my ear I touched a spot that made me wince in pain. I pulled my hand away and saw that it was covered in blood. I felt my neck again and found a small but deep laceration just above my ear. I moved my blood covered hand close to my face and stared at it, before wiping it on my pants leg.

Where was everybody?

I called out for some of the children, but nobody answered. I moved from shelter to shelter, calling out all the names I could think of, but still there were no answers. I sunk down to the ground on my knees, and then sat down.

"What are you yelling about, you crazy bastard?" someone said behind me.

I turned and saw Colonel Boynton standing several feet away with four soldiers armed with rifles.

"Where are they," I demanded. "What did you do with them?"

Boynton laughed, motioned to the soldiers and said something I didn't hear.

"You son of a bitch," I said standing. "You'll pay for what you've done, by all that is right, you'll pay dearly."

"You can dispense with the act, padre. Where are they?"

"Where is who?" I asked, confused.

"The children, where'd they go? Where are they hiding?"

"What are you, insane?" I said.

"I'm not going to ask you again," he said, "either you tell me right now or we'll force it out of you."

I turned and began walking away, wondering if it was me who was insane. Where were the children? If he didn't know, who did?

I was grabbed from behind and thrown to the ground. A young soldier who looked at me with a sheepish, embarrassed face, knelt on my back while another pulled my hands behind me and bound them together with a plastic tie.

"Last chance, where are they?" Boynton demanded.

"I told you, I don't know," I said. The soldiers yanked me to my feet.

Boynton stepped close to me, his face inches from mine.

"You're going to regret this," he said, slamming his fist into my stomach.

I buckled with the blow and was only prevented from falling by the soldiers that held me. When I looked up at Boynton defiantly, he asked me again where the children had gone and I began laughing. It was only then that it dawned on me. They were gone. All of them. Yet still, part of me didn't want to believe it. If they were gone, why had they left me behind?

Boynton half-heartedly struck me again, but I only laughed all the harder. He swore, and ordered, "Get him out of here."

I continued to laugh as they dragged me off, and he stood staring at me.

Two soldiers holding me by the arms lead me to the latrine building. They pushed me inside, securing the door closed behind me. I went to one of the sinks, turned my back to it, and with some difficulty was able to turn on one of the taps. I leaned over the bowl and put one side of my face in the water, and then the other, cleaning away the black soot and grime coating me. Then I put my mouth to the spigot and drank.

Outside, I heard the sound of voices and vehicles, and I stood on one of the commodes and looked out a window. A large truck, with a canvas tarp covering its rear section, was backing up close to the Burrow. Two men, dressed in orange containment suits with view-port hoods over their heads, climbed out of the truck. On their hands and feet were thick black gloves and boots that appeared sealed into the suits. They moved slowly toward a spot where several soldiers stood. As they approached, the soldiers parted and one of them pointed to something on the ground. The two men in the containment suits knelt down, and after a moment slowly stood in unison, each holding the handles of the metal case I had photographed along with the children just the day before.

The two carried the case to the truck where several soldiers, directed by Colonel Boynton, assisted them in placing it inside. I thought of the pink weapon inside the case, and had a momentary vision of the surprised faces when they saw it.

Movements near the Burrow's opening, which in the changing light now looked like a scream forged into the ground, caught my eye. Two figures were emerging from the darkness. It was Simon and Helen. When they stepped into the sunlight, Colonel Boynton spotted them and called out and waved them over to the truck. They briefly stopped to consider him, and then Simon called out something in return. Oddly, they moved quickly away from Boynton and the truck, toward the Heap's downed front gates and a waiting limousine.

A short while later, the door flew open and two soldiers carried an unconscious Airy Bender into the latrine. They dropped him on the floor next to me. "Someone to keep you company," said one of the men.

Airy's face was swollen with bruises and dark, ugly welts, and dried blood caked his nostrils. His nose looked broken and one of his eyes was purple-colored and swollen shut. After a moment, his good eye slowly opened and scanned the ceiling before coming to light on me.

Focusing, he said, "I hope I don't look as bad as I feel."

"I think you'll be all right," I told him. "What happened?"

"What happened?" he groaned, sitting up. "They beat the hell out of me is what happened. They wanted me to tell them where the children had gone."

"Where are they?"

"I wish I knew," he said, touching his nose gingerly. "They're gone is all I know. That's what I told them, but they weren't keen on hearing it."

He fumbled around in his shirt pocket and pulled out the

remains of a short reefer.

"But where?" I persisted. Someone had to know.

He shook his head and put the reefer in his mouth. "The last person I saw, late last night, was the Red Dwarf going into the Burrow."

"Is he still here?"

Airy shook his head again. "Gone with them, I guess. It's just you and me, Father. You wouldn't happen to have a match, would you?"

I shook my head and his tongue flicked out lifting the reefer from his lips to inside his mouth. For a minute, he sat chewing contentedly.

About two hours later, a soldier kicked the latrine's door open, and came in and cut the plastic ties on my hands. Turning to leave, he said, "It's over. You two can leave now."

It's over.

Outside, we walked to the downed gates and stood watching the tank with the battering ram push through the canvas shelter used by the Newspaper Nasties. The tank dragged several long pieces of canvas behind it, and small sheets of paper blew across the ground, set into motion by the tank's blustering exhaust. I bent and picked one of the sheets up. It was a torn page from a fashion magazine showing a model in an exaggerated pose.

It's over.

"Where are you going?" I asked Airy.

He nodded toward his house. Several of its windows were smashed out and its front door had been torn off at the hinges.

"To see what's left. Somewhere in there lie the secrets to eternal happiness. Yourself?"

I shrugged. I hadn't thought about it until that very moment. It was obvious I couldn't stay in the Heap.

What do you call it? Home.

"I suppose I'll return to the monastery," I said, without much conviction.

Airy held his hand out and I took it in mine.

"You did everything you could," he said.

"No, I did nothing. Nothing at all."

It's always the same.

"You're too hard on yourself. I suspect you did far more than you can imagine," he said, letting my hand go. He turned to go, and then turned back to face me. "Just remember, Father," he said, grinning widely, "love will never overcome the smell of sulfur."

Epilogue

ollowing that fateful week, I returned to the monastery. There I once again attempted to focus on my work concerning Simon Magus, but, as you may suspect, doing so was quite difficult. Concentration on any task was inevitably interrupted by thoughts of the Heap's children and my wondering where they had gone, and soon I found myself once again hospitalized. The strain of everything, combined with my learning that the entire Heap had been bulldozed into oblivion, was too much for me and I suffered a relapse into my strange malady.

On my first day in the hospital, the same doctor wearing his white lab coat came into my room, this time without the interns.

"Ah, a familiar face" he said. He took the penlight from his coat pocket and examined one of my eyes.

"You came back because you missed our food?" he joked.

"Hardly," I said, not feeling in much a mood to jest with him. "I'm not here by choice."

"Are you so sure?" he said, moving the light to my other eye.

"What do you mean?"

"Choice is not always a matter of thought."

After he finished examining me, he said, "You have obviously been through a lot of late, my friend, but I have an amazing cure for you."

"What's that?" I asked.

He winked at me and said, "It's called living for the future. It has worked remarkably well for centuries."

After several weeks of tedious recuperation, I was once again ready for discharge. My nurse, the same who had tended to me during my first stay, came into my room one morning and pushed the curtains on its sole window open, and announced, "All right, the doctor approved your release for the day after tomorrow."

Sunlight flooded the austere room, and I sat up in bed and asked her, for about the tenth time since I had been admitted, if any children from the streets had been brought to the hospital.

"Not a one," she replied. And then after a moment, "Mighty strange, if you ask me."

"Why is that?" I asked.

"They used to come in like clockwork, but not lately. Not a one in the past few weeks."

"Do you know why?"

"There are rumors everywhere throughout the city."

"Yes?"

"About something that happened in the Heap and other things."

"Other things?"

"Some say they have a new leader. An older boy they call the Prophet. Who knows what goes through the heads of these kids."

"Why do you say that?"

"Some of the rumors say they are arming themselves and that they are preparing for something."

"I doubt that," I told her. "I doubt that very much."

She had finished writing on my chart and was moving toward

the door.

"Well, I hope you're right," she said.

Throughout my last days in the hospital, when I wrote much of what you now have before you, many of the events that occurred in the Heap's final days came back to haunt me. But so too did images of my many other days in the Heap. And these were a welcomed haunting; one I hoped would cling to me for the rest of my life. Not an hour went by without me thinking back to the times when I would sit atop that pile of twisted metal and watch the children go about their daily routines. In summoning up images of my happier days in the Heap, I recalled the story Pockets had told me about the amazing abilities of dwarfs and their secret hiding places beneath the earth. I also remembered some of the children telling me about the tunnels beneath the Field of Heads and how they were thought to connect somehow to the Heap. Was that how the children had escaped? And if it was, where were they now? Why did they leave the bomb behind? Why did they leave me behind?

Urbain came to see me the night before I was to be discharged. I was sitting in a chair beside my bed, writing my account of the final days of the Heap, when the light on the ceiling flickered once, and then twice more.

"You are getting better, and will be traveling away soon, non?" Urbain said.

"Yes," I answered. I had made my decision days before.

"Where will you go?" he asked, sitting near me on the edge of my bed.

"To London, and then from there, I don't know."

Urbain gestured to the open journal resting on my lap. "And will you take that with you?"

"Yes, of course."

"Be very careful, mon ami, certain people will not like that you have made a record of things."

"It's all I have left of them."

"Are you so sure of that?"

"What do you mean?"

"One never knows what the future may hold."

"Do you know where they are?" I asked him. "Please, tell me, if you do."

He looked at me, and didn't say anything for a long time. Then he reached out with one of his blackened, charred hands and touched me lightly on the side of my face.

"Oh, Gabriel, you truly don't understand, do you?"

"What?" I said, taking his hand in mine.

"They haven't gone anywhere. They're here, as they always have been."

"Always?"

"Since long ago. When they once tried to save me, and long before that."

"I don't understand," I told him. "Why didn't they take the bomb with them?"

"They never wanted it to begin with," Urbain answered. "It was an unfortunate discovery."

"But Simon did, didn't he? He wanted it."

"Are you so sure of that?"

"No," I said, "I'm not sure of anything any longer."

"You are too hard on yourself, Gabriel. Simon only wants one thing. You, of all people, should know that."

I sat thinking, confused, unsure what he meant.

Inexplicably, Phaedra's words came back to me. *No, it's much more than that.*

"The Word," I said.

"Ah, now you are beginning to see things in the proper light," Urbain said.

"But, the children, they didn't know it, did they? How could—"

Urbain raised what was left of his scorched eyebrows, and I thought back to the day I had rushed breathlessly into the Burrow to warn the children the soldiers were coming. I remembered entering the Burrow's round room and noticing its remarkable floor with its countless pieces of tile, granite, and marble, and its strange symbols and letters. And then I thought of Simon's odd request that the children be removed from the Heap and resettled elsewhere.

"I didn't know," I told Urbain. "I didn't understand."

Urbain smiled and got up from the edge of the bed.

"Why didn't they take me with them?"

"There is still much for you to do here," he said, moving to the door. "I must go now, mon ami. Be very careful with yourself."

"What will you do?" I asked.

"Don't worry about me, Gabriel. I will be fine. I will remain here for a while to see what develops... and then... and then, who knows...maybe I will catch up with you."

"That would be nice," I said.

The day before I was to depart for London, I gathered up my manuscripts and books, and packed them in an airfreight box to be sent to London ahead of my flight. When I went to take one last look at my workroom, I found a small metal and copper flower situated in the middle of the desk. I stood staring at it for a long time. I picked it up and sat at the desk looking at it. Where had it come from? Had I placed it there? I had no recollection of doing so, nor did I have any recollection of taking any of Phaedra's flowers with me from the Heap. I put the flower in my pocket. When I stood up I looked out the window and saw a long, narrow plume of smoke rising from the spot of the Heap. I watched waiting for it to curve and form some odd, telltale shape but this plume only continued to slowly work its way skyward.

On my way to the airport in a taxi the next day, I picked up a newspaper that had been left on the seat and saw the bold headline, **DIPLOMAT DEAD IN BIZARRE ACCIDENT**. The story below it was brief and stated:

> Well-known and regarded diplomat Simon Driver was found last night hanging from the balcony trellis of the exclusive villa he occupied just outside the city's northern section. A spokesman for the police department said that Driver's death appeared to have been the result of a freak accident in which he somehow fell over a low railing and became entangled in the waist cord of the dressing robe he was wearing. According to people who witnessed the scene, Driver's body, discovered by a maid who had just reported for her morning shift, was discovered with the robe's cord wrapped around his neck. Colleagues close to Driver, who declined to be identified, said that he had not been depressed, or despondent, and that he was at the pinnacle of his career following a number of significant accomplishments. Other colleagues of the diplomat said they found "the circumstances of his death to be quite strange.
>
> Indeed, Driver's death does appear unusual in light of the seemingly unconnected, death of Helen Gray, a career foreign service officer, who worked closely with Driver in recent months as well as many of the locally based foreign consulates and embassies. Gray's body was found late last week bludgeoned to death in a marketplace less than a half-mile from Driver's villa. Reportedly, Gray's body also bore a large number of what appeared to be animal bite marks. Police have not identified any suspects in Gray's apparent murder, nor have they released details of her injuries or a final determination on the cause of her death. Police spokespeople would not comment

on either Driver's or Gray's death, citing policies concerning open investigations.

Beneath the story there was a brief article headed, **CONCERNS GROWING AGAIN ABOUT STREET CHILDREN**. This story was the usual rehash of words concerning the city's ubiquitous problems with homeless children, but it was its concluding sentence that most gave me pause. It read: "Recent reports that Colonel Daihen, former head of the special police squad formed to deal with street children, is about to be reappointed to that post remain unconfirmed at this writing."

It's always the same.

I set the newspaper down and looked out the window. The taxi was moving past the market area of the city now. Throngs of people were out and the hundreds of stalls selling anything one could imagine were enjoying a brisk commerce. I marveled at the thought that none of the final events that had taken place in the Heap had drawn any attention from the media—surely a deliberate act manipulated by persons working in alliance with Simon. Here and everywhere now, people went on as always completely unaware of what had occurred.

It's always the same.

Near one vegetable stall two men appeared to be engaged in a heated debate. One of the men raised his hands and began shouting at the other, just as a large black dog, with mournful eyes, sauntered by and disappeared into a group of people.

"Stop," I cried out to the driver.

"Here? But I thought you were—"

"No, please, stop here. And wait. I'll only be a minute."

I jumped out of the taxi and moved hurriedly toward the spot where I had seen the dog disappear. The crowd was thick and I had to maneuver myself around people. As I neared the stall, I caught a glimpse of the dog once more and then the familiar face of a young girl with bright red, braided hair.

Phaedra? Was it her?

"Phaedra," I yelled after the girl. I moved fast, pushing my way through the crowd, calling out, "Phaedra! Phaedra!"

I saw a flash of black to my left that I thought was Nameless and when I quickly changed directions I charged into a group of people, knocking down one man and stumbling and falling over another person who tried to prevent his fall. I stood up quickly and helped the bewildered men to their feet, apologizing profusely and looking about for Phaedra or Nameless. They were nowhere to be seen. I stood on top of a vegetable cart and scanned the marketplace, but couldn't see them anywhere.

At the airport I had an hour's wait before my plane was to board. My flight to London, with one stop, would take several hours. I sat down in the waiting area and fumbled about in my bag for something to read. My hand came on a small book and I pulled out Pockets' coverless copy of Lewis Carroll's *Through the Looking Glass*, remembering when Raoul had given it to me. I set it on my lap, and gazed down at its last page.

> Children yet, the tale to hear,
> Eager eye and willing ear,
> Lovingly shall nestle near.
>
> In a Wonderland they lie,
> Dreaming as the days go by,
> Dreaming as the summers die:
>
> Ever drifting down the stream—
> Lingering in the golden gleam—
> Life, what is it but a dream?

Postscript

Suffer little children, and forbid them not to
Come unto Me: For such is the Kingdom of Heaven...
—Matthew 19:14

According to the United Nations Children's Fund, or UNICEF as it is commonly called, worldwide millions of children live on the streets. The actual number is imprecise because it is growing daily, and because social scientists tend to quibble over "what constitutes a street child." It can be safely stated, however, that there are between one-hundred million and one-hundred-and-fifty million street children on our planet.

Once considered a problem confined to the dense populated urban areas of Latin America and India, large concentrations of street children are now everywhere throughout the world including the Far East, the Middle East, Africa, Eastern Europe, South America, and North America.

The International Labor Organization estimates that close to 250 million children between the ages of five and fourteen are working in developing countries, with about half this number being made to work 40 hours or more a week.

In recent years, a few forward thinking social scientists have seriously pondered what the future may hold for the world's street children. Some are very concerned about what they see as a certain pathology that is widely developing. Said one scientist, "God help us all if one day they come together and decide that they've had enough." Said another, "They will take revenge on society which is indifferent to their life."

In the civilized world's Western societies there are long-standing statutes concerning crimes that result in serious bodily injury and murder through depraved indifference and reckless endangerment. In regards to the world's millions of invisible street children, we are all guilty of violating these laws.

Et Verbum Caro Factum Est.

About the Author

H.P. ALBARELLI JR. is a writer, investigative journalist, and a third generation Vermonter, who currently lives in the Tampa Bay region of Florida with his wife Kathleen R. McDonald and dog, Cali. He has written numerous articles about the 9/11 anthrax attacks, biological warfare, missing and abused children, and the strange death of Dr. Frank Olson. His book *A TERRIBLE MISTAKE: The Murder of Dr. Frank Olson and the CIA's Secret Cold War Experiments* will be published next year. Readers may visit Albarelli at www.albarelli.net.